THE
SOWING
SEASON

THE
SOWING
SEASON

A Novel

KATIE POWNER

BETHANYHOUSE
a division of Baker Publishing Group
Minneapolis, Minnesota

© 2020 by Katie Powner

Published by Bethany House Publishers
11400 Hampshire Avenue South
Bloomington, Minnesota 55438
www.bethanyhouse.com

Bethany House Publishers is a division of
Baker Publishing Group, Grand Rapids, Michigan

Printed in the United States of America

ISBN 978-0-7642-3759-1 (paperback)
ISBN 978-0-7642-3782-9 (casebound)

Scripture quotations are from THE HOLY BIBLE, NEW INTERNATIONAL
VERSION®, NIV® Copyright © 1973, 1978, 1984, 2011 by Biblica, Inc.® Used
by permission. All rights reserved worldwide.

This is a work of fiction. Names, characters, incidents, and dialogues are products
of the author's imagination and are not to be construed as real. Any resemblance
to actual events or persons, living or dead, is entirely coincidental.

Cover design by Susan Zucker

Author is represented by WordServe Literary Agency.

20 21 22 23 24 25 26   7 6 5 4 3 2 1

To my dad

I still miss you.

CHAPTER
ONE

April 2019
Greenville, Washington

Cow manure spewed from the burst pipe and rained down on him like retribution. With a tight-lipped growl, Gerrit Laninga rolled up a flannel sleeve and exposed a clean bit of skin to wipe the muck from his eyes. This wasn't how he'd imagined his last day on the farm. But . . . well, it was fitting.

The sun had already passed its zenith. He'd better hurry if he was going to make it to Jim's office in time to sign the papers. If he didn't value his old Dodge so much, he'd be tempted to drive to the meeting exactly like this. Covered in crap. That would give Nicholsen an idea of how Gerrit felt about him and his so-called "deal of a lifetime." And an idea of what Nicholsen was getting himself into with this god-forsaken piece of property.

Gerrit trudged across the field with unwilling steps, the wind drying the manure so that it cracked and crumbled off him as he walked. After sixty-three years, he'd gotten so he hardly noticed the cow smell anymore—most of the time. But even he wrinkled his nose at the stench coming from him now. "Smells like money," he'd heard other farmers say. But he'd never made a dime off this place.

The farm was supposed to stay in his family forever. He'd meant to retire at the ripe old age of a hundred and be buried in the back forty under a cottonwood tree. But after last winter? Neither his old bones nor his bank account was going to make it through another year. Which he mentioned to the vet, who mentioned it to Grant Nicholsen down the road, who swooped in with an offer Gerrit couldn't refuse before sunrise the following day.

After cleaning up and changing his clothes in the office behind the milking parlor, Gerrit climbed in the Dodge and sat with his arms resting on the wheel. In a couple of hours, Nicholsen's crew would show up for the afternoon milking, and the farm would hum with steady progress, but for now it was quiet and still. Holsteins flicked lazy tails at fat black flies. Barn cats bathed themselves in the sun. The breeze blew bits of sawdust from the top of the pile.

Everything about this place felt like home and reminded him of his failures. He hated it, but he loved it. It was death, but it was the only life he'd ever known.

For the first time, he was glad Luke was dead.

GERRIT SHIFTED ON the fancy leather chair and stared at the manure under his fingernails. He still stunk. And his back was killing him.

Beside him to his left, his older brother's widow, Luisa, sat with the same sort of steady grace Luke had always had. She was surely no more surprised to be waiting on Jakob than he was. Gerrit had been waiting on Jakob most of his life.

"You've got manure in your hair, Gerrit," Luisa whispered, her Italian accent still strong even after thirty years in the States.

He ran a hand through his untamed brownish-gray mane. A dried clump of manure fell onto the lush beige carpet.

From behind his massive oak desk, Jim Dyk cleared his throat. "Okay then. Any idea where your brother might be?"

Gerrit shrugged. "Check the nearest casino."

"We can't wait much longer." Jim tapped his desk three times with a pen. "Nicholsen is anxious to—"

"Nicholsen can put a—"

"Gerrit." Luisa's rebuke was just sharp enough. "This was your decision. Don't take it out on Jim."

He grunted. He could take it out on whoever he wanted, but he forced his shoulders to relax. He wouldn't cause a scene in front of Luisa. She didn't deserve that, not after everything he'd put her through already. Yet he'd seen the smug look on Nicholsen's face as Gerrit passed him and his lawyer on the way into Jim's office, and part of him relished the fact that Nicholsen had to wait.

The door swung open with a thud. Jakob shuffled into the room looking twice his age and scrutinized Gerrit with bleary eyes.

Gerrit glared back. "Where you been?"

Jakob took the seat on Luisa's other side in silence, pulling his bright blue windbreaker tightly around him.

Luisa patted his knee. "Good to see you, Jakob."

Jakob nodded.

"All right." Jim straightened the papers in front of him.

"Time to get down to business. We covered all the details at our last meeting, so I just need you to warm up your writing fingers. There are a lot of papers to sign here."

Jakob leaned forward. "And what if I don't?"

Gerrit stiffened. "Then you can take over the farm all by yourself and run it into the ground." He wanted to add a few more choice words but held back for Luisa's sake. Jakob shouldn't even be here. Didn't deserve a penny. But their father had made sure years ago that Jakob would always have an equal share in the family business.

Such as it was.

Jakob huffed but offered no further resistance. Jim went over the pages of the sale agreement one by one, pointing out each place that required a signature or initials. He hurried them along as if afraid one of them might change their mind. And Gerrit considered it. He really did. Who was he without the farm? What would he do? But his back reminded him of the relentlessness of the work. The sunshine outside reminded him of the endless hours of labor ahead during the summer season. And his heart screamed that he had no choice.

It was time.

When the last piece of paper had been reviewed and signed, Jim shook hands with each of them in turn and dismissed them with a sigh of relief. Gerrit was the last to leave. In the hall, Nicholsen waited to take his place with an eager expression, and a strange feeling pressed against Gerrit's heart. *Take good care of her*, he wanted to say. *She'll need all you have to give.* Instead, he nodded, just once.

Jakob was long gone as Gerrit walked Luisa to her car. He held the door open for her and searched for the right words, knowing there weren't any. "I'm sorry."

"For what? Wanting to enjoy your life for once?" She patted him on the cheek. "Luke would not blame you."

He nodded, but inside he wasn't so sure. After all, who else was there to blame? Jakob, of course. But Jakob wasn't the one who decided to sell to Nicholsen.

He hung his head. "I wish it had been more."

She waved his words away. "A hundred and thirteen thousand dollars is plenty for an old lady like me. And I've got that money from my father. Don't worry."

"You're not old."

"Hmmph. Tell that to the bunions on my feet."

He lumbered to his truck, the numbers taunting him. One hundred and thirteen thousand each, all that was left for the three of them after paying off the farm's debts. All that was left of a lifetime spent believing his sacrifices would be worth it someday.

He heaved himself into the Dodge with an unshakable weariness. If he was careful, he could make the money last. Over the last ten years, he'd sunk his and Hannie's entire savings into keeping the farm afloat—a decision that haunted him now. But their mortgage would be paid off in a year, and Hannie brought in a little money from her shop. So long as nothing terrible happened, they would be okay. Right?

So long as nothing terrible happened.

"I'm tired, Luke." He scrubbed his face with his hands. "You don't know what it's been like all these years without you."

With a heavy sigh he turned the key in the ignition. Forty years of hard time could do something to a man. Could whittle his spirit down to a splinter of what it was and change him so that even his stride reflected the rigid structure of boundaries. Limits. Gerrit knew.

The Dodge hacked up some phlegm, pounded its chest, then roared to life. Gerrit gripped the wheel tightly. He was going home a free man, but he felt like a prisoner.

It took more to be free of a place than just driving away.

CHAPTER
TWO

It was six o'clock before Gerrit mustered the courage to point the Dodge toward his house on the hill. What a strange thing, to turn left at the junction. When was the last time he'd turned left while there was still daylight instead of driving on and getting back to work?

There was always work.

He parked the Dodge in the gravel next to the old pony barn and approached the house like a stranger. How long had Hannie been home? He quickened his step.

When he opened the door, his wife stood before him, her hair held on top of her head by some sort of clip. Her cobalt eyes downcast. She had one hand outstretched to turn the knob, the other gripping the handle of a faded blue suitcase with a white stripe around the middle. For a moment, her face registered surprise, and then she lowered her hand.

"You came home."

Gerrit blinked. "Of course I came home. Where else would I go?"

Her corgi, Daisy, peeked out from behind her legs. Hannie shifted. "The farm."

"Can't go there no more." He stared at Daisy, then at the suitcase. "I signed the papers."

Hannie's shoulders relaxed. Her grip on the handle loosened.

He jerked his chin at the offensive blue case. "Going somewhere?"

She chewed her top lip. "I didn't think you'd go through with it. When I got home from the shop and you weren't here, I thought you'd changed your mind. And I couldn't face another day, another month, another year . . ."

As her voice trailed off, he noticed her shoes. They were pink like rose petals. His muddy brown boots looked like filthy monsters beside them, ready to trample them into the ground.

He took a step back. "I don't understand."

"I didn't want to keep competing with the farm for your attention." She looked down. "I couldn't."

The hair on the back of his neck stood up. "How come you never said anything before? About the farm?"

"You make your own decisions, and you know it. You're as stubborn as a goat on top of a junk pile. Quitting had to be your choice."

Quitting? No, he hadn't quit. He'd been forced out by his traitorous, decrepit body. By unpredictable milk prices and unreliable laborers and Jakob's abandonment. But he'd never heard Hannie complain. At least not in so many words.

"Hannie, I—"

"Ever since the kids moved out, I've been living here alone." She raised her voice and jabbed her finger in the air for emphasis. "Just me and Daisy. You come and go at all hours. You're never here for dinner. And you're always angry."

He frowned. Yes, he'd been angry at times. A lot of times. That was Jakob's fault, but after what happened today, he would never have to speak to Jakob again.

"All that's over." His throat tightened. "Please. Don't go. I'm here now."

"You wouldn't even notice if I was gone."

He took another step back, his stomach clenching. "I would notice."

She looked him in the eye, and years of questions and memories and trials and joys passed between them. He struggled to hold her gaze. He had nothing to offer—no reason for her to stay—but he couldn't lose her. Not on top of everything else. Not his Hannie.

Daisy snuffled, sat on the linoleum, and looked up at her mistress, ready to follow her lead. The suitcase made no sound as Hannie set it down on the floor against the wall.

DINNER WAS QUIET. Gerrit wasn't sure what he was supposed to do. He couldn't remember the last time he hadn't come home late and pulled something from the fridge to heat up in the microwave. He'd almost forgotten what it was like to taste something fresh from the stovetop. Even if it was just spaghetti and green beans.

He cleared his throat. "Your cooking is better fresh."

Hannie stared. He swallowed. What had he said?

She stood to clear the dishes. "How nice of you to notice."

It was supposed to be a compliment. He should've known better than to say anything out loud.

He sat frozen in his chair as he watched her work, her movements like cornstalks in July. Steady and determined. The refrigerator droned louder than a cab tractor. Daisy stood sentry in the hallway entrance, following Hannie with her eyes as his wife went back and forth.

Gerrit's large callused hands lay idle on the table. "Should I help you?"

Hannie studied him until he squirmed. "If you'd like."

Suspicion scratched at him like a barbwire fence. Her words made out like it was up to him, but they sounded as though she'd already decided against it.

He remained at the table. "You work tomorrow?"

She looked at him again. "Yes."

Her voice was flat. Now what had he done? He considered asking what he was supposed to do all day at the house by himself but then studied the rigid set of Hannie's shoulders and thought better of it.

She draped the dish towel over the edge of the sink and snapped her fingers. "Come on, Daisy. Time for bed."

Gerrit glanced at the time. "It's early yet."

"Tomorrow's Thursday."

He stared. She stared back.

His shoulders tensed. Better get it over with. "So . . . ?"

Her nostrils flared. "*So* our biggest shipment comes on Thursday mornings. Every single week. At five a.m."

"Oh." The first milking started around four in the morning, so he'd always been out the door long before Hannie. "I forgot about that."

She smirked. "Right."

"Can't anyone else unload the flowers?"

"It's my shop, Gerrit. I'm the boss."

"Right."

Daisy was close on her heels as she strode from the kitchen. He strained to hear Hannie's steady footsteps ascend the carpeted stairs, followed by Daisy's bouncy ones.

That was that.

The house was quiet again.

He pushed against the table to lift himself from his chair, his stiff back protesting, and trudged through the living room. He stepped out onto the deck. Though it was as dark as used oil in the pan, he could still see the farm lit up at the bottom of the hill. He could make out the milking parlor and the loafing shed. And the big red barn. Even his father's old house, which had been empty for five years now.

What was he going to do? Never in his whole life had he gone to bed not knowing what he would do the next day. The farm had always been there. The cows had always needed milking. The work had never ceased. Even as a child, he'd been out there.

His throat tightened again, just as it had at the sight of Hannie standing by the door with a suitcase. He'd told her things would be different now. Would they? With a determined grunt, he went back in the house and climbed the stairs.

Standing outside her bedroom—their bedroom—he hesitated. He had taken to sleeping on the rickety recliner in the living room years ago due to his odd and unfortunate hours. He never wanted to bother Hannie with his coming and going, plus he'd had the distinct feeling she didn't want him in her bed. And he couldn't blame her. He smelled like cows.

His hand touched the doorknob.

Should he go in? Would she order him out? Was she sleeping

already? He had no idea how she spent her evenings. No idea how she would respond if he knocked.

No idea who she was anymore.

When had that happened?

He slipped back downstairs, avoiding the third to last step, which would creak under his weight. She used to wait up for him, eager to hear about his day and make sure he had enough to eat. Sometimes she would be wearing something short and made of satin. But how long could a man expect a woman to keep giving when she got nothing in return?

He heaved himself into the old recliner, the quietness in the house now breathing and pulsing in a way he'd never noticed before. This was the silence she'd been living with. This was the bed he had made.

Unable to bear it, he flipped on the TV. Voices. He needed voices. Life. He needed life. Hannie. He needed . . .

He fell asleep thinking about those pretty pink shoes.

CHAPTER
THREE

Rae Walters snapped her biology textbook shut and checked the time. Almost midnight. A long-haired gray cat yawned and stretched on the couch beside her. "This is the price we pay for straight A's, Mr. Whiskers." Not that she would need to know what peristalsis was to become a lawyer. She tousled the cat's scruffy head. "We'll go to bed in a minute."

She paused to listen for any noise. Mom and Dad had gone to bed over an hour ago. In socked feet, she crept down the hall and into the garage, Mr. Whiskers close behind.

He meowed.

Rae put a finger to her lips. "I know, I know."

She quietly opened the door of her mom's navy blue Ford Explorer and slipped in. Mom never locked it, which annoyed Dad to no end. But it worked out well for Rae. She reached over and opened the passenger door for Mr. Whiskers, who hopped onto the seat with a quiet dignity that bespoke his thirteen years and unending patience.

She grinned at him. "Buckle up."

He ignored her. Unimpressed. After securing her own seat

belt, she slid an invisible key into the ignition and pretended to turn it. With careful, deliberate moves, she went through the motions of sliding the shifter into reverse and easing her foot down on the gas pedal as she twisted to look behind her.

"All clear, Mister."

She closed her eyes and visualized it—driving out of the garage, turning onto the street, taking the Explorer all the way to school. Her heart began to pound. What if she forgot to check behind her? What if she ran a red light? What if she bumped another car in the school parking lot? What if—?

Her eyes flew open. Driver's Ed. started in two weeks. She might not need to know what peristalsis was to become a lawyer, but she *would* need a driver's license.

She'd gotten her permit three weeks ago. The small card had felt like freedom in her hand. For about two hours. Then Dad came home from work. In his best lawyer voice, he went over the driving basics with her, waxed eloquent about safety and responsibility, and insisted she drive around the block.

It wasn't until they got back to the house that her panic set in. She hit the gas instead of the brake as she pulled into the driveway, and in the split second the car surged toward the closed garage door, she discovered what it was like to lose control. And she didn't like it. She was a boat by the dock whose rope had been cut, with a giant wave bearing down on the shore. Her whole, perfectly ordered world had shifted. Dad patted her on the shoulder with a penetrating look.

"I know I don't need to remind you how important this is," he'd said. "Summer will be here before you know it."

She hadn't driven since, always finding an excuse whenever Mom or Dad brought it up. Always acting like it could wait.

That was the night the bad dreams had started.

Her knuckles turned white as she gripped the wheel, the inside of the garage suddenly dark and menacing. She blew out a hard breath. Somehow she needed to work up the courage to get back on the road before Driver's Ed., or she might find out what it was like to be bad at something for the first time in her life.

Maybe that should be what she wanted. Then everyone could stop treating her like she was perfect and only expect the same from her as they did from everyone else. But that wasn't what she wanted. She wanted to be good at it. She didn't know how to fail.

Not to mention what her parents would think. The Plan required her getting her license as soon as possible so she could get a job this summer. Dad said work experience would look good on her college applications, so that's what she must do. She would need every advantage if she was going to get into Columbia and follow in his footsteps.

She visualized herself and the Explorer driving back into the garage, then reenacted putting the car in park and removing the key. Her heart rate slowed back to normal. That wasn't so bad.

Driving was easy when you didn't go anywhere.

She unbuckled, scooped up Mr. Whiskers, and shut the driver's door as quietly as possible.

"It's a nice night." She hoisted the obese cat over her shoulder. "Maybe we should walk over to the barn."

Mr. Whiskers purred in her ear. He loved visiting that old barn as much as she did, and on such a mild evening, she couldn't resist. Walking to her favorite place under a moonlit sky would be much better than freaking out about her driver's license.

"Let's go in and get my shoes."

The door groaned as she slipped back in the house. Her sneakers were in her bedroom, and a sweatshirt wouldn't be a bad idea, either.

She set Mr. Whiskers on the kitchen table. "Wait here."

With practiced stealth, she tiptoed down the hall. As she passed her parents' bedroom, muffled voices slipped under the door. She stopped. That was different. They never stayed up this late.

"You're not being fair." That was Mom. "My mother needs me."

"And you're not being reasonable." Dad's voice had an edge. "I've worked too hard to—"

"*You've* worked hard?" Mom's voice rose. "*You?*"

"Keep your voice down. We've all made sacrifices."

Rae strained to hear as Mom lowered her voice to a tense whisper. "What have you sacrificed?"

"That's enough." Dad's tone transformed from lawyer to judge.

"I'm not one of your clients."

Rae leaned closer but couldn't make out her father's response. What were they talking about? She held her breath and listened but heard only the creaking of their bed and quiet footsteps.

Uh-oh. Time to make herself scarce.

She resumed her tiptoeing, praying their door wouldn't open. Five paces to her room. Four. Three.

"You still up?"

Rae spun around.

Mom leaned against the doorframe of their bedroom, a forced smile on her face. Eyes red. "You been studying this whole time?"

Rae dug her big toe into the carpet. "Um . . ."

"I've never seen a kid so dedicated." She closed the distance between them and gave Rae's shoulder a small squeeze. "Time for bed, though."

"Okay."

Rae waited until her mom shut the bedroom door before creeping back to the kitchen.

So dedicated. Well, she had to be. There was no room in The Plan for anything less.

She picked up Mr. Whiskers from the table and buried her face in his fur. "The jig is up, Mister." She settled him in her arms and headed back to her room. "We're not going anywhere tonight."

Another meow.

"I'm disappointed, too. Maybe next time."

Mr. Whiskers made himself comfortable at the end of her bed while Rae changed into her pajamas, her forehead furrowed. Why had Mom said Dad wasn't being fair? Something strange was going on. And what did other moms do when they caught their children wandering the house in the middle of the night? Probably not assume they had been studying. Other kids didn't live their lives beholden to The Plan.

"There's nothing wrong with being responsible." She switched off the light and slid under the covers. "If other kids want to text their lives away, that's their problem, right?"

Mr. Whiskers inched closer to Rae's pillow, ignoring the end-of-the-bed rule.

"I'm going to stick to The Plan. Even the driving stuff." Rae burrowed deeper into her blankets, unsure who she was trying to convince. "Are you even listening to me?"

Her loyal furry friend didn't answer.

Rae squeezed her eyes shut. Mr. Whiskers didn't understand how important this was. She'd been following The Plan her whole life, and she was on track. She had the highest GPA in her class. She was a member of the National Honor Society. By senior year she would be its president. The tiles were all falling into place—*tink, tink, tink*—forming the shape of her future.

All she had to do was hold on.

RAE'S ARMS JERKED, but she couldn't get them to move where she wanted. To grip the wheel. To turn the car. It kept going, speeding out of control. Careering down a hill, faster, faster toward two dark figures transfixed in the middle of the road. The brakes wouldn't work.

She cried out and awoke, sitting up in the dark, heart pounding. Mr. Whiskers lifted his head from where he lay on her pillow and sniffed, then went back to sleep.

She rubbed her face with her hands. It was a dream. Only another dream.

But why had it seemed so real?

CHAPTER
FOUR

The morning sun crept across the floor and tapped on Gerrit's feet. He awoke with a grunt. Morning? What time was it?

He strained to extricate himself from the recliner, each of his back muscles rebelling with practiced disdain. He checked his phone. It was seven o'clock. No wonder he was so stiff. He'd spent almost four more hours in this stupid chair than usual.

And he'd slept in his clothes.

As he worked the kinks out of his neck, Daisy appeared. She cocked her head to one side as if wondering what on earth he was doing. Well. It was none of her business.

Gerrit waved a hand. "Git."

Daisy did not git.

Gerrit put one hand on his lower back and pushed off the chair with the other. "I said git."

Daisy smiled. Gerrit didn't know dogs could do that.

He plodded to the kitchen, a hazy memory from the night before stinging in his brain. He had awoken with a start at some point, when it was still dark, his muscles tensed in panic that he had missed a milking. Certain his cows were going out of their minds waiting for him—before he remembered they weren't his cows any longer. And their milk was none of his concern.

In the kitchen, he found a note. *Please take Daisy for a walk.* He looked at Daisy, who had followed him into the kitchen.

"Did you put her up to this?"

Daisy barked once. Gerrit grumbled. How had he slept through Hannie getting up and leaving? Why hadn't she woken him to say good-bye?

Well, why should she?

He ate breakfast in silence. The clock on the wall ticked like impending doom. It was never like this on the farm. Peaceful, sure. But quiet? Not with three hundred bellowing cows meandering around, milking machines pumping, and equipment running at all hours of the day. But those were useful sounds. Productive.

What should he do? Taking Daisy for a walk was not an option. If she wanted exercise, she could run around in the yard. That's what it was for.

His boots were by the door, where Hannie's suitcase still sat, smug and contemptuous. *She's got no reason to stay*, it said. *I'm just biding my time.* Bah. He left the boots where they were and pulled on his old tennis shoes.

Daisy followed him outside, her stubby legs racing to keep up. Gerrit plowed ahead about thirty feet and stopped abruptly. Looked around. Where was he going?

Slowly he turned in a circle, scrutinizing his surroundings. For too long he'd neglected this place. Time to start taking care of business. He glanced at the barn first. Though twenty-five years old, it looked none the worse for wear for all the neglect it had received, aside from needing a fresh coat of paint. He had Luke to thank for that. Luke never did anything halfway. You wouldn't find a sturdier barn anywhere in the good state of Washington.

He could probably find an abundance of projects to tend to in that old thing, but he couldn't go in there. Wouldn't. Surely there were other things that needed his attention. Daisy waited patiently.

Though still early spring, a handful of weeds had already begun to sprout through the gravel in the driveway, evidence of the area's ideal climate for growing all manner of things. Gerrit walked the entire drive, extricating any he found. When he reached the end, he opened the mailbox. It was empty.

"When do they deliver the mail around here?"

Daisy was sniffing her way through the lawn and couldn't even be bothered to lift her head. Gerrit closed the box, listening for even the slightest squeak that would give him an excuse to oil the hinges, but it was silent.

Not far from his plain black box with gold numbers sat George and Agatha Sinnema's oversized antique car mailbox. You opened the hood of the car to retrieve the mail. It was ridiculous. But not as ridiculous as the bushes growing around the post, obstructing everyone's view of the road. How was Hannie supposed to pull out of the drive safely with that monstrosity blocking her sight line?

George should know better. He should. But he was an arrogant, thoughtless son of a gun for whom Gerrit had never found any use. It had been over twenty years since George had daily allowed his children to run amok all over the hill, destroying Gerrit's property while they were at it. Even longer than that since George had taken what should've been Gerrit's. But he hadn't forgotten. No, sir. Gerrit Laninga was not a man who could forget. And he would have some very particular things to say about those bushes next time he saw George.

Then again, why wait until then to do something about this problem? And why only talk when action was required?

He took his time on the bushes. He even used the handheld pruning tool he found in the shed rather than the chainsaw and trimmed the bushes as naturally as possible. No sense in doing a hack job. He'd done plenty of those on the blackberry bushes constantly threatening to overtake the back forty on the farm, sometimes even driving the loader tractor out there to rip piles of briars out. But this job required more finesse.

Daisy trotted over occasionally to check on his progress, sniffing his pant leg and appearing to shrug her shoulders each time he told her to mind her own business. He was in no mood to be criticized by a dog. And a corgi at that. She hadn't even been born back when George's man-sized German shepherd, Pal, would leave cat-sized piles of poop at the end of their driveway that George refused to acknowledge as Pal's.

What a punk.

After about an hour, Gerrit stepped back to admire his work. Much better. George might not even notice, but hopefully Hannie would when she saw how easy it was to pull out of the driveway tomorrow. She was going to be happy about this. He smiled to himself. He'd done her a favor, and she hadn't even had to ask.

That was good, right?

Gerrit put the pruners back and wiped his hands on his crusty jeans.

Now what?

A cursory glance at the time revealed lunch was still over an hour away. He wandered the perimeter of the house, checking the outside seals on all the windows. Did he even deserve to eat if he didn't put in a full day of work? They owned two acres in a part of the country where plants loved nothing more than to grow wild and free. Surely he could find a job to do.

What was Nicholsen up to on the farm? Had he remembered to check in with the breeder about next week's AI appointments? Did he know the milk replacement formula was running low?

Gerrit shook his head. Didn't matter. Wasn't his problem anymore. He had other things to worry about now. There *were* other things to worry about, right?

With a spark of inspiration, Gerrit remembered Hannie once saying something about the dryer. It wasn't getting clothes dry? Or did she say it was overheating? Better check it out.

Back inside, he walked with a renewed purpose now that he had a plan.

In the laundry room, he faced the dryer with his hands on his hips. "Well?"

The dryer exercised its right to remain silent. Gerrit pushed the start button and the dryer hummed to life, the drum smoothly spinning. It seemed fine. Why had Hannie complained? He put a hand on the side of the machine to feel for excessive shaking or heat and leaned closer when his fingers touched something stuck to the side.

He squinted. It was a service sticker from Frankie's Appliance and Repair. When had she called them? He looked closer. Two years ago.

Oh.

He glared down at Daisy, who had followed him inside. "Don't you say a word."

She did not.

An hour passed with similar results. He either remembered or dreamed up something around the property that might need his loving care, then glared at Daisy when he found Hannie had been ten steps ahead of him. No wonder she'd been about to leave. She didn't need him at all.

He paced back and forth in the kitchen, careful not to look out the deck window at the farm. Daisy joined him, her nails clicking on the laminate floor. *Click, click, click.*

"She spends a lot of time at her shop." He rubbed his chin. "There must be something left undone at the house."

Click, click, click.

He kicked at Daisy halfheartedly. "I can't think with all that racket."

She stopped.

He looked at her. "Wait a minute." He knelt beside her. "Let me see your foot."

Daisy whined.

"Okay, fine. Your paw."

She lifted a paw and placed it in his outstretched hand. He ran his thumb over her nails.

"These could use a trim."

Though his own personal hygiene regimen was nothing to write home about, he knew where the nail clippers were. In the small white cabinet above the sink. He slapped them against his palm as he surveyed the kitchen for the best light. If a man's going to do a job well, he's got to be able to see.

He pulled a chair from the kitchen table and swung it to rest beneath a light. "Come here, Daisy."

She approached him, but not too close.

He waved a hand. "I said come."

She scooted a little closer, her eyes never leaving the clippers in his hand. He huffed. How dare she distrust him?

He snagged one of her paws and studied it more closely. The nails were long, all right. She'd feel much better after he was through. With the confidence of a man long accustomed to working with animals, he slid her nail between the blades of the clippers and squeezed the lever.

A cow would never howl like that.

CHAPTER
FIVE

Rae narrowed her eyes at the bulletin board outside the counselor's office and tapped the paper with her pen. Driver's Ed. sign-ups. She'd waited until the last minute to add her name to the list, secretly hoping the spots would all fill up and she'd have no choice but to wait until the next session. But two blanks remained at the bottom of the page, and today was the deadline. She had no excuse.

Kylee nudged Rae's foot with one of her neon orange shoes. "Hurry up."

Kylee didn't like to wait. She smacked her gum and fidgeted with the colorful bracelets jangling from her wrists.

Rae stared at the board. Tutoring ads covered most of it, except for the Driver's Ed. sign-ups and a poster for some program called Community Hope. She scanned the poster quickly. Something about an after-school program at the church across the street helping at-risk students reach their full potential.

Hmm. Just this morning, Dad had reminded her that college admissions officers gave a lot of weight to a student's volunteer efforts.

Kylee clapped her hands. "Let's *go*."

Rae sighed and signed her name. "Here goes nothing."

"You act like you're signing up for boot camp." Kylee's bright blue eyes sparkled. "Don't you want your license?"

Kylee already had hers, like most of Rae's friends. Rae was the youngest in her class.

"It's a big responsibility."

Kylee's laugh filled the hallway. "You sound like my grandma."

"I'll take that as a compliment." Rae lifted her chin. "Grandmas are cool."

"Yeah, you *would* think that." Kylee tugged on her arm, and they started back to the cafeteria. "But you'll be glad when you don't have to ask for rides anymore."

Rae shrugged. "What if I don't pass?"

Kylee snorted. "When have you ever not passed?"

Rae didn't have to think about it. She'd never failed a test her whole life. Straight A's since kindergarten. Perfect attendance. Starting varsity as a freshman in basketball. She even had perfect 20/20 vision and the highest PSAT score in her grade. But she remembered how her hands shook after driving around the block with her dad, remembered the look on his face, and she shuddered.

Perfect attendance didn't make a girl perfect.

"There's a first time for everything."

"If you get anything but a hundred percent, I'll eat a whole salad." Kylee slid onto a seat in the cafeteria and pulled a yellow Sesame Street lunch box from her backpack. "With cauliflower on it."

Rae scrunched up her nose. "Gross."

Kylee's eyebrows bounced three times. "Don't let me down."

Her flamboyant friend's lunches always arrived in a brightly colored, wildly inappropriate-for-her-age lunch box and tended to consist more of Twinkies and Snack Packs than anything green. Rae plopped next to her at the table and pulled out a plain brown paper sack. Kylee didn't understand her anxiety about driving. She had failed many times at many things. She'd almost had to repeat sixth grade.

Rae's lunch—which Mom insisted on making in order to ensure its healthiness—was predictable. A tidy turkey-and-cheese sandwich on whole grain bread, a granola bar, a container of yogurt, and apple slices. She knew she was lucky to never have to worry about having good food to eat. Knew a lot of other girls would kill to have their moms even notice whether they went to school or not, let alone make them a lunch. But a tiny piece of her still had an unexplainable and wholly irrational desire to forget her lunch one day and take her chances with the cafeteria food. Just to see.

Kylee nibbled a powdered donut around double lip rings. "You eat like my grandma, too. The old witch."

Rae gasped. "Don't call her that."

A wicked grin split Kylee's face. "You know it's true. Just last week she told my mom she owed her a hundred and fifty bucks plus interest for the time she borrowed Grandma's car, like, two years ago. How's *your* grandma?"

It had been almost a year since Grandma Kate had become a widow, and since then her memory had begun its steady decline. Rae's mom was stressed about it, constantly making the hour drive to check on her and trying to make arrangements for her care over the phone.

"About the same, I guess. Yesterday she called my mom Gracie."

"Isn't that her dog's name?"

Rae cringed. "Yep."

"That sucks." Kylee frowned. "But that reminds me, my stepdad's dog had more puppies. Can you believe that?"

"Aw. I like puppies."

"You wouldn't like them if they were wandering all over *your* house peeing everywhere."

Rae chuckled. "Okay, maybe not."

"Guess what else?" Kylee lowered her eyebrows and gave her a sly grin. "I think Seth might ask me to the prom."

"Really?" Rae snuck a glance around the cafeteria, though Seth and his friends spent as little time there as possible. "Would you say yes?"

Kylee brushed a strand of dyed pink hair out of her eyes. "Of course. He's hot."

"He's wild."

"Oh my gosh." Kylee flicked her wrist in Rae's direction. "Spare me the 'boys aren't worth the trouble' speech, okay? I happen to like boys."

Rae crunched an apple slice. "I like boys."

"I happen to like *talking* to boys."

"I talk to boys."

Kylee huffed. "Right, I suppose you must talk to them when you're helping them with their algebra-two homework or proofreading their comp. essays. But you know what I mean."

Yes, Rae knew. She had plenty of friends who were boys but had never had a boyfriend. She didn't have time. Boys weren't part of The Plan.

"Hey, Rae."

A lanky boy with coffee-colored hair landed across the table from her with a smile. She sucked in a quick breath.

"Oh, hey, David."

"What are you doing?"

Rae looked down at the remnants of her lunch. "Um . . ."

"We're eating lunch, genius." Kylee crumpled a Hostess Ding Dong wrapper into a ball and threw it at David's head. "What does it look like?"

He grinned. "Nice hair. Pink this time, huh? Going for the My Little Pony look or . . . ?"

Kylee's mouth hung open in exaggerated indignation.

"I'm kidding." David folded his hands on the table in front of him. "It looks pretty. I like it better than the blue."

Kylee ran a hand over her head. "Thanks."

David turned to Rae. "So was that Driver's Ed. you were signing up for?"

Kylee scoffed. "Were you spying on us?"

Rae kicked her under the table. "Uh, yeah. Time for me to take the leap, I guess."

David nodded. "You don't sound too excited."

"She's afraid she's going to be terrible at it." Kylee stuck out a pierced tongue and made a face.

Rae gave Kylee a look she hoped would tell her friend to knock it off. She had known David Reynolds since she was six and he was seven. Back in first grade, he'd stopped another boy from sticking gum in her hair. He'd grown up to be a "nice young man," as Grandma Kate would say. Nowhere near as hot as Seth but not a gargoyle, either.

"Driving's not so bad once you get the hang of it." David's warm brown eyes matched his hair. "If you want, I could give you some pointers."

Her mouth went dry. Potentially screwing up behind the wheel in front of Kylee, her best friend in the world? Maybe. But in front of David? Not a chance.

"Parents always *try* to teach you," he continued, "but it never works because they freak out."

She looked away. Parents freaking out was something she could relate to. "Thanks, but I've already got someone helping me."

"Besides your parents?" Kylee asked.

Rae gulped and nodded. Why had she said that?

"Oh." David shrugged. "Cool."

She shoved another apple slice in her mouth so she couldn't say anything more.

Kylee gave her a skeptical look. "Who?"

Oh, great. Kylee was practically a lie-detector machine.

Rae swallowed. "A neighbor."

Kylee narrowed her eyes but kept her mouth shut.

David hopped up from the table and gave them a mock salute and a smile. "Well, I better run. See you later."

Rae gave a halfhearted wave and began packing up what remained of her lunch. She didn't look, but she could feel Kylee's questioning eyes staring at her. The truth was she had no one to help her, and she didn't want to drive with her dad again until she was confident she could perform up to his high standards. The last thing she needed was another "you only have one future" lecture. And she wouldn't drive with Mom until she could be sure she wouldn't scare her to death. Mom had enough to worry about already.

Rae would just have to rely on the Driver's Ed. instructor.

Kylee snapped her lunch box shut and leaned her elbows on the table. "A neighbor, huh?"

"Yep."

Kylee waited, but Rae wasn't about to explain. Kylee didn't need to know everything.

Her friend stood up. "If David asked you to the prom, would you say yes?"

Rae flinched. "He can't."

Underclassmen could only attend prom if asked by an upperclassman. That was the rule. Rae, Kylee, and David were all sophomores. Seth, of course, was a senior. And he could ask any girl he wanted.

"But if he could?" Kylee persisted as Rae followed her out of the lunchroom.

Rae shrugged. "But he can't."

They stopped at Kylee's locker, where she unloaded her lunch box. "There's always next year."

Next year? By then Rae would have her license, if she passed, and she'd be two months away from becoming a senior. Prom and David Reynolds would be the last thing on her mind. They were not part of The Plan.

But he *would* look pretty cute in a tux.

CHAPTER
SIX

Gerrit drummed his fingers on the kitchen table. Daisy lay on the floor on the other side of the kitchen, refusing to come near him. Shouldn't Hannie be home by now? He checked the time. Four o'clock. When did her shop close?

"I wonder what she's planning for dinner."

Daisy's ears perked up.

"Don't get too excited. It'll be hours yet."

He rose and scanned the kitchen, searching for clues. The Crock-Pot wasn't out, no meat thawed in the sink. He went and looked in the fridge.

"It's practically empty." He held it open with one hand and pointed at Daisy with the other. "Are you seeing this?"

She saw it.

He squared his shoulders and shut the door with resolve. He would go to the grocery store and visit Hannie at the shop. And then he would—did he dare?—make dinner for her. She would love that. Women loved that, right?

Last night, as he struggled to fall asleep in his chair, he

stumbled upon a cooking show on Netflix and watched an episode. Okay, he watched three episodes. Or four. It didn't look that hard. If he could bottle-feed a calf, surely he could make fettuccine Alfredo for dinner. That was what Chef Kellan had made in episode three.

What? He couldn't sleep.

Under Daisy's watchful eye, he made a grocery list. He would use salmon for his Alfredo, because what was the point in living in the Pacific Northwest if you're not going to eat salmon? Puget Sound was only a couple of miles away. Then he would need noodles, cream, Parmesan cheese . . .

The list complete, he looked at Daisy. "I'll be right back."

She sniffed.

"What?"

She sniffed again.

He pulled the front of his shirt up to his nose. "Oh. I see."

GERRIT SAT IN his truck outside The Daisy Chain, feeling like a teenager too chicken to ring his crush's doorbell. He was a grown man, for crying out loud. He'd been married to Hannie for thirty-five years. But the thought of going in that shop made manure-scented sweat seep from his pores. This was a mistake.

He would leave, but he'd seen her catch a glimpse of him through the window. She must have. She wouldn't have had that disturbed look on her face for anyone else.

He wiped his hands on his jeans and stepped out of the truck. Though he'd showered and changed, as Daisy had so subtly suggested, he still felt dirty. How long would it take to rid himself of the farm odor? Probably not as long as it would take to rid himself of sixty-three-years' worth of farm life. He didn't know how to be anything but a farmer.

A bell above the door jangled as he entered the shop. Sweet floral aromas swirled around him, stopping him in his tracks. It smelled like a garden. It smelled like Hannie.

"Welcome to The Daisy Chain." A perky young woman stepped in front of him. "Can I help you with anything?"

He took a step back, suddenly feeling like an intruder. "No."

"I'll take care of it, Jillian." Hannie appeared beside the young woman, wearing a look he couldn't interpret. "This is, uh, my husband."

"Oh!" Jillian smiled and stuck out her hand. "Nice to meet you, Mr. Laninga."

Gerrit stared at her hand. Why was Hannie frowning like that, cheeks pinker than a calf's tongue? And had she stumbled over calling him her husband or had that been his imagination? She stood in front of him like a sentinel.

Jillian dropped her hand, and Hannie sighed. "I'm sorry, Jillian. He doesn't get out much."

He quickly stuck out his hand, but Jillian had already bounced away.

"You too," he said.

Hannie put her hands on her hips. "What are you doing here? And what are you wearing?"

He looked down. Most of his clothes had been moved to the downstairs hall closet long ago, but he'd dared enter Hannie's room—*their* room—to look for anything he'd forgotten about that might be a little . . . fresher. He'd found this shirt in the back of her—*their*—closet. He had no idea where it had come from or what its purpose had ever been, but it had a collar and no holes.

Hannie tugged at a tag still hanging from his left armpit. "I remember this shirt now. Evi bought it for you for Christmas once. It doesn't fit."

His forehead scrunched. His daughter bought him this shirt? That must have been over ten years ago.

"Well?" Hannie waited.

"It's hard to breathe in here."

Her frown deepened.

He swallowed. "I mean—"

"Did you need something?" She smoothed the front of his shirt and nudged him closer to the door. "My goodness, you're a mess. Did you burn the house down or something? Is that why you're here?"

"I'm going to make dinner."

A half smile pulled at one corner of her mouth. "So you're *planning* to burn the house down."

"Yes."

She smirked.

"I mean, no." He threw up his hands. "I have to pick up groceries."

"We're going to have to get you some new clothes if you're going to be out in public."

"Fettuccine Alfredo."

She looked over her shoulder. "It's almost time to close up the shop. I need to get back to work."

The light caught her hair so it shimmered with streaks of silver. Some of it was still the deep golden color of late-summer hay, though much of it had turned to gray when he wasn't looking. His fingers itched to touch it, but he would never.

She turned back to him and gave the door a pointed look.

He flushed and nodded. "I'll meet you at the house."

At the grocery store, he filled his cart with salmon, noodles, self-loathing, and second-guesses as he bumbled around searching for garlic salt. Why had he ever thought it would be a good idea to visit Hannie at her shop? When was the last time he'd set foot in that place? That was her world. Her domain. And even—yes, he'd admit it—her refuge. From him.

He chose the shortest checkout line and dumped his items on the belt, grumbling to himself about the price of butter. He'd never be able to make his nest egg last at $3.49 a pound for butter. And where did they get the nerve to charge so much for salmon they caught two miles away? The stiff collar of his shirt grew tighter as he neared the front of the line until he could barely breathe when his turn came.

"Hi, there." The woman at the register wore a black vest with a name tag and gave him a chipper smile. "How are you today?"

He grunted. Did he know this person? She acted like she knew him.

"Have you been enjoying the sunshine?" she asked.

"Uh . . ." He floundered. How exactly did one enjoy the sunshine?

"This salmon looks amazing." She slid each item over the scanner and into a bag with practiced movements. "I love salmon."

So much talking. All he wanted to do was go home and make dinner for his wife. Did Hannie know how much butter cost?

"Ahem." The cashier looked at him expectantly. What had she just said? "Your total's $28.75."

He flushed. "Fettuccine Alfredo."

CHAPTER
SEVEN

A strange, tight feeling gripped Gerrit's throat when he pulled up to the house and found Hannie had beat him home. He thought of the blue-and-white suitcase and braced himself.

She was waiting for him with her arms crossed when he entered the kitchen. "I got a call from Agatha. As soon as I got home."

He set the grocery bags on the counter.

"It's been one day, Gerrit." Her voice rose. "You can't stay out of trouble for one day?"

His brow furrowed. He hadn't seen Agatha in months. "I didn't talk to Agatha."

Hannie rubbed her forehead. "George is livid about the bush."

Oh. That. He let out his breath. And here he'd thought he was in trouble. George should be thankful for what he'd done. That bush was a danger to society.

He concentrated on pulling food out of the bags. "I wanted to help."

"You can't trespass on private property. What were you thinking?"

Gerrit snorted. "Technically, mailboxes belong to the federal government. They're not private property."

Hannie's nostrils flared as she watched him deposit the cold items inside the fridge. "And why is Daisy limping?"

He hid behind the open fridge door. Good thing he'd already cleaned up the blood. "I wanted to help."

"What did you do?"

"Her nails were long."

He avoided looking at Hannie as he pulled a large pot and a saucepan from the cupboard. He kept his back to her as he filled the pot with water and set it on the stove to boil.

"Was that before or after you took her for a walk?"

He could not safely answer that question. He opened the package of pasta and examined its contents carefully.

Hannie sighed behind him. "She's got special clippers. For dogs. They're in the top drawer of the dresser by the back door."

That was good to know, although Gerrit was pretty sure Daisy would run and hide if she saw him holding clippers of any kind ever again.

He dared a glance at Hannie as he pulled out the butter and caught her yawning. "You were up early."

"Every Monday and Thursday."

"I'm making dinner."

"Yes." She blinked. "I can see that."

The butter sizzled when he dropped it in the saucepan. Why had he said that? Her nearness was making him nervous. He could feel her eyes on him as if she was waiting for him to mess up. The tension in his shoulders rose with the bubbles in the pot.

She took a step back and turned away. "I'm going to work in the flower beds until it's ready."

His shoulders relaxed.

THE SAUCE WAS lumpy, the noodles mushy. Gerrit ate with his head down, occasionally sneaking a peek at Hannie's plate out of the corner of his eye. She was eating it, as far as he could tell.

"The salmon's good," she said.

He sat up straighter. "I bought the freshest package I could find."

She nodded, covering up another yawn. "I used to get it all the time. The kids loved it."

He considered mentioning they could hardly be called kids anymore but took a drink of milk instead. Evi was, what, twenty-nine? No. She was thirty! When had that happened? And Noah was twenty-seven. The milk turned sour in his stomach. When was the last time he'd seen them? Spoken to them?

"We should invite the kids over for Memorial Day weekend."

Hannie gaped. "*Our* kids?"

He swallowed. "I'll cook."

She set her fork down and opened her mouth twice before speaking. "They're very busy."

He gripped his own fork with unnecessary force, trying to picture Evi and Noah at the square wooden table, all of them eating together like they used to.

"They don't want to see me."

Hannie sighed. She sure did that a lot. "Can you blame them?"

Though her tone was gentle, the words hit him like a kick from the back hoof of a Holstein. "I did the best I could."

The muscles in her jaw tightened. "Did you?"

"It was up to me." Luke's face flashed in his mind. "I was the only one left."

Hannie stood and carried her plate over to the sink. She leaned against it, looking straight ahead out the window. He watched and waited.

Her voice sounded deflated. Resigned. "You loved your cows more than you ever loved our children."

A shock shivered up his spine. No. That wasn't true. He loved Evi and Noah more than anything. The farm just required a lot of attention. It was a relentless, demanding place. He thought they understood. But had he ever talked to them about it? Ever tried to explain?

"I'll barbecue ribs." It couldn't be as bad as Hannie seemed to think. The kids would come. "And bake a pie."

She dumped the water out of her glass and set it on the counter, then called for Daisy. "Come on, girl. Let's go sit on the deck for a while."

Gerrit watched them go, clearly not invited.

It took him hours to clean up the mess he'd made in the kitchen and scrub the noodles off the bottom of the pot. At least it felt like hours. And with each minute that passed, he thought of Evi and Noah. What did he know of them anymore? He scoured his mind for details Hannie might have shared during their brief moments together over the past year.

Evi was living in Everett, working at Boeing. But what did she do there? And was she seeing anyone? He shuddered. She was a grown woman. Who knew what she was up to in *that* department.

And Noah. Gerrit was sure Noah still lived in Seattle. He was not sure, however, whether Noah was still attending community college, because it seemed like his school status changed every time Hannie brought it up. Taking classes, taking a break. Taking classes, taking a break. That boy didn't appreciate the opportunity he had for higher education, the way he was dragging it out like he had all the time in the world.

He stalked through the living room to the back deck to take his turn. Hannie and Daisy had gone to bed. The last light of dusk tinged the horizon, and the air was cool. Soon an evening mist would climb the hill and cover his backyard. He could smell it. He looked down at the farm.

He hadn't appreciated his opportunity for higher education, either. Hadn't respected the gift he'd been given when Luke said, *"I'm not cut out for college life. Besides, you're smarter than me."* Neither of those things had been true, but regardless, Gerrit had gone to college at Luke's insistence. In Luke's place. He'd even had the audacity to believe things would be different when he returned. That his father would see him in a different light. Maybe even respect him.

It wasn't until after Luke died that Gerrit learned the college fund had not come from his father at all.

"You were such a fool, Luke." He spoke to the falling darkness and the rising mist. "Such a fool."

Back in his recliner, he squirmed in discomfort, searching for relief for his back. He hadn't set a single foot on the farm, but his body still felt like he'd spent the day wrestling cows. He clicked the TV on. A man with wiry eyebrows and spiky hair was making a lemon meringue pie. He whipped the meringue until it was so fluffy it looked as if it might float away.

"Now, how did he do that?"

Gerrit leaned forward. If he was going to impress his kids with his cooking on Memorial Day, he'd better start paying attention.

CHAPTER
EIGHT

Rae waited by Kylee's locker with a grin on her face. Kylee scowled as she walked up. "I hate it when you're perky. Especially on Monday."

Rae liked Mondays. She got a kick out of watching her classmates drag themselves around like zombies. She wasn't like that. She had purpose and determination.

Kylee pulled a book from her locker and shoved it in her backpack. "Why do you always have so much energy?"

Rae flinched as Kylee slammed her locker shut. "Rough day?"

"The usual."

Rae fell into step beside Kylee as they exited the high school. They'd been best friends since Kylee's family moved to Greenville five years ago, and Rae couldn't remember a school day Kylee hadn't been thoroughly disgusted with. Rae had the nerve to actually like school, which only made it worse. But they were both an only child and had bonded like sisters the first time they met.

"Want a ride home?" Kylee asked.

"No, thanks."

"You taking the bus?"

"No." It was Rae's last week of freedom before Driver's Ed. started. "I'm going to volunteer."

"Oh my gosh." Kylee rolled her eyes. "Not that again."

"What?"

Her friend stopped walking and faced her. "You're already a shoo-in for a scholarship to any college you want."

"There's no such thing as a shoo-in at Columbia. And that's not why I volunteer."

Kylee gave her a look.

"Okay, it's not the *only* reason I volunteer."

"Then why?"

Rae tucked her thumbs under the straps of her backpack. "I like to help people. It makes me happy."

"You're already happy. All. The. Time."

She smiled.

Kylee scoffed. "See?"

"You should come with me." Rae pointed across the street. "I'm going to check out that Community Hope thing."

"No way. I need a nap."

"Okay." Rae shrugged. "Then I guess I'll see you tomorrow."

"Fine. Bye." Kylee trudged off to find her car in the jumbled mass of vehicles parked helter-skelter around the school.

Rae watched her go for a minute. Many people had remarked over the years how strange it was that she and Kylee could be such good friends when they were so different. So mismatched. But their friendship had been forged in the loneliness of two sibling-less homes and the fact that neither of

them really fit in anywhere else, except with each other. Rae
didn't always understand Kylee, but she never doubted Kylee
would be there for her.

She dodged careless teen drivers and weary school-bus drivers and crossed the street. She'd always found it paradoxical
the high school was located on Fallow Drive. No one else ever
appreciated the irony.

She studied the unassuming brown building as she approached it. Greenville Community Church. *All Are Welcome Here*, a white sign with black letters said. Her family
had attended a church across town a couple of times when
she was younger, but they hadn't been there in years. Dad
said he was too busy. Mom said she wouldn't go without
Dad.

The same Community Hope poster she'd seen on the bulletin board at school was taped to the glass front door. At the
bottom, someone had written *Room F* in black Sharpie. She
entered the building and looked around. While she couldn't
see Room F, the low din of voices pointed the way.

The door to Room F was propped open, and she paused
in the hall to peer inside. At least two dozen kids filled the
space, along with three adults. One man and two women.

The man spotted her and waved. "Come on in."

A couple of kids glanced at her as she walked in, but most
of them paid her no mind. A basket of snacks sat at the end
of one table next to a cooler of bottled water and Gatorade.

The man walked over to her with a smile, a clipboard in
hand. He was one of those hipster types with skinny jeans and
a beard, and he was obviously the guy in charge. "Welcome.
I'm Mark. What's your name?"

"Rae Walters."

He checked the list on his clipboard. "I don't see your name here, Rae. Were you referred by one of your teachers?"

"No." She slid her backpack off and dug around inside it. "I want to volunteer."

She pulled the Volunteer Information Sheet she'd printed off the internet from her bag and held it out.

"Cool. We need all the help we can get." Mark took the paper from her hand and skimmed it over. "Looks like you filled everything out. This is impressive."

She lifted one shoulder. The sheet had all the standard questions on it—name, address, birth date, and school information—but it also had questions about previous volunteer experience and why the applicant was interested in the Community Hope program. She'd felt a little weird listing all the random places she'd helped out before, like she was trying to show off or something.

Mark added her paper to the pile on his clipboard. "You've got a lot of volunteer hours racked up already. You going for an award at school or something?"

She raised an eyebrow at his red flannel shirt. "You going for the lumberjack look or something?"

He gave her a dimpled grin. "I have just the job for you."

RAE TAPPED THE open math book with her pencil. "You still have five more problems, Taylor. Come on, you're running out of time."

The petite girl with mousy brown hair wrinkled her nose. "I don't care."

"You'll care when you fail math and have to repeat seventh grade."

Taylor scoffed. "That doesn't really happen."

"Yes it does." Rae scooted her chair closer. "Now, let's go. Number seventeen. Write it down."

"Fine." Taylor gave an exaggerated sigh. "But only so you'll shut up."

She looked like an ordinary shy middle schooler on the outside, but Rae had discovered in the past hour that Taylor was unlike anyone she'd ever met. She reminded Rae of a woman she used to know at the nursing home named Betty who would cheat at cards and then blame Rae.

Before introducing them, Mark had hinted that Taylor's family life was less than ideal. Based on the language she'd heard from the thirteen-year-old's mouth, Rae could only imagine what that meant.

Taylor scrunched her lips to one side as she concentrated, and Rae glanced around the room. More kids had arrived after her, but none were volunteers. As far as she could tell, only the three adults, Rae, and one other student she knew was a senior at her school were there to help the kids referred by teachers for extra help. It wasn't near enough to give everyone the attention they needed.

A kid about her age sat as far into the corner as possible with his back to the room. His stringy black hair fell in his face as he hunched over his work. Something about his posture, about the way he focused on whatever was in front of him as if it were the cure for cancer, tugged at her heart. What was his story?

"One more minute," Mark called out. "Wrap it up, guys."

Rae felt Taylor flinch beside her. The girl whose feistiness had known no bounds only moments before tossed her pencil on the table and slumped in her chair.

"What are you doing?" Rae picked the pencil up and held it out to Taylor. "You're almost finished. Let's do the last problem."

Taylor stared at the math book. "Why?"

"Because." Rae waved the pencil under her nose. "Don't you want to complete your assignment?"

Taylor grabbed the pencil and snapped it in half.

Rae nodded once. "Okay then."

"Time's up." Mark positioned himself by the door and pointed with his clipboard. "You don't have to go home, but you can't stay here."

Students groaned as they shoved books and papers into backpacks. They nabbed snacks from the basket on their way to the door so that there was nothing left on the table by the time they filed out. The kid with the black hair kept his head down as he slipped out of the room without a word.

Rae hung back, waiting for all the referred kids to leave before approaching Mark. "More volunteers are coming, right?"

He combed his fingers through his scruffy beard. "Here? Probably not."

"But we need more help."

"Tell me about it." He held the door open for the two women volunteers and gestured for Rae to go ahead of him. "We had twice as many kids this week as last. And more will probably come as the word gets out that we have food."

She stepped into the hallway. "You're going to have to do something about it."

He locked up Room F and walked with Rae toward the front door. "What do you suggest, Miss Volunteer of the Year?"

She felt her face flush. "I don't know. That's your job, isn't it?"

"Not my *job*, per se. I'm a volunteer, too."

Oh. She looked at him out of the corner of her eye with new appreciation. He was kind of old, like thirty at least, so he had to be out of school. But he still volunteered? That was pretty cool.

Wait. She knew how this worked. Dad was a lawyer, after all.

"You have some court-ordered community service hours to complete?"

He laughed. "Nope. I just like helping people."

The words sifted down into her gut and stung a little. She'd said the same thing to Kylee. And she'd meant it, hadn't she? But when Mark said it . . . well, it seemed different.

She stepped outside and saw several of the kids from the program milling around the parking lot. "Do you have to wait with them until their parents come?"

Mark gave her a look that made her feel like a little kid. "Their parents don't come. Most of them probably don't even know their kids are here."

She kicked at a rock. "So do they walk home?"

"I'm not sure. I always offer rides, but most of them put off going home for as long as possible. I think some of them don't want me to see where they live."

"Oh."

Rae lived in the nice part of town. In the biggest house on the block. And she could be anywhere at any time, and all she'd have to do was send a quick text, and her mom would come for her. In fact, her mom always knew exactly where she was.

A Ford Explorer pulled into the parking lot as if to prove the truth of what she'd been thinking, and Rae suddenly felt embarrassed. "There's my mom. I—I'll be back Wednesday."

"Look, Rae." Mark gave her shoulder a gentle punch. "Volunteers are hard to come by. If you have any brilliant ideas about recruiting more, let me know."

She nodded and slipped into the passenger seat of the Explorer.

Mom gave her a big smile. "Hi, sweetie. How was your day?"

Rae looked at the other kids through the window. Almost invisible in the shadows behind the building, the boy with the black hair leaned against the church, hands in his pockets. Alone.

Rae pulled on her seat belt. "Better than I thought."

CHAPTER
NINE

Gerrit peered through a gap in the curtains of the dining room window. Daisy sat at his feet and gave him a dubious look.

"What?" he whispered. "He doesn't need to know I'm home. It's none of his business."

The postal truck appeared, and Gerrit checked his watch. 1:42. He had learned the mail was delivered between one-thirty and two every afternoon. He had also learned Hannie didn't appreciate his opening mail with her name on it. It had been a mistake, but one he would surely never make again. When the truck drove away, he sprang into action.

Daisy jumped up from the floor to follow him outside.

"You don't need to come."

She wagged her undocked tail. Hannie had insisted the breeder leave the tail alone when she was born, not caring whether Daisy ever met the AKC standard.

"I'm only getting the mail."

Daisy barked.

"Fine." Gerrit opened the door and let her out ahead of him with a grand gesture. "After you. But this counts as your walk."

He strode purposefully to the end of the drive, pleased with the crisp, fresh air and the daffodils and tulips leaping to life around him. Not to mention the rhododendrons. After spending the majority of the day indoors watching cooking shows and scraping the seal around the downstairs bathtub so he could recaulk it, the outdoors put a spring in his step. Hadn't he spent most of his life in the open air? It's where man was meant to be.

As he passed the barn, Daisy by his side, a vague memory sharpened into focus. He was agile and unwrinkled. He held two-year-old Noah's hand on one side and Evi's on the other. She made up a song as she skipped beside him.

"Daddy and me on a walk, walk, walk. Checking for mail in the box, box, box."

He grinned at her and lifted her from the ground with one arm.

She squealed in delight. *"When's the pony barn gonna be done, Daddy?"*

He set her back on the ground. *"Uncle Luke's coming this weekend. We'll finish it then."*

"Then we can get a pony and play in it all the time?" Her eyes were big and bright and full of hope and faith.

"Yes. All the time."

The memory faded. His time-ravaged, worn body returned. He had never played in the barn with Evi. And they'd never gotten that pony.

He slowed his steps. He had time to play now, but it was too late. Evi was all grown. And Noah. There had been a time when Gerrit hoped Noah would take over the farm one day. Follow in his footsteps.

That would never happen now.

He reached the box and pulled a small stack of mail from inside, remembering a movie trailer he'd seen during the commercial breaks on the cooking channel this morning. It was for a movie about a man who discovers a fantasy world inside his mailbox. Huh. He might want to see that movie. When was the last time he'd gone to the theater?

He turned to head back to the house and froze. Wait a minute. He looked down. Something was wrong.

The end of the drive had a strange ridge of gravel scattered with trash that hadn't been there the day before. What had happened here? Daisy looked up at him with a question in her liquid brown eyes, and he drummed his chin with his fingers. It was almost as if someone had raked all the dirt, gravel, and litter from the road and the ditch into a pile at the end of his driveway. But who would—?

His hand clenched into a fist.

George.

Unbelievable.

He picked up an insect-infested beer can and hurled it in the direction of his scoundrel neighbor's house.

George would pay for this.

GERRIT STRUTTED AROUND the kitchen as he put the finishing touches on the broiled pork chops with rosemary beans and potatoes and biscuits made from scratch. He had outdone himself this time, he was sure.

The back door banged, and Hannie called from the mud-room. "Smells good."

Daisy sprinted to meet her mistress, grinning from ear to ear.

Gerrit rushed to set the table. "It's almost ready."

Tomorrow was Thursday. If Hannie had to go to bed early on Wednesday nights in preparation for Thursday morning deliveries, the least he could do was have dinner ready on time.

Hannie swept into the kitchen, Daisy at her heels. "I'm starving."

He eyed the pork chops warily as he set them on the table, a pinch of dread biting his chest. It was easy to overcook pork to the point of dryness. Hadn't that guy on TV said so at least a dozen times? Gerrit gave the chops the same look he used to give the kids when they were little that said, *Don't even think about it.*

Hannie set her purse on the counter and knelt beside Daisy to give her a good scratch behind the ears. "It looks great. Biscuits are my favorite."

His palms began to sweat. He had been gun-shy about tak-ing any risks with dinner after the fettuccine Alfredo—opting for the safety of grilled-cheese sandwiches and tomato soup, chicken Caesar salad, and the like—but tonight was a big night. It had been one week since he signed the farm papers. One week since he became a free man. He needed to convince himself that was something to celebrate. And he needed to talk with Hannie about Memorial Day.

They sat at the table in silence, and he waited with anticipa-tion as Hannie took a bite of her meat. He held his breath. She chewed. Her expression was inscrutable. He waited.

She was not going to comment.

He quickly cut a bite of pork from the outer edge of his chop and ate it. It was . . . fine. Not amazing, but not dried out. Definitely passable. His shoulders relaxed. It wasn't a disaster.

If he was waiting for a good omen, this was the best he was likely to get. He cut a potato, studying it as if it were the most interesting spud he'd ever seen. "So have you talked to the kids yet?"

After a long moment with no response, he looked up.

Hannie swallowed. "About what?"

"Memorial Day weekend. Are they coming?"

She chose a biscuit from the tray and admired it. "I didn't think you meant it."

He speared a bean. Of course he'd meant it. Why would he have brought it up if he hadn't meant it?

"I'm not sure it's such a good idea." She buttered the biscuit with deliberate movements. "And they probably already have plans."

"But I'm going to barbecue ribs."

She sighed. "Look, honey, I'm not sure how to tell you this."

He narrowed his eyes. "What?"

"Evi's a vegetarian now."

He sat back in his chair, hard. It couldn't be. She loved meat. Hamburgers, buffalo wings, rump roast. Pulled pork.

"How could—when did—I can't—"

"Don't take it personally."

His fork dropped to the table. It was beyond all comprehension. He hadn't worked—*slaved*—on that thankless piece of land for sixty-three years so his own daughter could shun the very animal that had put food on their table her entire life. How could he not take it personally?

"She still eats fish." Hannie waved her biscuit in the air. "Sometimes."

Gerrit didn't know what that meant. Couldn't process it. "Does she still drink milk?"

Hannie studied the table. "Almond milk."

He threw up his hands. "You've got to be kidding me."

"Like I said." Hannie brought the biscuit to her lips. "I don't think Memorial Day's a good idea."

He helplessly watched her bite into the biscuit. Evi must hate him more than he figured.

Hannie's face twisted for a second as she chewed her biscuit, then smoothed back into place. Uh-oh. Gerrit snatched a biscuit from the tray and took a big bite, the pinch of dread in his chest a fistful now. Fresh biscuits were one of Hannie's most beloved foods. He had counted on them being his ace in the hole.

He spit the bite out. "It tastes like cardboard."

Hannie set her biscuit down with a disappointed sigh and folded her hands on the table in front of her. "I think you forgot the salt."

His ace had turned into a joker. He retraced his steps in his mind, trying to recall the biscuit recipe and what ingredients he'd used. Yes, it had called for salt, but only half a teaspoon.

"How much difference could that little bit make?"

The crow's feet around Hannie's eyes appeared. "Sometimes it's the little things that make the biggest difference."

She wasn't talking about biscuits anymore. He knew that much. But what exactly she meant was not something he was willing to consider.

CHAPTER
TEN

Rae looked up from her laptop as her dad entered the kitchen. He was usually deep into *The Wall Street Journal* by this time of night. She glanced over at her mom, who was scouring a pot at the sink. Mom caught her eye and gave an almost imperceptible shrug.

Dad sat down across from Rae. "What are you working on?"

She sat back in her chair. "Just an essay for comp. class. Nothing major."

"Every assignment is major, Rae." Dad leaned his elbows on the table and gave her an intent look. "Every grade matters."

"I know." She shifted. "I just meant it's easy. Only three pages."

"Make it five."

Mom tossed her dishrag on the counter with a thwack. "Give her a break, Wade. It's one assignment."

Dad threw up his hands. "I just think it's time to start taking her future more seriously, that's all. She's almost sixteen."

"I think we take it seriously enough."

"I'm not sure we all do." He gave Mom a pointed look.

Mom narrowed her eyes. "What's that supposed to mean?"

Rae looked back and forth between them and forced a smile. "I can make it five. No problem."

Mom shook her head. "You don't have to do that, sweetie."

"I want to."

Dad stood with a nod. "That's my girl."

As he left the kitchen, Rae watched Mom from the corner of her eye. Dad had always been a little on the demanding side, yet it wasn't like her parents to talk like that in front of her. Mom's face as she turned back to the sink seemed pensive. Like she wasn't sure what to make of it, either. Like something Rae couldn't see had changed and the conversation wasn't over.

Rae squirmed.

GERRIT SHIFTED ON his feet. "What are you looking at me for?"

Daisy inched closer with a whine.

"I said come on." Hannie put her hands on her hips. "Time for bed."

Daisy turned her back on Hannie. Hannie blanched.

Gerrit winced. "I think she knows I'm going"—his voice dropped to a whisper—"outside."

The stout corgi's ears perked up at the magic word.

Hannie smirked. "Well, she certainly does now."

"Go with your mom." He shooed Daisy with his hands. "Up the stairs with you."

Daisy didn't budge. He nudged her with his foot.

Nothing.

He knew how to get a cow moving when it didn't want to,

but he didn't think that strategy would work here. Especially not with Hannie watching. He pled with Daisy to go with his eyes.

Hannie's shoulders drooped. "Okay. I can't blame her for wanting to play outside. It's a nice evening. But I need to get to bed."

Gerrit was afraid to move. Afraid to keep encouraging the dumb dog to go, in case she didn't. Afraid to let it appear he was fine with her staying, in case Hannie believed that. So he stood there like a fool as Hannie ascended the steps. As she rounded the corner at the top, he lifted a hand.

"Good night."

He thought he heard a muffled "good night" in response, but it might have been "yeah, right." He knew which was more likely.

He turned on Daisy. "This is all your fault."

Daisy smiled and took a step toward the door as if they'd been planning this all along. Great. She thought they were in cahoots.

"I don't like it." He pointed a finger at her. "You better not get mixed up in anything out there."

He pulled on his boots and unrolled the sleeves of his flannel shirt, buttoning them at the cuffs. Then he stepped outside. Hannie was right. It was a nice night. The heady smell of spring was in the air, and a hint of gold remained on the horizon. He could even hear the lowing of Holsteins as he closed the door behind him. If only the language Hannie spoke was as easy to understand.

Daisy took off at a trot toward the pony barn. Why did he still call it that? He shoved his hands in his pockets as he stared at the structure, his brother's face flickering through his mind. Luke had been gone almost twenty-five years now.

Gerrit started walking, his boots crunch-crunching across the gravel drive. Maybe Luke had been the lucky one. He had died young enough to be immortalized in fond memories. Young enough that he'd never struggled to get the work done, never doubted his purpose. He died forever strong and ambitious.

Gerrit stopped, watching Daisy sniff at the door of the barn. He'd spent the past twenty-five years trying to fill Luke's shoes, trying to carry the torch—and for what? To hand the farm over to an opportunistic interloper without a drop of Dutch blood. His father would turn over in his grave. Not that he'd worked his life away on the farm for *him*.

Daisy's sniffing became more intent, and a low growl warmed the air.

Gerrit tensed. "What're you doing?"

His voice stabbed the falling night like a pitchfork through hay. Daisy's growl intensified. The hair on Gerrit's neck stood at attention.

Something—or some*one*—was in the barn.

DESPITE HIS UNWIELDY girth, Mr. Whiskers leapt into Rae's arms with the agility of a feline half his age. She clutched him to her chest and slid deeper into the shadows, her heart pounding.

A tall man with broad shoulders appeared in the doorway of the barn with a shovel in his hand. "Who's there?"

Rae froze in stunned silence. This was her special place. Her refuge. The only place on earth she had no pressures or expectations hanging over her head and no parents to worry about. An overwhelming sense of being violated washed over her.

Mr. Whiskers squirmed as a dog ran up to them barking. The man raised the shovel with one hand. "Come on out."

A spark of indignation lit in her chest. She wasn't a criminal. Maybe technically this barn belonged to someone, but it had obviously been abandoned for years. She's the one who'd spent hours tidying it up. And in the three years she'd been coming here, she'd never seen this man. Occasionally, she'd glimpsed a woman in the buttercup-colored house in the evening, sitting alone, but no one had ever come near the barn. Never given it so much as a passing glance, as far as she could tell.

She took a step forward, buoyed by righteous indignation. "What do you think you're doing?"

The man swung his other hand above his head until it connected with a ratty old string hanging from the rafters. He pulled the cobwebbed cord, and a bare bulb clicked on in the middle of the barn. She flinched at the sudden bright light.

"How did you get in here?" The man's face appeared as astonished as she felt.

"You look upset."

His nostrils flared. "Of course I'm upset. I just found a stranger trespassing on my property. You're lucky I didn't take your head off with this shovel."

The dog stopped barking but remained vigilant. It was cute the way it acted tough. Mr. Whiskers yowled.

She patted his back. "You're scaring my cat."

The man's eyes bulged. His mouth opened and closed. He leaned the shovel against the wall with a thunk and looked around the barn.

"Did you move all this stuff around?"

He didn't sound pleased. She nodded reluctantly. "I like your dog."

"It's not mine."

"Sure looks like yours. What's his name?"

The man shook his head. "What are you doing in here, kid?"

She took a long, slow breath, buying time. He didn't need to know how long she'd been coming here. Didn't need to know she fled to the quiet solitude of this barn as often as she could, trying to escape the relentless forward progress of her life.

She shrugged. "Just thinking."

He scowled. "You can't think on your own property?"

She wrinkled her nose. He would never understand. Sometimes she got tired of people watching her every move, waiting for her to slip up. Tired of Dad's unending ideas about her future. "I'm sorry, I didn't think anyone—"

"Owned this barn?"

"—cared about this place."

The man took a step back, like someone had struck him. Something in her stomach twinged. She didn't know why or how, but an invisible line had been crossed. The concluding words of Edna St. Vincent Millay's "Bluebeard" poem rang in her mind: *This now is yours. I seek another place.* Her secret hideout had been trespassed upon, and yet something told her she had unwittingly committed an even greater offense than intrusion.

The barn was special to this man, too. Whoever he was.

She shifted so that Mr. Whiskers lay cradled in her arms like a baby. "You live here?"

"Of course." He threw his hands up in disgust. "Why else would I be here?"

"I've never seen you before."

His eyebrows shot up. "You've been here before?"

Oops. She searched for a way to answer that question without causing more trouble but came up empty. Instead, she jerked her chin toward the door. "I guess I'll be going."

The man stepped aside so she could pass. "Don't get any ideas about coming back."

She paused with her back to him, her heart sinking. No other haven would ever be as good as this. But it had been nice while it lasted.

She sighed. "Okay."

The dog trotted behind her, smiling now as if they'd been friends all along. She stepped onto the gravel drive and turned to go behind the barn, where the shortcut trail was hidden.

The man called out, "It's a she."

Rae stopped. "What?"

"The dog. Daisy. It's a she."

"Oh." Rae knelt beside Daisy to pat her on the head. "Good girl."

Daisy licked Rae's hand and sniffed Mr. Whiskers's rear end, much to the cat's dismay.

Rae laughed. "She's just saying hello."

She sensed the man close-by, watching, but was afraid to look at him. He was old and seemed harmless, but something about him was a little frightening. Intense. She stood and turned to go again.

The man cleared his throat. "Why'd you really come here?"

She hesitated. She'd never told anyone about this place. Not even Kylee. But the man's voice demanded the truth.

"It's peaceful." She slowly spun to face him. "For some reason, whenever I'm in the barn, I feel safe. And happy. Like that's what it was made for, to make people happy."

And when she was inside, she could be herself. She didn't have to be the best. Didn't have to have all the answers.

"I didn't mean any harm."

It was dark. The light from inside the barn shone on the man's back, shrouding his face in shadow. She strained to see whether he was still angry.

He crossed his arms. "You take that cat everywhere?"

She half smiled. "Not to school."

The air had cooled considerably since she first arrived, but Mr. Whiskers was like a heating pad in her arms. He nestled against her, his confidence apparently restored now that he was out of Daisy's reach. Rae took one last longing look at the barn and exhaled sharply. She was sure going to miss it.

The man grunted and muttered something.

"Pardon me?" Rae asked.

"I said I guess it's okay if you use it." He waved an arm at the barn. "It's just sitting there, after all."

Rae suppressed a squeal. "Really?"

His arms hung at his sides. He didn't seem so intimidating anymore. "Just for now. But you've got to stop moving stuff around."

She bounced with delight. "I promise I won't touch anything."

He pressed a button on his watch and it lit up. "Don't you have school tomorrow?"

It couldn't be later than nine o'clock. She stifled a grin. "Yes."

He waited expectantly. "Well? It's late. Go on now."

"Right." She patted Daisy again on the head, then gave the man a salute. "See you later. And thanks."

She slipped around the barn before he could change his

mind. If she was careful, he would never even know she was there. She wouldn't give him any reason to rescind his offer.

Once she was well into the trees, she paused and looked back. In the dark, there was no way the man could see her, but she could see him. He had turned off the light in the barn and now stood by the back door of the house, one hand on the doorknob. Daisy stood beside him, looking up at his face.

Rae waited. What was he doing? A minute marched by. He raised his chin and looked at the upstairs window above the door, then hung his head. Even from fifty feet away, the weight on his shoulders was visible.

Where had he come from? Was he married to the woman with the blond hair who sat at the table alone? Why had Rae never seen him before?

"He looks sad."

Mr. Whiskers meowed.

"Shh. Let's go home."

The trail back to her neighborhood was black as pitch, but Rae knew it by heart. With every step she took closer to her house, the weight on her own shoulders grew. She was worried and scared about driving. That was true. But it was more than that. Something was going on with her parents. And something else had been bothering her more and more lately.

She knew where she was headed. The Plan was set. And everyone else in her life knew who she was and what she should do and how her future would turn out.

But what if she failed?

"God's got big plans for you," Papa Tom always used to say.

She reached her house and stole quietly into the garage. Mr. Whiskers fought to get down so she set him gently on his feet.

"What if He doesn't, Mister?"

The old cat rubbed against her legs, his fur the color of thunderclouds in the dim light.

"What if He's just got regular, ordinary plans for me?"

No. She couldn't think like that. Couldn't let Papa Tom down—the late, great Judge McDaniel.

Her throat tightened. She missed him. Missed the way he used to tug on her ear with a smile and say, *"I'm praying for you,"* even though she had no idea why he did that. Why he thought God had some kind of special purpose for her.

She just added it to the list of expectations she needed to meet. *"God's got big plans for you."* How do you live up to that? Somehow she would find a way. She thought of her parents' standoff in the kitchen earlier and drew a determined breath. Yes, she would find a way.

Mr. Whiskers pawed at the door as if he suddenly remembered his food dish. She put her hand on the doorknob and pasted on a smile. She didn't know how, but she would do it. For Mom and Dad. For Papa Tom.

"Okay, Mister." She twisted the knob. "Time to shine."

CHAPTER
ELEVEN

Friday morning was dreary and wet. Gerrit could feel the damp chill in his aching bones.

He looked out the window and frowned. "Don't forget your umbrella."

Hannie rinsed her coffee mug in the sink. "My coat has a hood."

Gerrit scoffed to himself. A hood could not compete with an umbrella for protection from the rain. She should keep an umbrella in her car at all times, in fact. He wanted to tell her so. The resolute look on her face as she punched her arms through the sleeves of her jacket and flipped the hood over her head dared him to tell her so.

He did not dare.

"About Memorial Day . . ."

She tensed. "You are welcome to call the kids and ask them about it if you like."

It was the same overly polite tone of voice she used when someone from the shop called her after work hours. He wasn't the sharpest tool in the shed, but he was smart enough not to engage in that particular conversation.

"Maybe we can go see a movie tonight." Surely this was a safer topic. "You know that one about the mailbox?"

She finished lacing up her shoes and stood to face him. "What?"

He swallowed hard. "That mailbox movie . . ."

Her crow's feet appeared. "You want to go to a movie."

It wasn't a question, he knew that, yet her tone was indecipherable. She looked at him like he'd spoken Chinese. What did she have against the movies?

"It looks funny."

She took a long moment to answer. "I'll probably be home pretty late. I've got a gal out sick right now."

He leaned against the wall, trying to act casual. "Oh. Okay."

She threw the strap of her purse over her shoulder. "Is that the one with that Steven Douglas guy in it?"

He blinked. Who the heck was Steven Douglas? Aside from Clint Eastwood, Gerrit probably couldn't name a single actor. But the mailbox movie did have a guy in it. He could easily be named Steven. "Um . . ."

"That guy's annoying." She opened the door and stepped into the rain. "See you tonight."

Then she was gone.

Gerrit stared at the closed door for a minute or two. Did that mean she didn't want to see the movie? The idea of going to the theater alone made his chest hurt.

Daisy grew impatient and wagged her tail for attention. It thumped against the blue-and-white suitcase propped against the wall. He ought to throw the stupid thing in the garbage, but he couldn't touch it. He had no right. Daisy eyed the suitcase and rammed the top of her head against his leg.

He looked at the suitcase. Looked at the dog. "I don't want to hear it."

Well, she certainly hadn't meant anything by it, if you could believe the innocent look on her face. Which he didn't.

Back in the kitchen, he paused in front of the calendar hanging next to the fridge. April 12. He jabbed the calendar with his finger and counted. *One, two.* Flipped to May and continued. *Three, four, five, six.* Six weeks until Memorial Day weekend.

Hannie had not talked to Evi and Noah about coming, and he couldn't blame her. She'd been busy with work, and the kids might not believe her if she told them it was his idea. Maybe calling them himself was the answer, after all. But what would he say? Would they even answer the phone if they saw his number?

Only six weeks. Plenty of time to plan a feast, but was it enough time to convince his children to give him the time of day? Luke had always been good with kids. Knew how to talk to them, even when they were little. He'd been a good farmer and a good man, and he would've been a great father.

Gerrit needed to check in on Luisa. He had a responsibility to make sure she was okay. She and Luke had never had the chance to have children.

That was Gerrit's fault.

He looked again at the calendar, the muscles in his neck tightening. "I can't call them. They hate me."

His words rippled through the empty house.

"Come on, Daisy." His voice was gruff and lost and sounded like the past. "Let's see what's on TV."

THE MAIL ARRIVED at 1:51. Gerrit studied the sky with the practiced eye of a farmer. The rain had downgraded to a drizzle.

He hobbled to the back door like a ninety-year-old man, his back stiff and painful. He'd hoped it would get better once he wasn't working every day, but the opposite seemed to be true. What on earth had he retired for, then? He thought of the cows, the hay, the fields. The smell of iodine on udders and sawdust in pens. He had labored alongside hundreds of pregnant heifers, grunting his approval each time a calf slid headfirst into the world like it was supposed to, but all that life . . . well, he wasn't sure how much it meant anymore. What kind of life did he have now?

He opened the back door and stuck his hand out to test the dismal gray sky, then turned to his canine shadow. "Might be as good as it gets today."

Daisy took a step back.

Gerrit gaped. "Are you kidding me? It's just a little water. Get over here."

The furry creature refused.

"What's wrong with you?" He wasn't above the shaming approach. "Your mother doesn't mind the rain. She didn't even take an umbrella."

At the word *umbrella*, Daisy perked up. Harrumph. As if she knew what an umbrella was.

She pranced over to the low dresser next to the coatrack and nudged the top drawer with her nose. Gerrit harrumphed again. He knew the umbrella was in there, but there was no way *she* knew that.

He threw on his coat and glared at her. "Fine. You can stay here."

She whined at the drawer.

"No. It's just the mailbox. We don't need an umbrella. It's hardly even raining anymore."

Her eyes grew bigger as she waited.

"I said no."

It required a certain amount of balance to hold the umbrella over the dog and not break his stride, but by the time they reached the end of the drive, Gerrit had gotten the hang of it. He opened the mailbox and blew out a huff at the three pieces of junk mail.

"What a waste."

He tucked the mail in his coat pocket, repositioned the umbrella over Daisy, and turned to go back.

A voice stopped him. "Did you already give her a shampoo and shine this morning?"

Gerrit tensed and looked over at George's place. "What are you talking about?"

George leaned on the fence between their properties and smirked. "Is that why she can't get rained on?"

Gerrit's eyes narrowed. He would not be cowed. Instead, he held his head high. "She prefers to remain dry."

George laughed. "I didn't know she was such a princess."

Gerrit happened to believe it was rather ridiculous himself, yet he was loath to let on in front of George. The tips of his ears burned as he glanced up at the red-and-white polka-dotted umbrella, grasping for the last remaining fragment of his dignity. He turned up his nose and took a step toward the house, but George wasn't finished.

"The gravel in your drive sure looks nice. Don't know how you keep it so clean and smooth."

The blood in Gerrit's veins warmed considerably. What

nerve, bringing that up. George's payback would need to be soon.

"Same way you keep your bushes trimmed, I guess."

The smile on George's face never wavered. "How's retirement treating you, by the way? You keeping busy? Other than dog sitting, I mean."

"Yes. There's plenty to do." Gerrit shifted on his feet, his blood cooling in a hurry. "And I'm, uh, planning a big party."

"Oh?"

Why had he said that? "For Memorial Day weekend."

"I see." George folded his arms. "Evi and Noah coming and everything?"

He did not like hearing their names launching from George's lips in such a familiar way. Still, he gave a hesitant nod. Surely they would come.

"Well, that's real nice." George pushed off the fence. "And Jakob?"

Gerrit stiffened. It was a low blow, bringing up his brother. Especially when Gerrit had spent the last couple of weeks trying to forget he even existed. Trying not to imagine him walking around Greenville with fistfuls of Gerrit's hard-earned money. "No."

"I see."

"No," Gerrit growled. "You don't."

"I suppose you heard about Mallory?" George raised his eyebrows.

What? Gerrit scoured his mind for a clue about what he was supposed to have heard about George's daughter. Hannie talked about her sometimes. She was the same age as Evi. But he didn't know anything else.

He shrugged.

"I'm going to be a grandpa in June." George grinned pointedly at Daisy. "To a child, not a puppy. Don't that beat all?"

Gerrit's blood now turned from cool to glacial. The word *grandpa* was like a heavy chunk of ice falling from the sky and pinning him to the ground. Would he be a grandpa someday? Even if Evi or Noah did have kids at some point, they probably wouldn't want his influence in their lives. Him? A grandpa? His heart turned inside out, exposed.

"Con—uh—congratulations," he stammered.

"Thanks, neighbor." George turned and began strutting back to his house, calling over his shoulder, "Keep up the good work with that puppy."

Gerrit's grip on the umbrella tightened. His blood was warm again. Boiling, in fact. But he would not dignify George's remark with a response. And any halfway intelligent person could see that Daisy was not a puppy. She was almost ten years old, for crying out loud.

He began walking back to the house, head down, plotting his next move. George needed to be put in his place. Taught a lesson. But how?

Daisy barked, and Gerrit jerked to a stop. "What is it?"

She appeared to be looking at the pony barn.

"Yes, we had a bit of an adventure out there the other night, didn't we?"

He considered the barn for a moment. He never should've caved on giving that girl permission to come back here. He checked his watch. 2:19. She wouldn't be out of school already, would she?

Not that he cared or anything. Made no difference to him. But maybe he should check in the barn and make sure she hadn't caused any damage. He hadn't had a good chance to look around the night he found her in there.

He changed course and headed toward the barn. He was *not* interested in finding out if the girl had been back. Definitely not. He just wanted to make sure he hadn't unintentionally allowed a vandal to return to his property, that's all.

It was dark and quiet inside the barn. Good. No one was here. He didn't have time to deal with some kid, anyway. He had a lot of other—uh—*important* things to do.

Daisy sat as he searched for the pull-cord in the dim light and tugged on it, illuminating a large square room filled with boxes. The girl must have stacked them like that, because when he threw them in here all those years ago, he certainly hadn't put them in neat piles. Unless Hannie had done it, though he doubted she would come in this place. There was enough baggage thudding around in their house without adding these boxes to it.

Speaking of their house, he should head back.

But . . .

Each step he took deeper into the barn felt like an affront to the sacredness of what could've been. What could never be. He stopped beside the shortest stack of boxes and rested his hand on the top. The box read *Luke, High School* in hurried black letters. Had he written that? Or Luisa? That whole month was a blur. A hazy, swirling nightmare.

The cardboard seemed to heat up under his fingertips as memories turned up the dial on the anger always simmering in his heart. He'd taken all the blame for Luke's death. Bore all the burden. Made all the arrangements and taken on all the work Luke's absence left behind. And Jakob had shown up drunk to the funeral. Gerrit had wanted to lay him out, and he'd been mad enough to do it, but Hannie had known his thoughts and held his hand.

Had their father been upset at Jakob for his disrespect? No. No, he'd put his arm around Jakob's shoulders and then turned to Gerrit and criticized him for failing to convince Luisa to have an open casket.

"So we could say good-bye," he'd said.

The box grew warmer. Part of him longed to open it and drown himself in the past. Destroy himself with it. But a greater part of him resisted. He shouldn't even be in here.

His finger traced Luke's name, and he thought about what George had said about being a grandpa. Evi and Noah hardly knew what a grandpa was. Hannie's father had died before Evi and Noah were born, and his own father? He'd been a dead man walking for decades until five years ago, when he collapsed from an aneurysm in the milking parlor and made it official. Right in the middle of cussing out a stubborn heifer.

Almost against his will, Gerrit's hand pulled his cell phone from the pocket of his jacket. It was the old flip-style variety. No smartphone for him. Hannie had programmed in all their family's important phone numbers. He pushed a couple of buttons, and there was Evi's name on the screen.

The air in the barn grew oppressive. She wouldn't want to talk to him. But it was only six weeks until Memorial Day.

He pushed the call button and jumped when the phone began to ring.

And ring.

"Hello?"

Her voice was bright and eager, full of hope.

His heart constricted. "Evi? Is that you?"

Silence.

"Dad?" The eagerness was gone. The hope deflated. "I—uh, didn't recognize this number. I thought it was someone else."

"Oh." He cleared his throat. "Well, how are you?"

"Fine, Dad." An edge crept into her tone. "What do you want? Is Mom okay?"

A sour taste filled his mouth. This girl—*woman*—was a stranger. He forced the words out. "Can you come for a visit? Memorial Day weekend?" After a long, painful moment, he tried again. "I'm going to try this spicy marinade and barbecue—"

"I'm a vegetarian, Dad."

He slapped himself on the forehead. What an idiot. He had forgotten.

"Look, I gotta go." She sounded distant now. He was losing her.

"Evi, wait."

"I'm pretty busy with work right now. Might not have time for a family gathering. You of all people should be able to understand that."

The words hit their mark. His lungs fought for air. "Evi . . ."

"Bye, Dad."

Click.

He let his hand drop from his ear and hang at his side, clutching the phone. What had he expected? He deserved her resentment. But he'd done the best he could, hadn't he? He hadn't been around much, but he'd given his family a nice home on a two-acre lot with flowers and trees and a view. He'd kept them clothed and fed. His eyes returned to the box filled with memorabilia from Luke's high-school days.

What would Luke do if he were here? What would he say to Evi?

Didn't matter. Gerrit was on his own.

The barn walls began to close in on him. With the low growl of a cornered animal, he spun on his heels and strode toward the door. Only to slam into a petite girlish figure.

"Ow." The girl stumbled backward, a cat falling from her arms.

Gerrit shook his head to clear the fog of memories. "Oh. Sorry."

She rubbed her right shoulder. "You in a hurry?"

"Uh . . . no."

She frowned and picked up her cat. "You okay, Mister?"

"I'm fine. What are you doing here?"

"You said I could come back. And I was talking to my cat."

He stood awkwardly in front of her. He wanted out, but she was blocking the door. Why was she looking at him like that?

"I was checking my mail."

"Oh." She shrugged. "Cool. Have you seen that movie about the mailbox?"

His eyebrows rose. "I've heard of it."

"It looks funny."

He grunted. "Yes. I was hoping to see it tonight, but my wife . . ."

Well, that was certainly none of this kid's business. Nothing was ever anyone else's business actually, as far as he was concerned, so why did he keep opening his big mouth?

"She turned you down, huh?"

"No." His cheeks grew warm. "She has to work late."

The girl tilted her head. "My best friend didn't want to see it, either. She thinks that guy's annoying."

He did everything he could to keep the corners of his mouth from turning up, but he failed. "I've heard that. But I still want to go."

"Me too."

She stared at him. He stared back. What was she waiting for?

She leaned a little closer. "I'd go with you."

He blinked and opened his mouth. Closed his mouth. Cleared his throat. Scratched a phantom itch on the top of his head.

"There's a three o'clock show." She whipped out her phone and pointed the screen at him. "We could go right now."

Words finally loosed themselves from his throat. "What about your parents?"

"What about them?"

"I would think—I mean—wouldn't they—?"

"I'm not a little kid. They trust me."

"They don't know you're here."

She shrugged. "Here's what we do. You drive me to my house. I drop off Mr. Whiskers, then we go to the theater. There's enough time if we leave right away."

"But . . ."

"I'll text my mom. I promise."

It was absurd. But he did want to see the movie. "Wouldn't you rather hang out with someone your own age?"

"I've been volunteering at the nursing home since I was thirteen."

He huffed. "I'm not *that* old."

"Kids my age are too much work. My grandpa used to take me to the movies, and he would say—"

"What?"

She looked away. "Never mind."

Gerrit narrowed his eyes. This was getting crazier by the minute. "I don't even know your name."

She slung the fat cat over one shoulder and stuck out her free hand. "Rae Walters. At your service."

"Isn't Ray a boy's name?"

"Rae with an *e*."

"An *e* makes it for girls?"

She shrugged. "I guess so."

"Okaaay." He shook her hand. "Gerrit Laninga."

"As in Laninga Family Farm?"

He cringed. "Not anymore."

She looked long and hard in his face as if searching for something. He squirmed under the scrutiny. What could she see? Probably nothing. Or maybe everything.

"Well." She smiled. "Let's go."

Rae's stomach hurt by the time the movie ended. She hadn't laughed that hard in a long time. Kylee would've thought the movie was lame and complained the whole time, but going to the movies with Mr. Laninga was like going with Papa Tom before he died. They both snorted more than laughed, and they both sat stick-straight in their seats as if their enjoyment of the movie depended on their posture. They even ate their popcorn the same way, dumping one small pile at a time onto a napkin on their laps.

Maybe that was why she'd brought up going to the movies on a crazy whim. Because Mr. Laninga reminded her of her papa. Whenever she thanked Papa Tom for taking her, he'd say, *"That's what papas are for."*

Plus, she had been desperate for a reason to stay away from her house.

Outside, the rain had stopped, and the sky had brightened. They'd had to park at the outer edge of the parking lot because it was so crowded, but the long walk back to Mr. Laninga's truck couldn't keep a grin from splitting Rae's face. This was *way* better than facing her parents.

"Where does your wife work?"

Mr. Laninga startled as if he'd forgotten she was there. "Huh?"

"Your wife. Where does she work?"

"Oh." He stuck his hands in the pockets of his jacket. "At The Daisy Chain."

"Cool. Flowers, right? Does she like it there?"

He scrunched up his face. "I guess so."

"You don't know?"

"I never asked."

She studied his face from the corner of her eye. He was rough around the edges, no doubt about that, but he didn't seem uncaring. Crusty? Yes. Awkward? Definitely. But heartless?

"Maybe you should ask her sometime."

He looked straight ahead, not altering his course when he reached a puddle but stomping through it as if it had deliberately set itself in his path and needed to be put in its place. His face was grim. Apparently, the subject of his wife was a touchy one.

Rae pictured the tall, slender woman she'd seen at his house, sitting alone at the table. Had they been married a long time? Maybe they'd lost some of their spark and needed to get it back. Or maybe something happened between them. That could explain his response.

She resisted the urge to rub her hands together. This was a project she could get behind. The old man was clearly miserable, and the lady was clearly lonely. Maybe she could help them if she could get some answers. Dad always said the best lawyers ask the best questions.

Mr. Laninga cleared his throat. "How old are you?"

Her growing excitement stalled out. She was supposed to be the one asking questions. She needed to pry, by golly, and show no mercy.

"Fifteen and three quarters."

"So you don't have your license yet?"

Her smile disappeared, all thoughts of coaxing information out of him gone. Driver's Ed. started on Monday. "Permit."

When they reached his black Dodge truck, Gerrit paused. "You been practicing?"

"Yes." It was technically true. She "practiced" almost every night.

He held out his keys. "Want to drive back?"

Panic seized her stomach like a menstrual cramp. She wasn't ready. What was he thinking? That movie must've put him in a good mood. Yes, he was just like Papa Tom.

She held up her hands and stepped backward. "No, that's okay."

He dangled the keys in her face. "You need road experience, don't you?"

Fear and dread sent chills through her body, but she watched the keys swinging from his finger. She *had* told Kylee and David she had someone helping her learn to drive. She'd even said it was a neighbor. And if she had to find out how bad of a driver she really was, it might as well be with someone she barely knew. Someone who wouldn't make fun of her at school. Or tell her parents.

"Okay." She snatched the keys. "I'll try."

He raised his eyebrows. "You'll try?"

"I mean, I'll do it."

She forced herself to climb in the driver's seat before she

could change her mind. *Be cool. Fake it till you make it. You can do this.* She'd never met a challenge she couldn't overcome. Dad said success could always be achieved with hard work and determination.

This was not a good idea. Her palms were sweating. People didn't fake something like this. Yet the drive back to Mr. Laninga's house was short and straightforward. Though they lived close to each other, she would have to make several turns, change lanes, and even—*shudder*—navigate a roundabout to get to her house because of the hill. But Mr. Laninga's house was almost a straight shot. Then she could take the shortcut home from there.

What could go wrong?

She buckled her seat belt and inserted the key. At least he had backed into the parking space so she could pull out easily.

Her hands trembled.

It's all part of The Plan, Rae.

They were both going to die.

GERRIT WAS PLEASED when Rae turned on the truck's headlights even though it wasn't yet dark. He appreciated the extra measure of caution. She appeared to have a good handle on everything. Kind of like Luke. Always self-assured.

But he didn't want to think about that.

He looked out the window as Rae started the truck and chuckled again, remembering the scene in the movie where a rooster from one world managed to slip through the mailbox into the other world and cause all kinds of trouble. Ha. Maybe he should get a rooster. Yes, that could be exactly what he needed to exact his revenge on George.

Cock-a-doodle-doo.

He slammed into his seat belt as Rae slammed on the brakes.

He snapped to attention. "What are you doing?"

Her face was pale. "Uh, sorry."

He watched her with wary eyes as she drove the Dodge forward. It had been a moment of weakness, offering her those keys. He never let anyone drive his truck. But she had gotten him out of the house, made him laugh. It was like he'd been given a gift, and he wanted to give something back. What had he been thinking?

The truck crept through the parking lot slower than the sun across the sky. He'd learned to drive a tractor before he was ten and had been in charge of the silage truck every summer since he was twelve, handling its crotchety stick shift and spontaneously combusting engine with ease. He'd never thought about how other people learned to drive. Kids just . . . knew how to drive, right?

What about Evi or Noah? If they'd needed help learning, they must've turned to Hannie. His only memory involving his kids and their driving skills was when Evi screamed at him to leave her alone after he made a comment about where she had chosen to park the car.

Had his kids had a hard time learning to drive? He didn't know. He had missed it. He had missed everything.

They reached the point where the parking lot met the road. Rae came to a jerky stop and waited.

How had he gotten himself into this?

He tried to keep his voice even. "Blinker."

She quickly switched it on.

"Look both ways."

She complied.

"Now ease on out there."

She hesitated.

"Go ahead."

Still she waited, concentration etched on her face.

"Any time now."

Her lip began to quiver. "I—I'm too scared."

He shifted in his seat. "You said you've been practicing."

"I know, but not on the road."

His forehead wrinkled. "Where else would you—?"

"Just in my driveway. Well, in the garage."

His eyes bulged. "What?!"

She flinched, and he was fifteen years younger, blowing up at his teenage daughter for wearing his boots to work in the garden and not putting them back. Didn't seem like such a big deal now.

Rae's eyes filled with tears. Oh no. Please, no. If she started crying . . .

"Okay, it's okay." He lowered his voice and spread his hands in a placating way. "Why don't you put it in park, nice and easy, and we'll trade places. Everything's okay."

Her shoulders drooped as she adjusted the shifter. Her face took on a desolate look. "I'm terrible, aren't I?"

He didn't answer as he hopped out and switched sides with her. He was in way over his head here. Why was she asking him if she was terrible? Surely she could see that for herself. His stomach twisted. Maybe she was looking for something else from him, but darned if he had any idea what it was.

She looked dejected in the passenger seat, head hanging low, all self-assurance gone. No hint of Luke remaining. Only a few minutes ago they had been laughing their heads off at that crazy movie, and now she was acting like her life was over. But it wasn't his fault she didn't know what she was doing. Wasn't his responsibility to teach her.

Evi's face popped into his mind, and he sighed.

He pulled onto the road. "I'll get us closer to my house, and then you can try again."

She looked up. "But you think I'm terrible."

He grunted. "I never said that."

"I could hurt someone."

"Now you're being dramatic."

She groaned. "You don't think running someone over is dramatic?"

He fought to keep his eyes from rolling. "There won't be anyone on the road by my house."

She didn't answer. Good. They drove in silence for a few minutes until he maneuvered to the side of the road and put the Dodge in park.

"Your turn."

She hesitated.

"You've got to learn sometime."

She didn't smile, though her eyes brightened a tiny bit. She unbuckled. They made the switch.

He pointed. "You see where my driveway is?"

She nodded.

"Drive down and turn in. That's all you have to do."

"Okay." She shifted on the seat and gripped the wheel, resolve showing on her face. "I can do this."

His driveway was only about a hundred yards away. The length of a football field.

He blew out a breath. "Nice and easy now."

She put the truck in drive and crept down the road. At some

point she would need to be able to drive the speed limit, but this probably wasn't the best time to mention that.

They reached the halfway mark, and he pumped an invisible brake pedal with his foot when the truck started veering toward the ditch.

"Straighten out."

She jerked the wheel.

He raised his hands in protest. "Where are you going?"

"Sorry." She shrugged. "I'm a little tense."

Unbelievable. No wonder he never let anyone drive his truck. His shoulders began to ache. And she thought *she* was tense.

"Almost there. You think you can make the turn?"

She set her lips in a determined line. "Yes."

The driveway was ten feet away. He gripped his knees and pressed his back into the seat.

Rae screamed. The truck bumped over something. She slammed on the brakes, only it wasn't the brakes. It was the gas.

The truck surged forward. She jerked the wheel.

Bang. Crunch.

The front wheels of George's antique-car mailbox rolled down the street in a satisfyingly straight line as the post holding the box tipped to a forty-five-degree angle.

Rae yelped.

"Huh." Gerrit rubbed his chin. He may no longer have need of a rooster. He weighed his options. "Put it in reverse and try again."

"But . . . but . . . I ran over an animal or something. And hit a mailbox."

He smirked. "Serves him right."

CHAPTER
THIRTEEN

Daisy's ears perked up at the sound of Hannie's car pulling into the driveway.

Gerrit gave the dog a wry smile. "Good, your mother's home. Now you can quit following me around."

She wagged her tail. He quickly donned two floral oven mitts and pulled the lasagna from the oven with a flourish. His face fell. He'd been forced to guess at Hannie's return time, which meant the lasagna had finished cooking about a half hour ago and had been warming ever since. And it showed.

The back door banged shut.

He set the pan in the middle of the table, wrinkling his nose at the overly crisp edges.

Hannie swept into the kitchen. "Hello."

He nodded. "Hello."

She eyed the table. "Lasagna?"

He nodded again. "If I would've known when you'd be back, I wouldn't have overcooked it."

She set her purse on the counter and gave him a solemn look as if he'd just announced he had six months to live.

He fidgeted. Cleared his throat. "I just meant if you would've given me a call . . ."

She pressed her fingertips to her forehead, and his words faded away. He waited.

Uh-oh. There were those crow's feet again.

Her eyes fixed on him. "You mean like all those times you let me know when you'd be home for dinner?"

He swallowed. There was no safe answer. He used to call her from the farm when he knew what his evening was going to be like. Sometimes. But when was the last time he'd done that? Ten years ago? Twelve? How had she ever known if he would be home for dinner?

He grunted. She hadn't known. So she and the kids had gone about their lives without him. Never expecting. Never waiting. And then the kids had grown up, and Hannie had opened her shop and kept right on living without him.

Hannie sat down at the table. "I do appreciate your making dinner."

He quickly filled her glass with water from the sink, his chest inflating. "I put a lot of work into this lasagna."

Her mouth twitched. "I can see that."

He joined her at the table and glanced at the two empty chairs, a nearly forgotten image filling his mind. He and Hannie and the kids holding hands around the table, praying. Thanking God for their food as Luke had taught them to do. It had been so easy to believe in God back then.

Hannie leaned her elbows on the table and gave him a sideways look. "I got an interesting text from Agatha about an hour ago."

Oh, great. Gerrit hid a grimace as he scooped a medium-sized piece of lasagna onto her plate. There were no secrets around here.

"Apparently there was a hit-and-run on their mailbox." Hannie picked up her fork and pointed it at him. "You wouldn't know anything about that, would you?"

He mumbled something about drivers being crazy these days and shoveled the biggest bite of pasta he could manage into his mouth. The tips of his ears began to burn. But Hannie didn't need to know, and the mailbox would be easy to fix. After what George had taken from him back in the day—the nerve he'd had then—he could hardly complain now. Besides, it had been an accident.

He chewed harder, covering up his satisfaction. An accident that saved him the purchase of a rooster. Ha. What a day it had been. He couldn't remember the last time he'd had so much excitement.

The girl's question from earlier sprang to his mind. About whether Hannie liked working at The Daisy Chain. He finished his bite and glanced at his wife, who was giving him a suspicious look.

"Did you have a good day at work?"

The faintest hint of a smile appeared. "It was good *and* bad. The good part was that even though I was shorthanded, we still had one of our biggest days since Valentine's weekend."

"Good." He spoke around a lump in his throat. "That's real good."

He used to buy flowers for Hannie on Valentine's Day. Luke had insisted. *"Gotta treat your lady right,"* he'd always say. Luke was probably the only reason Gerrit had managed to marry Hannie in the first place. He'd picked out Gerrit's clothes, made suggestions about where to take her for a date. He'd even helped Gerrit select Hannie's engagement ring and forced him to practice his proposal out loud in the old red barn with a hundred cows looking on.

Was there anything Hannie had ever seen in him that Luke hadn't put there?

"What was the bad part?"

Hannie leaned her chin on her hand and groaned. "The boiler's on the fritz again. The guy who came to look at it thinks it needs to be replaced, but getting a new one installed would cost at least five thousand dollars."

He whistled.

"Tell me about it." She sat up and tilted her head at him. "How about you? Did you have a good day?"

He caught Daisy's eye and could've sworn she winked. He ignored her. "Uh, yes. It was good." He stabbed at his food. How many times could he use the word *good* in one conversation?

"Well, *good*." Hannie's eyes twinkled a little as if mocking him. "What did you do?"

"I called Evi."

Her eyes widened. "Oh?"

"She said she's busy."

Hannie stared at him as if she knew that wasn't all their daughter had said. "That's too bad. What about Noah?"

He shook his head and stared at his plate. "Maybe I'll try him tomorrow."

If he could work up the nerve. At least Noah wasn't a vegetarian, so he couldn't mess that up. A thought struck him. What if Evi talked to Noah before he did? Would she convince him to turn Gerrit down?

Hannie set down her fork and laid her hand over his. He started at her touch, the soft pressure of it somehow seeping through his leathery hide like a salve until he could feel it all the way to his bones.

"It's going to take some time." She gave a small squeeze and moved her hand away again. "The kids have a right to be angry."

The gentleness of her voice touched his heart. He watched her hand reach for her glass, longing for it to touch him again. To heal him.

"Okay."

He didn't know what else to say.

She took a bite of the broccoli that had been steamed beyond recognition. "What else did you do today?"

He pushed the lemon pepper toward her plate. If she was going to eat the broccoli, she might as well season it. "Nothing, really. Checked the mail. Helped Rae with—um—something."

She raised an eyebrow. "And who's Rae?"

His palms began to sweat. Why had he brought that up? It was like his mouth was conspiring against him.

He shrugged. "A kid who lives on the other side of the trees. Down in that fancy Evergreen neighborhood. She, uh, is interested in our barn."

Hannie looked reflective. "I thought I'd seen a young girl snooping around back there before."

"Why didn't you say anything?"

"I didn't want you to freak out. She wasn't causing any trouble."

"I wouldn't freak out!" He sat back, his outburst hanging in the air like an incriminating cloud. He mashed his lips together. Yep. Definitely a conspiracy.

Hannie gave him an amused look. "You're right. My apologies."

One corner of his mouth twitched. He chanced a glance at her.

She was smiling as she finished her meal and began clearing the table. "Anyway, now that we've cleared that up, what were you doing with Rae? Calculus homework?"

His head shot up in surprise. Was that a joke? She knew he despised math. Was she teasing him? Her grin confirmed his suspicions.

He smiled back, warmed by the memory of long conversations with Hannie in the silage truck when they would laugh and laugh. "I don't think she's old enough for that. We just went to the movies."

Hannie's grin faded. "The movies?"

His body stilled. Her voice had changed. Something was wrong. "Yeah, the mailbox movie."

She dropped the dirty silverware in the sink. "But I thought we were going—"

"You said you didn't want to go."

His words were pinched. Desperate. She *had* said that, hadn't she? He frantically tried to remember their conversation, tried to remember exactly what she'd said, but the only thing he was sure of was the gut instinct he'd struck out big-time.

Her eyes locked on his, disappointment as clear as a winter morning flashing inside them. "No I didn't."

The words were soft and low, almost a whisper, but they hit him like the business end of a pitchfork. He forced his mouth not to open, not to speak, sure he would only make it worse. This was the longest conversation they'd had in years, and he'd seen her. The Hannie he used to know. The one who used to love him.

But he'd messed it up.

He watched helplessly as she slowly, deliberately covered the leftover lasagna with aluminum foil, set the pan on the top shelf of the fridge, and walked away.

CHAPTER
FOURTEEN

The bell rang, and Rae sprang from her seat. If she hurried, she could beat the other students to Room F and help set up the snacks again. On Monday she'd managed to be the first student there, and Mark had appreciated her help getting ready. Especially since they'd lost two volunteers last week.

Someone pulled on her backpack as she dashed through the crowded hallway. "Whoa, slow down. Where's the fire?"

She turned to find David walking behind her, a relaxed half smile on his face. Was it her imagination, or was he cuter today than yesterday?

She gave a small wave. "Hey. Just trying to beat the crowd."

"Where are you going?"

"Across the street." Maybe if she walked faster, he'd give up on her. "I've been volunteering at that Community Hope program."

He picked up his pace to keep up with her. "I saw a poster for that on the bulletin board."

She slowed down—a hair—and gave him a pointed look. "They need more volunteers. . . ."

He shrugged. "Sure, I could probably do it."

She dodged a freshman and tried to hide her surprise. Bringing up the program was supposed to be a surefire way to end the conversation. Most boys she knew had no interest in taking on extra work, especially at a church. Of course, David had never been like most boys she knew.

"It's basically just tutoring other kids, right?" He chuckled. "I'm not as smart as you, but I could at least point someone in the right direction."

Today would be her fourth time at Community Hope, and she'd been enjoying it. None of the students there cared that she was a straight A student or star athlete. None of them cared about The Plan. They only knew she was one of the few people trying to keep them from failing out of school. She wasn't too sure she wanted to risk David coming in and changing that.

"You have to fill out a volunteer application." She pushed open the door at the end of the hallway and stepped outside. "You can download it from their website and bring it on Monday."

"Don't they have any applications on hand?"

She pictured Mark's clipboard. "Maybe."

David smiled. "Then I'll tag along and see if I can find one. If that's all right with you."

She didn't know if that was all right with her actually, but she could hardly turn away a willing-and-able volunteer. Not after complaining to Mark about the lack of help.

"Okay."

They skirted the crowd of students waiting to be picked up, slipped between two buses, and jogged across Fallow Drive.

"You got Driver's Ed. tonight?" David asked.

"Yes."

It had started Monday. Seven to nine every weeknight for three weeks. The first two days of class had been uneventful, boring even, but that hadn't prevented her recurring nightmare from getting worse. The one where she's driving down a hill out of control toward two people shrouded in shadow.

They reached the front door of the church, and David rushed to open it for her. "How's it going so far?"

She held back a shudder. "Fine."

The incident on Friday with Mr. Laninga, which had ruined an otherwise happy day, hadn't helped with her nightmare situation. Now, in her dream, the two people were surrounded by mailboxes, and she could hear them crying out as she careened wildly down the hill. Lovely.

Mr. Laninga had assured her his neighbor's mailbox would be fine, but she hadn't been back to his house to check on it. She was nervous about facing him again.

She led David to Room F, where Mark was scrambling to set eight chairs around each table. David jumped in to help while she got to work on the snack table. Other students would arrive any minute, and they always went for the snacks before doing anything else.

A small group of middle-school girls, including Taylor, came in first.

Rae waved. "Hey, Taylor. How'd your English test go today?"

They'd spent the whole session on Monday studying for it with little progress. Taylor kept spouting wrong answers even after they'd gone over the material a hundred times, but Rae suspected this wasn't because she didn't get it.

Taylor shrugged. "Got a D."

Rae frowned. Taylor was capable of more. She was sure of it. But why wouldn't Taylor apply herself? Why didn't she care about school? She didn't seem to care about anything except maintaining the protective attitude she wore like a bulletproof vest.

Taylor walked away, and Rae dragged David back over to Mark and asked if he had any volunteer applications printed out.

He grinned. "Sure do." He took one from his clipboard and handed it to David. "Here you go. But there's no time to work on this now. We're swamped."

Rae looked around at all the kids waiting for help. "But he can't volunteer without the application."

"Rules are the difference between order and chaos," Dad always said. He had taught her to ignore them at her own peril.

Mark wagged his unkempt eyebrows. "Can you vouch for him? Just for today?"

He must assume she knew David pretty well. Her cheeks warmed. "I guess so."

"Great." Mark held out his hand for David to shake. "Welcome aboard. Let's get to work."

Rae watched Mark lead David to a table of rowdy middle-school boys and leave him there to fend for himself. She felt a little guilty for getting David into this, but it had been his choice to jump right in. Now he'd have to sink or swim.

She made her way to the table where Taylor sat and plopped down beside her. "What happened with that English test?"

Taylor shoved some pretzels in her mouth and rolled her eyes.

"Did you study last night?"

She shrugged. "I was busy."

"You need to make schoolwork a priority, Taylor."

How many times had Dad told her that?

"Yes, Mother." Taylor smirked.

"I'm serious." Rae hated to nag, but this was important. "You could fail seventh grade."

"Ugh, you keep saying that." Taylor finished off the bag of pretzels and took a swig of Gatorade. "I got a D. I passed."

The Gatorade left a red mustache on her petite, waifish face. Rae couldn't hold back a smile.

Taylor scowled. "What's your problem?"

It was Rae's turn to shrug. "Nothing."

"Can we get to work already?" Taylor pulled a couple of books from her backpack. "You're being weird."

WITH TWENTY MINUTES left in the session, Taylor's homework was finished, including three makeup assignments.

Rae clapped her hands twice and grinned. "See? I knew you could do it."

"Whatever." Taylor put everything back in her pack. "Can I get my phone out now?"

The rule was no phones until all the work was done. When Rae nodded, Taylor pulled out a new-looking iPhone.

Rae leaned in to look at it. "Wow. Sweet phone."

Taylor waved her away. "Steve got it for me. My mom's boyfriend."

She said the name *Steve* as if it were a curse word. Rae had never heard that hollowness in her voice before.

"That was nice of him."

Taylor shrank into herself, her already tiny frame nearly

disappearing as if engulfed in shadow. "It's just so I'll stay out of his hair."

Rae knew she had no right to make a snap judgment, and she had nothing to go on aside from the look on Taylor's face, but she decided she didn't like this Steve guy.

She waited for more of the story, but Taylor was done sharing. With a barely suppressed sigh of frustration, she left Taylor to Snapchat on her brand-new iPhone in peace, thinking about what Mark had said about kids not wanting to go home. To what lengths would a thirteen-year-old like Taylor go to avoid going home?

David was engaged in a lively discussion about NBA players at his table, but he caught Rae looking at him and gave her a playful smile. She smiled back. Maybe it wasn't so bad having him here.

She looked around for a new job, since Taylor had dismissed her. Mark was in the hallway doing a routine shenanigans check, as he called it. No matter how many times he told the students that only one person was allowed to go to the bathroom at a time, a group of kids always managed to sneak off and cause trouble.

She stuck her head out of the room to see if he was on his way back. He was standing between two shouting boys with his arms out, keeping them from swinging at each other. She pulled her head back into the room. That looked serious. Might take a while. She was on her own.

In his usual corner, the boy with black hair sat alone with his back to the rest of the kids. He was bent over a red notebook, earbuds in his ears. Everything about him screamed *Stay away*. She should leave him alone, yet something unexplainable pulled at her. Like he was calling her name. Or *someone* was.

Before she could think it through, she found herself walking up behind him. Pulling out a chair. Sitting down. And waiting.

He didn't look up. Didn't speak. She should move along, but it was too late. She had committed. He worked away in his notebook, his pencil scritch-scratching the paper.

After a long minute, she scooted her chair a little closer. "Hi."

Even with the earbuds in, he had to know she was there. Why was he ignoring her? Probably because he didn't want to be bothered, of course. She should leave him alone.

"What's your name?"

She spoke loud enough to be heard over whatever music was blasting his eardrums. His pencil paused for a second, then resumed its scribbling. She looked around the room. There were plenty of other kids she could be helping. Kids who were desperate for attention. She was about to concede defeat and stand up when the boy's pencil stopped again.

"Morgan."

She leaned back in her chair slowly, as if any sudden movements might frighten him away. "Hi, Morgan. I'm Rae."

He didn't look up. "I know who you are."

"You go to Greenville High?"

Mark had told her the students in the program came from three different middle schools and two high schools, Greenville High and Stillaguamish. She'd assumed this boy went to Stillaguamish, but he nodded in answer to her question.

She looked at him closely. Behind the hair, his face *was* vaguely familiar. They certainly didn't have any classes together this year, but maybe they'd been in the same class when they were younger.

"Are you a sophomore, too?"

He pulled one earbud out. "Senior."

Oh. She didn't interact with many seniors. How would he know her?

"But we were in third grade together," he continued. "Mrs. Baker."

A faint memory of a quiet blond kid who was afraid of his own shadow took shape. "Morgan West?"

He nodded.

"You dyed your hair."

He looked up. His sharp blue eyes took her in, daring her to back down. She held his gaze.

"Wait a minute." She folded her arms on the table. "We were in third grade together, and now you're two years ahead of me? And everyone says *I'm* smart."

The hint of a smile flashed across his face and was gone. "They moved me up a grade in sixth, then when I got to high school I started doing independent study classes so I could graduate early." He pulled out his other earbud. "And I took a few community college classes last summer to get more credits."

Why had she never thought of that? Dad would probably salivate at the idea of Rae graduating early. One less year to wait before he had the summa cum laude Columbia graduate daughter he dreamed of.

Morgan set his notebook on the table, and she shifted, trying to get a look at what he was working on. He snatched it away.

Okay, okay. She could take a hint. She leaned back and looked around the room. "If you're graduating early, what are you doing *here*?"

He fiddled with his pencil and bounced his knee, staring at his earbuds as if itching to put them back in.

Mark called from the doorway. "Time's up, guys. It's five o'clock. You don't have to go home—"

"But you can't stay here." The students finished the now-familiar line, rolling their eyes.

A shadow darkened Morgan's face. He quickly closed his notebook, shoved it in his bag, and stood.

She jumped up, too. "I guess I'll see you next week."

He glanced back over his shoulder, his piercing eyes scrutinizing her from head to toe. She fought the urge to inspect her clothes. Was she a mess? No, she was fastidious about her appearance. Dad had drilled it into her head that lawyers needed to make a good first impression at all times. But then what was Morgan looking at? Or for? He gave an almost imperceptible nod and strode from the room.

David appeared at her elbow. "Hey. That was fun." He followed her gaze to the figure disappearing into the hall. "Make a new friend?"

She looked into David's soft brown eyes. So welcoming and gentle. So unlike Morgan's. Part of her wanted to tell David who Morgan was. He'd been in Mrs. Baker's third grade class, too. But something held her back. While Morgan hadn't said anything about keeping it a secret, it felt almost as though it would be a betrayal of his trust to say anything.

"I've been trying to meet all the students." She gave him a smile. "How'd your first time go?"

"Great. But there's not enough of me to go around. Some of these kids need a *lot* of help."

Her eyes darted back to the door where Morgan had gone. *And some apparently don't need any.*

At the door, Mark held a fist out to David for a pound and nodded at Rae. "You got any more helpers up your sleeve?"

She shook her head. "I'm working on it."

"We decided to add another session on Fridays, but only for hanging out. There seems to be a real need for a safe place to hang out after school."

"So you don't need volunteers on Friday?"

"No." He nodded for them to go ahead and then locked the door behind them. "But we still need more on Mondays and Wednesdays. And you guys are great and all, but we could use some more mature help, you know?"

David grabbed his chest as if hurt by the remark. "Are you saying we're not mature?"

Mark shooed them down the hall and laughed. "I meant older. These kids need positive adult influences."

Rae and David stepped outside and said good-bye to Mark. She scanned the parking lot for her mom's car but didn't see it. When she checked her phone, a text told her Mom was running a few minutes late because she'd been with Grandma Kate.

"Need a ride home?" David asked.

"My mom's coming."

"I'll wait with you."

She gave him a sidelong glance. "You don't have to."

He caught her looking and grinned. "I don't mind."

She looked away and peered down the road, hoping to see a navy blue Ford Explorer. No such luck. David's nearness made her feel tingly. What would it be like to hold his hand? Feel his arm around her waist? Her cheeks grew warm. For heaven's sake, what was she thinking? She and David had been friends a long time. She'd never felt awkward around him before.

"You really had fun?" She fought to keep her tone light, her expression unconcerned. "Those middle-school boys didn't scare you off?"

"No way." He nudged her shoulder with his. "You can't get rid of me that easily."

She swallowed hard. That was exactly what she was afraid of.

CHAPTER
FIFTEEN

Friday. Finally. Rae waved her appreciation to Kylee for the ride and hurried into the house. She wasn't usually so glad for the school week to be over, but her first week of Driver's Ed. had her nerves frayed. Thank goodness for early release on Fridays.

Mr. Whiskers was waiting inside the door, and she scooped him into her arms. He clearly had no stress in *his* life.

She rubbed his ears. "You lucky duck."

So far, all they'd done in class was watch a few instructional videos and sit around listening to Mr. Fletcher lecture them about safety. Still, knowing she had to go to another Driver's Ed. session after dinner almost made her break out in hives. It was the last thing she wanted to do on a Friday night.

"Mr. Fletcher's always staring right at me," she muttered. Mr. Whiskers craned his neck to look up at her. "It's like he knows about the mailbox."

The lethargic feline yawned.

"Thanks a lot. Your breath smells like rotten fish." She set her backpack down and carried the fat cat into the kitchen. "Mom?"

She grabbed a granola bar from the cupboard and glanced at the calendar on the wall, her heart rate rising. At the end of class last night, Mr. Fletcher had said, "Make sure and sign up for a drive time on your way out." She had seen other kids huddled around the clipboard, eager to choose a time and date on the schedule and write down their names, but she had left without looking at it. If she went on an assigned drive, her secret would be out. And yet if she didn't sign up, she'd fail the class.

She'd have to sign up tonight.

"Mom?"

Her mother was usually only a couple of steps behind Mr. Whiskers with a greeting after school. Where was she? Rae walked down the hall and peeked into the living room. No Mom. She checked her phone. No messages.

She turned on her heels and walked to the other end of the house. Her parents' bedroom was off-limits. Nevertheless, she put a hand on the door, and it swung open.

Mom was sitting on her bed, holding her wedding ring in her palm. She stared at it as if searching for something important.

"Mom?"

She looked up, startled. "Oh. Hi, sweetie." She slid the ring back on her finger and pasted on a smile. "Home already?"

Rae eyed her suspiciously. "Early release on Fridays, remember?"

"Oh. Right." Mom stood and joined Rae in the hall. "Can I get you a snack?"

"I had one." Rae walked with Mom back to the kitchen. "What were you doing?"

"Nothing. Just . . . thinking."

Rae noted the dark circles under her mom's eyes. "How was Grandma today?"

"Fine, sweetie. Everything is just fine."

RAE TRUDGED THROUGH the woods toward Mr. Laninga's barn, Mr. Whiskers tucked snugly inside her zipped-up hoodie. Everything was most certainly *not* fine. The long hairs on the tips of the cat's ears tickled her chin, but she was too distracted to find it endearing. Something was up with Mom, and whatever it was, Rae didn't like it. Not one bit.

A cold feeling bloomed in her chest as she pictured the way Mom had looked at her wedding ring. Could she and Dad be thinking about getting a . . . No. She wouldn't even think the *D*-word. Mom was upset about Grandma Kate. That was all.

The back of the barn came into view through the trees. She began to relax. It was the perfect place to hide from her life.

As she rounded the barn, she spotted Mr. Laninga standing in the middle of the driveway, staring at a piece of paper. He faced the house as if he had meant to go in but then something had stopped him. His profile was grim. The crunch of her shoes on the gravel didn't catch his attention. Daisy trotted over to her, tail wagging, and still he didn't notice. Whatever was on that piece of paper must have been important.

She considered sneaking into the barn and leaving him to his reverie, but she never could leave well enough alone.

"Hello, Mr. Laninga." She stopped a few feet away to give him space.

He whirled around, crumpling the paper in his fist. His eyes flashed for a second, then dropped to the ground. "Oh. It's you."

"Nice to see you, too. What have you got there?"

He shoved it in his pocket. "Nothing."

"Okaaay." She jerked a thumb at the barn. "I was heading in there. Is that all right?"

"Sure, sure." He waved an arm absent-mindedly. "Do whatever you want. I was just leaving."

He was clearly in a sour mood. Even so, she couldn't help but ask, "Where are you going?"

He looked at her for the first time. Squinted at her bulging cat-filled hoodie. Rubbed his chin. "I need to find a rooster."

"A rooster?"

"Yep."

She had no experience with farm animals. "Do they sell those at the pet store or . . . ?"

He hesitated. "I'm not sure."

"Have you tried Craigslist? You can find anything on Craigslist."

His eyes narrowed. "Who's Craig?"

Oh, this was just too much. She smiled. "No one. It's an online thing. People post stuff for sale or for free so other people can find it." She pulled out her phone and brought up the website, then held it out to him. "See?"

"Well?" He raised his eyebrows. "They got any roosters on there?"

A quick search revealed several possibilities. Two that were local.

"There's one on Meadow Lane for free. And one down at Cole's Corner, but I don't think you'd want that one."

He perked up. "Why not?"

She pointed at the screen. "Says here they're getting rid of it because it's too loud and obnoxious. 'Would be more comfortable out in the country.'"

"That sounds perfect." A mischievous light sparked in his eyes. "Let's go. And you can call me Gerrit."

He jogged over to his back door before she could wonder how she had gotten roped into this strange adventure. He'd hardly even heard her address him when she'd first arrived and now they were teaming up for something? With a sudden spring in his step, he grabbed a set of keys from inside the door and strode to his truck.

She watched him. "I don't think my mom would approve of my calling you Gerrit."

Rae's mother had spent her whole life insisting Rae use the proper terms of respect for everyone, just like the great Judge Tom McDaniel had taught her. Good practice for the courtroom and all that. Rae was used to it by now, and even kind of liked it. When she addressed the folks at the nursing home by their proper titles, it gave them some of their dignity back.

He reached the driver's door and looked back at her. "When someone tells you what they prefer to be called, it's impolite to refuse them, *Miss Walters*." He held up the keys and shook them. "Get in. I'll drive."

Well, that was unnecessary. She sucked in her lips. He had some nerve bossing her around. All she wanted to do was duck into the barn and contemplate life with her cat. But her curiosity won out.

"Better call me Rae, then." She opened the passenger side door. "And Mr. Whiskers gets to come this time."

Gerrit looked at her squirming sweatshirt. "Is he trained?"

She got into the truck with a smirk. "He won't poop in here, if that's what you mean."

She adjusted the seat belt so the lap strap tucked underneath Mr. Whiskers and the shoulder strap fit above him. He protested mildly when Gerrit turned the key and the engine fired up, but then he settled in.

As they pulled onto the road, she peered through the window at the neighbor's mailbox. It was standing upright as if nothing had ever happened. She should say something about it, maybe thank Gerrit for fixing it for her, but she hated to bring it up. Especially when his mood seemed to be improving.

Maybe she should talk about something else instead.

"How was your day?"

He concentrated on the road as if he hadn't heard her. He could at least turn on the radio. She fidgeted in her seat.

"Is your wife working today?"

Nothing. It was worse than talking to Morgan at Community Hope. In fact, the two of them had a lot in common. Surliness, for one thing. Well, she wasn't giving up that easily.

"What's her name?"

He made a right-hand turn and glanced over at her. "Hannie."

She tilted her head. "That's a pretty name. Unusual."

"It's Dutch."

"Do you have any kids?"

As soon as the words left her mouth, his face clouded over. Did his strained relationship with his wife have something to do with their kids? She couldn't help him if she didn't have all the facts. Dad said it was in her blood to interrogate people.

"What are their names?"

He frowned. She was prying, but he's the one who wanted her to come along. If he had wanted to make the drive in utter silence, if he'd wanted to avoid all her questions, he should've gone to find a rooster all by himself.

"How old are they?" She was doing it on purpose now. "Do they live nearby?"

They were close to Cole's Corner. He would need her to tell him the address soon or the whole trip would be a waste. He gave her a questioning look, and she raised her eyebrows. She wasn't giving him anything until he answered at least one question.

"Evi is thirty and Noah is twenty-seven, okay?" He huffed. "Happy?"

She stuck her nose up in a self-satisfied way. "Turn left on Bower. We're looking for number eighteen. Green house."

He made the turn. Her thoughts drifted to the piece of paper he had stuck in his pocket earlier. What could it have been?

At house number eighteen, they pulled up to find a buxom woman waiting by the garage. Rae had texted the number from the ad and let them know they were coming. The woman wore heavy-duty work gloves and held a trembling cardboard box in her arms.

Gerrit stepped out of the truck.

The woman hurried over and thrust the box at him before he could even close the door. "There's Bernard. He's all yours."

From her seat, Rae nodded her approval. Bernard was the perfect name for such a regal creature as the one she'd seen pictured in the ad. The cardboard box shook and an unholy cacophony came from inside, like the woman had trapped an evil spirit in it that would burst forth if you said the magic words. But of course the bird would be making a fuss after being trapped in a box. He would probably calm down once they let him out.

Poor Bernard.

Gerrit clung to the box, struggling to keep hold, and looked at it like it might detonate. "Uh, thanks."

The woman shooed him away with a gloved hand. "Hope you have lots of space." She turned to go back to her business, calling over her shoulder, "Never approach him with bare hands. I learned that the hard way."

Gerrit's jaw clenched. The box screamed, and Rae shrunk back. Gerrit stood at the open door of his pickup truck, glancing back and forth between the bed of the truck and the cab.

"You can't put him in the back," she said. "What if he escapes while we're driving?"

He gave her a hard look. "And what if he's in here with us and escapes while we're driving?"

She scrunched her lips to one side. Good point. The transportation of an ornery rooster was not something she'd ever had to worry about before. She'd feel a lot better if the woman had taped the box shut. Instead, she'd only crisscrossed the box's flaps over each other.

Gerrit nodded as if he'd made a decision, then set the box down in the truck bed. "I don't want any distractions up there. Especially since you're driving home."

She stared. "Uh . . ."

"Slide on over." He gestured with his hands. "You need more practice."

He walked around the front of the truck to the passenger side and opened the door. She had not moved.

He motioned with his chin. "Scoot."

"Have you forgotten what happened last time?" She couldn't look him in the eye.

"Like I said, you need practice."

"I ran something over."

"I went back and checked. It was only a raccoon." He shrugged. "I hate raccoons."

Her voice rose. "It could've been a child."

He stood motionless with one hand on top of the cab until she looked up. "It wasn't." He jerked his chin again. "Now scoot."

Rae slowly slid across the bench to the driver's seat. This was not how she'd imagined the end. Careering to her death next to a man who was little more than a stranger. Taking the innocent Mr. Whiskers down with her. Not to mention Bernard. That was not how it happened in her recurring nightmare.

If only she'd gone to see what was happening in Room F instead of letting Kylee drive her home and then trying to visit the barn. Though Mark had said he didn't need volunteers on Fridays, she had considered dropping by the church to say hi to the students. To check in on Taylor. Now she would never have the chance. Who would tutor Taylor once she was gone?

She sat there for a long moment, unmoving, her hands gripping the wheel.

"You might want to take him out of there." Gerrit indicated her sweatshirt. "You don't want anything disrupting your focus while you're driving."

Another good point. She unzipped the hoodie and pulled Mr. Whiskers out. He blinked in the sudden light. She held him out to Gerrit. "Will you hold him?"

His eyes flashed, reminding her again of Morgan. "No."

She frowned. "Please, *Gerrit*?" It felt weird calling him that.

He curled his lip. "Fine, *Rae*." He grabbed the cat. "But this will be the only time this happens."

As if there were going to be other times they would be riding around in the truck together with a cat. She chuckled to herself. Well, who knew? Maybe there would.

She buckled up and turned the key in the ignition, her life flashing before her eyes. How was she supposed to back out of this driveway?

"There's no one around." Gerrit was matter-of-fact, his hands resting on Mr. Whiskers's back. "You know what to do."

It should be easy. Press down on the brake pedal, shift the truck into reverse, and back out onto the road. But her arms and legs were paralyzed.

"What are you waiting for?" Gerrit asked. "You want me to promise you ice cream or something?"

She wrinkled her nose. "I'm not a little kid."

He didn't answer. She looked in the rearview mirror, thankful to see no other vehicles on the road.

"So . . ." She looked at him out of the corner of her eye and was pretty sure he was rubbing Mr. Whiskers's ears. "Do you *have* ice cream or . . . ?"

"Just drive." He scowled at her, but there was laughter in his eyes.

"Fine, but only on one condition." An idea began to take shape in her mind. "I want to stop somewhere on the way back."

"Oh, for crying out loud, I was joking about the ice cream." He huffed. He sure did that a lot.

"No, not that." She put the truck in reverse and took a deep breath. This was either a terrible idea or a genius one. "There's someone I think you should meet."

CHAPTER
SIXTEEN

Gerrit grabbed at the door handle for security as Rae took the turn too tight, ran over the curb, and drove the truck into an almost-empty parking lot. In his anxiety, it took him a second to recognize their destination as a church. It sure didn't look like one. But the name Greenville Community Church was unmistakable, right there on the white sign.

"What are we doing here?"

It had been a bumpy ride from Cole's Corner, but overall, Rae's driving had been passable until turning in here. Not great, but they hadn't crashed.

She inched into a wide open parking space with three empty spaces on each side. "I told you. There's someone I want you to meet."

He hadn't gone to church since Luke's funeral. He didn't plan to start now. "I'll wait out here."

She turned off the engine and looked at him. "We had a deal."

He didn't remember making any deal officially. He should've given in on the ice cream.

"Someone has to stay here with the animals."

"We'll move the box into the truck while we're gone, just in case." She reached over and slid the fluffy, decrepit cat off his lap. "Mr. Whiskers can babysit Bernard. They'll be fine for a couple minutes."

She hopped out and reached down into the truck bed, trying to grab the rooster box. It shrieked like a banshee and waggled out of her reach. She stood on the back tire and tried again but couldn't get the leverage she needed. He sighed.

Fine.

He got out and grabbed the box, flipping it and keeping a wary eye on the top, where an evil beady eye peered at him through a small opening between two flaps. He set the box in the cab and slammed the door.

"I'm not interested in being preached at by some self-righteous pastor who thinks he knows about life because his dog died once."

Rae gave him an inscrutable look. "I don't think the pastor's even here on Fridays. We're not here for church."

He signaled for her to lead the way and followed her into the building. He only had himself to blame for this one. It had been his idea to go after the rooster. His idea to bring her along. His idea to let her drive. She stopped at a door marked *Room F* and smiled back at him. Uh-oh. Girls only smiled like that when trouble was coming.

Loud and rowdy kids were everywhere when she opened the door. His eyes widened. Was this where the exorcisms took place?

A young man approached. "Rae, what are you doing here?"

Rae grinned. "Just stopping to say hi. I brought a friend."

"I see that." The young man held out his hand. "I'm Mark."

Gerrit stared at him. How did he walk around in pants that tight? And did he not own a razor?

Rae nudged him.

What? Oh, right. He shook Mark's hand. "Gerrit Laninga."

"I'm impressed." Mark turned back to Rae. "Two new volunteers in one week?"

Gerrit shivered, the word *volunteers* casting a cold shadow. What was this guy talking about?

Rae gave Gerrit a sidelong glance. "Well, I—"

"Let me see if I can find another volunteer application," Mark said, then gestured at the feral creatures climbing the walls, "while you introduce Gerrit to some of the kids."

As Mark walked away, Rae tugged on Gerrit's arm. "Come on."

Gerrit followed dumbly. It was like one of those horror movies where you scream at the person to run because you can see the monster coming for them, but they're frozen in fear. And then they get eaten.

Rae waved at a tiny slip of a girl sitting against the wall, who looked like she would blow halfway to Canada on a windy day. "Hey, Taylor. Got any homework this weekend?"

The girl hung her head, her face stricken, and wrapped her arms around her knees.

"Everything okay?" Rae asked.

The words that came out of the little girl's mouth next shocked Gerrit out of his daze. What foul pit of hell was this? It was worse than a milking parlor on a hot summer day. He had to get himself out of here.

Rae grabbed his arm as if sensing his intentions. "I'm going to need to talk to her. But first let's go say hi to Morgan."

Gerrit was too dumbfounded to protest. He didn't know

anything about a world where people just "go say hi." For no reason. Or where little girls cussed as if the barn were on fire. But before he could express his dismay, he was standing at a table in the back of the room occupied by a boy with black hair. He appeared . . . sullen.

"Hey, Morgan," Rae said.

The boy gave her a slight nod, then looked at Gerrit with suspicion.

Rae was either oblivious or pretended not to notice. "This is my friend Mr. Lan—uh, Gerrit. Gerrit, this is Morgan."

The boy met his gaze. They stared at each other, sizing each other up. The boy—what had she said? Morgan?—looked about Rae's age. Was it true kids could smell fear like sharks could smell blood?

"I need to talk to Taylor for a minute." Rae patted Gerrit on the elbow. How condescending. "Be right back."

The boy, Morgan, watched her walk away almost as if . . . was that fear on his face, too? Gerrit cleared his throat. He was the adult here.

"Got any homework this weekend?" He borrowed Rae's question.

Morgan stared at him. "What are you doing here?"

He shrugged and pointed a thumb at Rae across the room. "She brought me."

Morgan looked down, pondering Gerrit's answer, then relaxed his shoulders as if accepting it. "What kind of dog do you have?"

Gerrit's forehead wrinkled. "What?"

"There's dog hair on the bottom of your jeans."

"Oh. Well, I don't have a dog."

Morgan waited.

126

"I mean, it's my wife's."

"Uh-huh."

"She's a corgi."

The boy's face shifted ever so slightly. "I like corgis." His voice was quiet. "What's her name?"

This was rather ridiculous. Talking about dogs with some strange kid in some random church that some meddling girl had dragged him to.

"Daisy."

Morgan waited. Expecting something.

Gerrit shifted on his feet. "Uh . . . do *you* have a dog?"

"I used to have a golden retriever." His expression darkened. "Her name was Fangs."

A golden retriever named Fangs? Could this day get any stranger?

"Did she die?"

Morgan flinched. "No."

If he wanted Gerrit to pull the details out of him, it wasn't going to happen. It was none of Gerrit's business what happened to this kid's dumb dog. He shifted again and glanced around the room. Where could Rae have gone?

Morgan stared at the bottom of Gerrit's jeans. "Maybe you could bring Daisy next time you come."

Gerrit shook his head as if to clear it. No, he wouldn't be coming here again. And he definitely wouldn't be bringing that ratty creature. Morgan glanced up at him and narrowed his eyes. It was as if he knew Gerrit didn't want to be there. Knew to expect disappointment. In fact, it was almost as if he was testing him.

Before Gerrit could answer, Rae reappeared with a piece of paper in her hand, and Morgan's face changed. A curtain dropped over it, his sullenness returned, and he looked down at the table.

"We better get going." Rae waved at Morgan. "See you Monday."

Morgan didn't respond. As Gerrit followed Rae down the hall, he couldn't get the boy out of his mind. Why was he testing him? Why had he shut down around Rae? What was this place?

"What are those kids doing here?" he asked.

Rae stopped at the door and looked at him. "On Mondays and Wednesdays they come to get help with their homework. Tutoring and stuff. They get referred to the program by teachers who don't want them to fail. I'm one of the volunteers. On Fridays, Mark just opens the room up to give them a place to hang out after school."

"So that Morgan kid. He's failing his classes?"

"I don't know." She hesitated. "He's really smart. He's only sixteen but he says he's graduating this year."

"Then what's he doing here?"

She shrugged. "I'm still trying to figure that out."

They stepped out into the fresh air, and he was relieved to be free of that place. He and churches didn't mix. But what was the deal with that Morgan kid?

An eerie wailing sound rent the air, and he frowned. It sounded like a—

"Mr. Whiskers!" Rae shouted and took off running toward the truck. "Something's wrong."

He picked up his pace to keep up with her. When he got close enough, he could see feathers flying inside the cab of his truck and hear Bernard's banshee scream. Great. Just great.

Rae lunged for the door.

He held his hand out. "Wait!"

Too late. She opened it.

Bernard rocketed past her in a black-and-green blur aimed straight at him. He crossed his arms in front of him and braced himself, but the rooster flew right past and headed for the bushes lining the parking lot.

He glanced back at the truck. Rae had Mr. Whiskers in her arms and was gently petting his blood-smeared face.

"You poor thing. What did that nasty rooster do to you?"

Gerrit's lip curled. This wouldn't have happened if she hadn't insisted they stop here. That rooster might be more trouble than he was worth. Maybe bringing it home wasn't a great idea, after all. But he couldn't leave it here. It might carry off a small child.

He headed for the bushes.

"Where are you going?" Rae called after him.

"I've got to catch him."

He turned his back on her and tromped ahead. Steam would be pouring from his ears if that sort of thing happened in real life. Of all the stupid, harebrained, ridiculous . . .

"Here, rooster, rooster." He stepped into the bushes, moving with quiet deliberation. "Come on out."

He used the voice that usually worked on cows that had been injured and needed to be approached for treatment. Except the only treatment he was considering for this creature was a pot of boiling water.

"I'm not going to hurt you. I just need to get you back in your box."

The bush two down from where he stood shook.

"Come here, rooster, rooster."

"Maybe if you call him by his name."

Gerrit jumped and spun around. "What are you doing?"

Rae tilted her head. "I'm going to help you."

"I don't need help."

"Mr. Whiskers is fine. Just a couple scratches."

"Great." He turned back to the shaking bush. "Wonderful. Go wait for me in the truck."

"Remember what that lady said about gloves?"

He looked at his bare hands and scowled. A rooster's talons could be vicious. That dumb cat was lucky he still had both his eyeballs.

Rae took a step closer. "You'll never catch him by yourself."

He'd never been a patient man. He used to blow up at his kids for being too loud. For being too slow. For needing more than he could give. He'd shouted at Noah that very morning when they'd talked on the phone, and Noah had said he would only come for Memorial Day weekend if Evi did.

Gerrit had been trying to avoid thinking about that call all day. He turned on Rae, ready to lose it on her, but his anger fizzled out at the expectant look on her face.

She was just a kid.

Like Evi and Noah had been. All those times.

"I have a plan," she said, hopeful.

His shoulders drooped. The raging swirl in his chest morphed into a tight fist of remorse. "There's a pair of gloves tucked under the driver's seat. Go put them on."

"What about you?"

He pulled his sleeves down over his hands. "I'll be fine."

Her plan was a good one. She returned with the gloves and the box and showed him a spot in the bushes where it was like a wall, too thick for the rooster to get through. They positioned the box on its side next to the wall, then closed in on the beast from the other two sides until he was forced into the open box.

Rae grinned in triumph. "We just have to close it."

He cringed. Sure. Just reach on in. No problem.

He opted for the Band-Aid approach. Rip it off quick and get it over with. He managed to get the box sealed up with only two scratches on each hand to show for it.

"There now, Bernie." Rae patted the box. "We're not going to hurt you. Everything's fine."

Gerrit gave her an incredulous look.

"What?" She lifted her hands. "He was just scared."

"Bernie, huh?"

She nodded.

"Pfft." He muttered to himself. "More like Bernard the Terrible."

She grinned and headed toward the passenger side of the truck.

Gerrit shook his head. "Oh no, you don't." He pointed. "Driver's seat."

Her nose wrinkled in disgust, but she acquiesced.

They settled into the truck with Mr. Whiskers on the bench between him and Rae. Gerrit held the box on his lap upside down with both arms set on top so there was no possibility of escape. Focused as she was on the task at hand, Rae didn't ask any more invasive questions as she drove ten miles per hour under the speed limit.

Well, maybe it was her turn to be interrogated, then. He could ask her a bunch of personal questions and see how she liked it.

If he could think of any.

What did people talk about? What could he possibly ask

about her life? She lived in a house, went to school, and volunteered at that wildlife preserve for feral children. What else was there? He thought of Evi. What would he ask her if she were here?

"Do you have a boyfriend?"

He imagined his baby girl in the arms of some shaggy-haired bum and shuddered.

Rae concentrated on the road. "No. Boys aren't part of my plan right now."

His brow puckered. "Your plan? You have a plan?"

"Of course. First, I have to get my license, obviously. Then a job. Then I have to keep my spot on the varsity basketball team and break the record for most three-pointers in a season. After that, I have to ace the SAT, become president of the National Honor Society, and graduate valedictorian so I can get into Columbia. And then . . ."

Her voice wavered. Certainty turned to doubt.

"Then what?" he prodded. "What will you study?"

"I'm going to be a lawyer."

He narrowed his eyes at her. "Sounds like you've got it all figured out."

"I know exactly where I'm going to be in ten years. But I'm not completely sure after that."

"I don't think you need to plan any further than that."

Something shifted in her expression, though he didn't know what.

"Tell that to my dad."

She said it so quietly, he wasn't sure if it was meant for him or not. He decided to let it go.

"See my driveway?"

She sat up straighter. "I won't miss it this time."

She slowed the truck to a crawl and gave herself an hour and a half to make the turn. Felt like it, anyway. His hands grew clammy, and his heart rate rose as he glanced up and down the road for other cars, but there was no rushing her. Had he mentioned he wasn't a patient man?

They pulled up to the house without incident. Rae tucked her cat back into her sweatshirt, then turned to him. "How'd I do?"

He nodded. "You didn't kill anything."

"I need to keep practicing."

Her hint was so obvious, even he couldn't miss it. But he didn't know how far he wanted to take this. He wasn't responsible for this girl.

"You should ask your parents for help."

She looked down. "Yeah."

"You did good."

"Here." She took a piece of paper from her pocket. "It's a volunteer application for Community Hope. Where we went earlier. You should fill it out."

He eyed the paper as if it were a calf with a bad case of newborn diarrhea.

She held it closer. "We need more volunteers. And it's not like you have anything better to do."

He scoffed. Nothing better to do? What did she think he did all day? Watch cooking shows, talk to Daisy, and wait around for the mail to show up?

The kid with the black hair came to mind. Morgan. That look on his face . . . it was clear he never expected to see Gerrit again. He had the look of someone all too accustomed to being disappointed.

Gerrit had seen that look before.

Rae waved the paper in his face. "At least think about it."

He snatched it from her hand. "Fine. I'll think about it."

She smiled and gave her cat a hug. "Come on, Mister. Let's go home." She waved at him. "Bye, *Gerrit*."

He managed a small nod. He'd almost be able to like the kid if she wasn't so infuriating. She hopped out, strolled into the woods, and disappeared down the shortcut trail before he could ask himself what he was doing sitting in his Dodge with a rooster on his lap.

Daisy was waiting when he climbed out of the truck, carefully holding the box with one hand on each end. Bernard the Terrible had been quiet during the drive home, but one small bark from Daisy got him riled up again. The rooster clawed at the box like he was buried alive. Gerrit had not considered the repercussions of introducing Daisy to a rooster.

Bernard's unnatural screech sent a chill down his spine as he shut the truck door with his foot. What should he do now? Why had he ever thought this was a good idea?

"Gerrit."

He turned to see George huffing and puffing down his driveway, one arm raised as if hailing a cab. Ah yes. That was why.

George's face was not exactly friendly. "I need to talk to you about something."

The box gave a violent shudder and slipped from Gerrit's hands. Bernard exploded from the torn-up cardboard the instant it hit the ground and immediately became entangled with Daisy. Daisy yelped in surprise. Gerrit kicked at the rooster.

It wasn't how he pictured exacting his revenge on George for leaving that ultrasound picture of his granddaughter in his mailbox.

No.

It was a hundred times better.

Bernard took off down the drive like a jet on the runway, flapping his wings and heading straight for Mr. I'm-Going-to-Be-a-Grandpa. George's eyes bugged out, and he took a step back, then tripped over himself as he turned to run like all the demons of hell were after him.

Gerrit hadn't laughed that hard in a long time.

CHAPTER
SEVENTEEN

Gerrit never even knew what an éclair was before this week, but the batch turned out quite nicely. He whistled as he applied the last of the chocolate frosting, glad he'd had the foresight to make both it and the filling earlier in the day. Chef Kellan hadn't been kidding when he said this was a time-consuming recipe.

Dinner was reheated leftovers, but he hoped the éclairs would make up for it. He checked the time. Hannie had said she'd be home "around six." It was 6:09.

He glanced out the window every thirty seconds. Had Hannie done the same thing back in the day? When they'd first met, he couldn't imagine keeping a woman like her waiting. She was so perfect and beautiful. So out of his league. He'd fallen for her the first day but had kept his distance in the beginning, afraid of what might happen when she met Luke. What woman would choose him when there was a man like Luke around?

His father had not been subtle about his desire for Luke to settle down, give him grandsons to carry on the family name, and run the farm. Hannie would've been the perfect match for him. A good churchgoing girl. Strong Dutch heritage. Just what his father wanted for Luke.

But Hannie had chosen him.

He looked out the window again. There she was. His stomach did a funny little swoop, and he ran a hand through his hair.

His wife was home.

"THESE ARE AMAZING." Hannie took another bite and closed her eyes. "It's like eating heaven."

Gerrit nodded to himself. The leftover clam chowder had been uninspiring, but the éclairs were going over better than he'd hoped.

Hannie licked frosting from her lips. "If we had these at the shop, we'd have to turn customers away."

Well now. He squared his shoulders and lifted his chin. "They're pretty good for my first try, I guess."

She laughed. "They're delicious. And you look like that rooster I saw when I was coming in, strutting around like that."

A chuckle stalled out in his throat. He'd completely forgotten about Bernard. He hadn't realized the psychotic creature had shown back up after running George off the property.

"Uh . . . rooster?"

"Yeah, he was sitting on the fence and acting like he owned the place. He must've escaped from somewhere."

A small bead of frosting clung to her chin. He stared at it, struck by the smoothness of her skin and how it was the color of thick cream. How her dark rose blouse brought out the pink in her cheeks. Could she really be nearly sixty? Looking at her, it was almost as if they were in their twenties again, sneaking kisses in the barn and skinny-dipping in the river by moonlight.

Gerrit's eyes moved from her chin to her lips, and something long forgotten twinged in his chest.

He stilled.

Her phone buzzed, and she reached for it.

The distraction brought a flood of both relief and disappointment. He shook himself free from the desire to kiss her.

"That's strange." Hannie indicated a text message on her phone. "Agatha seems to think that rooster is ours."

Right. Bernard. He'd forgotten again. What would be the best way to break the news?

"There's something you're not telling me." Her crow's feet appeared as she laid her phone on the table. "You have that look on your face."

He had no idea what look that was, but he'd never get away with lying. She was way too smart for that, and he knew better than to mess with the crow's feet.

"Tell me we don't own a rooster, Gerrit."

He picked up an éclair and studied it with great interest. "He needed a good home. He was free."

She sank a little deeper in her chair. "And what are we going to do with him?"

"I don't know yet. Rae found him."

"Rae again, huh? So this is her fault?"

"Uh . . ."

"Is it true the rooster attacked George?"

Attacked was a strong word. The dumb fowl was in a panic, and George happened to be in the way. It wasn't Bernard's fault George had come over uninvited at precisely the wrong time.

"Not exactly."

"What is it with you and George? This isn't still about the money, is it?"

Gerrit's jaw clenched.

"I can't believe this." Hannie huffed. "That was years ago. Why do you keep insisting on causing trouble?"

He blinked. He didn't *want* to cause trouble. Did he? "I . . . uh . . ."

"Here." She went and grabbed a paper plate from a drawer in the kitchen and placed the remaining éclairs on it. "You can bring the rest of these to him as a peace offering."

Gerrit stared at the plate. No way was he going over there to grovel. George was the one who wouldn't stop bragging about his grandbaby. George was the one who came running over without warning. He'd been trying to make Gerrit's life miserable for years. Ever since . . .

"Fine." Hannie sighed. "I'll do it myself."

Daisy followed Hannie out the back door, and Gerrit jumped when it slammed shut with a bang. Why did it feel like no matter what he did, he was letting someone down? He thought of his earlier conversation with Noah. *"I don't know, Dad,"* he'd said. *"But if Evi decides to go, I'll try to make it."* When had he become someone who had to beg his own children to visit him? He would call his daughter again tomorrow.

A piece of paper on the counter caught his eye. The volunteer application for the Community Hope program. He snatched it up. The look that Morgan kid had given him, the one that said he'd given up expecting anything from anyone . . . it reminded him of Evi.

CHAPTER
EIGHTEEN

Hannie stood in the hall in a floral dress, her shoulder-length hair curled. Her red open-toed shoes matched her purse and made Gerrit wonder what she would think if she could see the state of his bare feet. He'd need a chisel to trim up his toenails. That was if his back was having a good day and he could even reach his toes.

She looked like one of the bouquets from her shop. "Are you sure you don't want to come? It's Easter Sunday."

He glanced down at the clothes he was wearing. Everything he owned looked disheveled and misshapen. She had mentioned they would need to go shopping if he was going to be out and about in public, but it hadn't happened.

He shook his head. "I've got to read the paper yet."

"You can read the newspaper anytime." She stared at him with reproach. "It might do you some good to go back to church, you know."

Ha. Little did she know he'd been in a church only two days ago. It certainly hadn't done him any good.

She eyed his wrinkled shirt. "There's got to be something decent in this house you could wear."

There wasn't. He'd looked. He picked at his fingernails.

"All right, then." She raised one hand and headed out the door. "See you in a couple hours."

He watched through the window to make sure she made it to the car without being accosted by Bernard. To say that feathered beast was temperamental would be like saying the Sound was a mud puddle. Gerrit had heard him loud and clear that morning, announcing the sun's arrival at the top of his lungs, but he was nowhere in sight now.

Hannie slipped gracefully into her old gray Toyota Corolla and drove away. How much longer was that thing going to run? It had already been used when they bought it fifteen years ago. He scowled. One more expense to worry about.

She disappeared down the road. Part of him admired her dedication. Her faith. She went to church every Sunday without fail, as if tragedy had never struck. As if their lives hadn't been crumbling around them for decades. As if it mattered.

Luke used to have faith like that. He used to tell Gerrit there was nothing the world could offer that was worth giving your life for. He'd said God was the only thing worth everything. But God's reward to Luke for his unwavering devotion was to crush him like a caterpillar under His almighty foot.

Gerrit forced his shoulders to relax, his fists to unclench. He didn't want God to see how it still affected him, after all this time. Wouldn't give God the satisfaction. Instead, he shifted his attention to more important matters.

It was now only five weeks until Memorial Day weekend. He'd chickened out on calling Evi yesterday, but this morning was the perfect opportunity with Hannie gone and Evi off work. He could use Easter as an excuse.

His phone waited for him on the counter. Hannie's phone had all sorts of fancy buttons on the screen that could perform all sorts of wizardry, while he only used his for making calls. As far as he was concerned, that was what a phone was supposed to be for. Alexander Graham Bell would roll over in his grave if he could see the newfangled devices these days.

Hannie used to try to talk him out of his flip phone and convince him of the virtues of a smartphone, but she'd given up on that. A sharp stick of discomfort fell into his stomach straight from his heart, like a branch falling from a tree with a crash. With regard to her husband, was there anything left Hannie *hadn't* given up on?

She hadn't given up inviting him to church. Stubborn woman.

His mother used to say the only person more stubborn than a Dutchman was a Dutchman's wife. Ha.

He picked up his phone and plopped into an armchair to make the call. He punched the correct buttons, then braced himself.

"Hi, Dad."

He tensed. She'd answered. And she knew it was him.

"Hello."

Silence. Daisy sat at his feet, giving him a supportive look. More silence. Why would his daughter answer the phone if she didn't plan to talk to him?

"What do you want?" she asked.

"What?"

"You called me, remember?"

"Oh."

"Unbelievable." Her voice was muffled now, like she had turned away from the phone and was talking to herself. "He doesn't even know how to talk on the phone."

He cleared his throat. "Happy Easter."

"Really?"

It was a perfectly normal thing for a parent to call their child about, wasn't it?

He tried again. "I found a recipe for baked ziti."

This time the silence buzzed with tension.

"You called to tell me about a recipe you found?"

"It's vegetarian."

"Okaaay."

He pressed the phone to his ear. "I'm going to make it for Memorial Day."

Daisy's face went from supportive to downright sympathetic. He didn't know how much more silence he could handle.

"You have the day off work, right?" He squeezed his eyes shut to concentrate, not wanting to miss any sound, any clue that might give him a hint about what she was thinking. "There's no reason you can't come up—"

"I can think of a few reasons."

He knew better than to ask.

"Please, Evi. Your mother wants to see you."

Daisy laid her head on the floor and covered her face with her paws.

"I see. So this is all to make Mom happy?" Evi's words came fast and strong. "*You* don't actually care whether I come or not."

He pressed a fist to his forehead. "I care."

"Since when?"

The question was like a torpedo. He was the target. He'd always cared. He still remembered the day Evi was born and how small and delicate and beautiful she looked in his callused hands. How he'd loved her so much he thought he would die from it. But what could he say now? He'd never stopped caring about her. Only about making sure she knew.

"I care." He said it again, no other words coming when he needed them most. It was like his heart and mind might burst with all the things he knew and felt and feared, yet his mouth could not accommodate them all.

He strained to hear a response, any response, but instead heard only a man's voice in the background.

Evi sighed. "I gotta go, Dad. Travis is here. Bye."

Click.

She kept doing that to him. Hanging up. It wasn't as though he was asking for much. Just a short visit over a long weekend. He wanted to see his kids and talk to them. Tell them he was sorry he hadn't done better. Been better. They deserved that.

He was beginning to see how little was left of him now that the farm was gone. Maybe there hadn't been much there before, either. He'd just hidden the emptiness of his life behind stacks of hay and a herd of cows. Maybe he deserved to be hung up on.

Oh, Evi. His baby girl.

Wait a minute. He pressed a fist against the arm of the chair. Who was Travis?

CHAPTER
NINETEEN

Four minutes wasn't much time to get from one class to the next. Rae hurried to her locker to fetch her math book and found Kylee waiting there.

Kylee half smiled. "Have you run anyone over yet?"

"That's not funny." Rae pulled the locker open and scrambled to organize her backpack. "My first official drive is next Monday morning."

"I'll be sure to stay off the roads until after lunch."

"Ha-ha."

Rae shut the locker door and checked the time. Two minutes. Not enough time to stop at the bathroom if she was going to get all the way to B Wing. She fell into step beside Kylee, who was headed to B Wing, too.

"Rae, wait up."

She looked over her shoulder. David. She tried to keep her face from revealing anything, but Kylee was looking right at her with a knowing smirk. She and David were just friends. Still, she liked hearing her name on his lips.

She slowed her step. "Hey, David."

The color of his shirt made his eyes look like chocolate. She loved chocolate.

He smiled at her. "Are you going to Community Hope today?"

Kylee turned to face him, walking backward now. "What do you care? Are you stalking her or something?"

Rae glared at her. She was trying to get a rise out of David or Rae or both of them. That was how Kylee operated.

"Stop it, Ky."

David held up his hands. "No stalking, I promise. I was just wondering because I'm volunteering now, too."

"Is that so?" Kylee raised her eyebrows at Rae as she continued walking backward, plowing over anyone unfortunate enough to be in the middle of the hall. "For some reason, Rae hasn't mentioned that."

Rae reached for Kylee's shoulders and spun her back around. "Watch where you're going. And I didn't say anything because I didn't know if he was going to come back or not."

"Well, I am." He hooked his thumbs in the straps of his backpack. "Are you?"

She avoided his tantalizing eyes. She was pretty sure his next class wasn't in B Wing. He was going to be late. "Yes, I'll be there."

"Cool. I'll meet you out front after school, then."

"Okay."

"And maybe I'll see you at lunch."

He peeled off and headed in the other direction before she could answer. She watched him go, hoping he wouldn't look back and catch her. He did. She gasped and bumped into an upperclassman.

"Sorry," she mumbled.

Kylee's eyes glittered with amusement. "Watch where *you're* going."

She could feel her face burning but was powerless to stop it.

Kylee gave her a smug look. "This is an interesting development."

She tried to appear casual. "What?"

"You know what. You and David."

"There is no me and David. You're the one who wants to go out with Seth." She quickened her pace. If she could get to her class before—

"Oh, please." Kylee was grinning like a goose. "Seth is old news. And you're trying to change the subject. David's obsessed with you."

Five feet to the classroom. "He's not obsessed."

"Okay, well, he likes you. And I'm pretty sure you like him."

She reached the door and stopped. Tried to refute it. Felt her lips turning up and fought to keep them from giving her away.

Kylee wagged her eyebrows. "That's what I thought. See you later."

Rae ducked her head and opened the door just as the bell rang. "Later."

She hurried to her seat. Kylee was always making outlandish claims and pushing people's buttons for fun. It was like a sport to her. She shouldn't pay attention to anything Kylee said. In fact, it was easy to discount her friend's words after years of listening to her blow smoke.

But it was much harder to ignore the huge smile on her face and the butterflies in her stomach.

RAE KNEW THE one thing she absolutely must not do under any circumstances was look around the cafeteria to try to spot David. Not with Kylee sitting next to her, the girl who never missed anything. And yet she couldn't help but scan the room out of the corner of her eye when Kylee bent her head to check her phone.

No David. But he hadn't made any promises. He'd said *maybe*. And Kylee would only cause problems if he showed up, anyway.

Kylee wrapped an entire Fruit by the Foot around her finger and sucked on it. "I'm tired. Why are you never tired?"

She shrugged. "I'm tired."

Kylee rolled her eyes and rested her head on the table with a groan. "Wake me when it's time for class."

She closed her eyes, her fruity finger still in her mouth. Rae didn't know anyone who slept as much as Kylee, but she wasn't dumb enough to think Kylee was checked out. Oh no. Just because her eyes were closed didn't mean she wasn't aware of everything going on around her. She wasn't someone who let her guard down easily.

Rae dropped her bag of grapes and glanced around the room again when she reached down to pick it up. A boy who was most definitely not David caught her eye. Morgan. He was sitting with his back to her in the corner in his usual slumped position, hood pulled up over his head. She would've never noticed him, never known it was him, except for the red notebook in his hand.

She put the grapes back in her lunch sack and stood. "I'll be right back."

Kylee yawned and opened one eye. "Where are you going?"

"To say hi to someone."

"Is it David?"

"No. Someone else."

"Okay." Kylee tucked her arm under her head. "Well, if he comes by, I'll be sure and let him know you're in love with him."

Rae walked away shaking her head. Kylee would never do that. For all her quirks, she was a loyal friend. Rae's only *true* friend, in fact. But sometimes she didn't know when to let something go.

No one paid Rae any attention as she approached Morgan's table and slid onto the bench beside him. Including Morgan.

"Hey."

She spoke just loud enough to be heard over the din of the cafeteria.

Morgan kept his eyes on his notebook. "What are you doing?"

"I saw you over here." She faltered. His tone was less than welcoming. "I thought I'd say hi."

He looked up for a second, his eyes guarded, searching. Then looked back down. "Hi."

The implication was clear, but she resisted the urge to flee. "What're you working on?"

"Nothing."

"Did you have a good weekend?"

He shifted in his seat, and she heard her trying-too-hard voice through his ears. He must find her annoying. But she was just trying to be friendly.

"You want to come sit with me and Kylee?"

The word *harrumph* was the only way she could describe his response. She almost chuckled over how much he reminded her of Gerrit at that moment.

A figure appeared behind them, and Morgan tensed.

"Hey, guys." David put a hand on Rae's shoulder. "Whatcha doing?"

She looked back and forth between David and Morgan. Morgan didn't look at David or give any sign that he intended to respond.

She tried to smile. "I was just saying hi to Morgan."

"Mind if I join you?"

She glanced at Morgan, cringing inwardly. He sat unmoving, like David's words had frozen him in time. She'd tortured the poor guy enough for one day.

"I was heading back to Kylee, actually." She rose from the table. "See you later, Morgan."

She didn't expect an answer.

David followed her across the cafeteria. "Quite the chatterbox, isn't he?"

She shrugged. "I think he's focused on his work."

"I heard his dad's in jail for stabbing some guy in an alley."

She frowned. "Where'd you hear that?"

They reached the table where Kylee was sprawled out like a toddler who had crashed after a sugar high.

It was David's turn to shrug. "From some of the guys."

She nudged Kylee with her elbow as she sat down beside her. "Wake up, Sleeping Beauty."

Kylee groaned. "Do I have to?"

"Only if you want to pass English."

She sat up and stretched. "Passing is overrated."

David leaned on the table next to her. "No it's not."

"Oh. It's you." Kylee waved a hand as if dismissing him. "What do you know?"

"Only that I don't want to repeat sophomore year. And

that I have a better chance at getting a scholarship if I get good grades."

"You sound like her." Kylee pointed at Rae with her chin.

David grinned. "Is that a bad thing?"

Rae smiled back at him. "According to Kylee, I'm too boring for words."

"I don't think you're boring."

Rae could see Kylee making a *Gag me* gesture with her finger from the corner of her eye, but she ignored her. It was true she'd never been one to do anything that exciting. Aside from basketball, she spent all her time focused on The Plan, something Kylee found exceedingly dull. But as she locked eyes with David . . . well, suddenly, her life felt anything but boring.

CHAPTER
TWENTY

Gerrit scrunched up his face. "What's that noise?"

Hannie, at the wheel of her Toyota Corolla, shrugged. "It's been doing that for about a month."

"Why didn't you tell me?" He sat up and strained to listen. "Sounds like a belt."

She pulled into the parking lot without responding. He should take the car to the shop, but who knew what the mechanics might find once they started digging around? Who knew what it would cost?

Surely he could fix it himself.

As Hannie turned off the engine, he shifted his attention to his surroundings. Was it too soon to regret this decision?

Hannie grabbed her purse and put a hand on the door handle. "Ready?"

He hesitated. "I still don't understand why we couldn't go to Bill's."

"Because Bill's doesn't sell anything but flannel shirts and work pants."

"But I know where everything is."

She opened the door. "Come on, this was your idea."

That wasn't technically true. She'd been the one to first hint at his need for a new wardrobe, and there'd been nothing subtle about her hint. But he was the one who'd brought it up again this morning after spending the night filling out the volunteer application for Community Hope.

If he was going to show up there again, he didn't want to look like he came straight from the farm. And it wouldn't hurt to look the part of a changed man when Evi and Noah came for Memorial Day. *If* they came.

He slid out of the passenger seat with a groan, his back protesting. It was easier to ride in his truck because he didn't have to bend over as far, but Hannie had insisted on taking her car. She said his truck smelled like moldy hay and dried-up cow manure.

He liked that smell. But her car, dilapidated as it was, smelled like daylilies and strawberry shampoo. So. She drove.

He followed her into the mall, keeping his head down and trying to shrink himself as much as possible. When you're four inches over six feet tall and built like you've been doing hard labor your whole life, you tend to stand out. He didn't like standing out.

Hannie strode purposefully ahead, oblivious to his discomfort. "Let's try Macy's first."

He grunted. By the look of the window displays, Macy's was much too fancy for his needs.

"The men's section is over here." She looked back at him as he lagged behind and waved a hand. "Come on. We don't want to be here all night."

He'd seen the sign on the door. "They close at nine."

He wasn't sure what the look she gave him was, something between amusement and exasperation, but he liked it.

When they reached the men's section, Hannie immediately began digging through racks as if she knew exactly what she was looking for. He stood behind her and waited.

"If you see anything you like, grab it." She flashed him a smile. "Once you have a few things, you can try them on."

He made a face. He hadn't anticipated trying anything on. Couldn't he hold it up and decide?

She must've read his expression. "They're just clothes, dear. They won't bite."

He swallowed. The idea of undressing in a fitting room with people walking by and mirrors all around made his mouth dry. But she'd called him *dear*. "Okay."

Clothes of every color surrounded him, all looking sharp and crisp in their newness. He looked down. The knees of his pants were threadbare, the cuffs of his shirt frayed.

Hannie held a dark purple polo up to his face and squinted. "Hmm. I think this color would look good on you."

He shrank from the shirt. "Purple's a girl color."

"Hmmph."

Twenty minutes later, he found himself at the entrance to the fitting room area with an armload of clothes. Only one pair of pants—plain old denim jeans—had he chosen himself. The rest were Hannie's doing.

He eyed the pile nervously. "It would take me months to wear this many clothes."

She gave him a gentle push in the right direction. "Try them on and see what happens."

There was nothing for it. He had once milked thirteen cows in a row by hand when the power went out and the generator ran out of gas. His hands and arms had been sore for weeks. Surely he could try on a couple of shirts.

He shuffled down the long hall to the first available stall. Was this how the cows felt stepping into the parlor?

Well, *moo*.

Inside the stall, he carefully locked the door and hung the shirts on hooks. He set the pants—and who needed more than one pair of pants?—on a stool in the corner. A full-length mirror caught every movement. He turned his back on it. He didn't know who that sour-looking old man was, but he had other things to worry about.

He took a deep breath.

Taking off his pants resulted in banging his elbow hard against the wall. Removing his shirt left his thinning hair sticking straight up from static. He tugged a polo shirt—a gray one, *not* the purple one—from its hanger and quickly pulled it on. There. He smoothed his hands over the front. That wasn't so bad. He buttoned the three buttons with stiff fingers.

Why not? He turned to look.

He started. He hadn't seen legs that white since they'd taken the kids to see the polar bears at the zoo when they were little. Grabbing the pants from the stool, he stuck his feet in them, one after the other.

Yank.

Yank.

He checked the size on the tag. Seemed about right, yet these jeans weren't like the ones at Bill's. Somewhere between his knees and upper thighs, the pants came to a grinding halt. Maybe Mark from Room F could handle pants this tight, but Gerrit Laninga was not about to squeeze his ham hocks into fabric this unforgiving.

He pushed down. The pants wouldn't give. He made some adjustments and tried again with more force.

"Aargh!" He couldn't keep the exclamation from coming out as blinding pain stabbed at his lower back.

"Gerrit?" Hannie's voice floated through the air to his stall with a note of concern. "Everything okay in there?"

He grimaced, forcing the words out through clenched teeth as fresh pain washed over him. "I'm fine."

The pants would have to wait. He carefully straightened, breathing heavily, and concentrated on relaxing his back muscles. Yes, that was better. Reaching up didn't cause him nearly the trouble reaching down did. Maybe he should focus on the shirts for now.

And to think women did this kind of thing for fun.

With cautious movements, he took hold of the bottom of the gray polo and lifted the shirt. The pain was minimal. He could do this. His arms rose to chest height, then shoulder height. Easy now.

When his arms reached the point where they were level with his head, he let out another brief cry of distress. He had forgotten to undo the buttons.

"Are you sure you're okay?" Her voice came from directly outside his door this time.

Sweat broke out on his forehead. "Fine."

His voice was muffled by the shirt covering his face. The best course of action would be to pull the shirt back down and take care of the buttons, but one of his elbows was caught. When he tried to pull it free, a back spasm jolted his body.

"Oooh," he groaned.

His body jerked, and he stumbled because of the awkward

position his pants had put him in. Unable to see, he ran headfirst into an empty hook.

"Yow." His nose smarted.

"That's it." Hannie knocked on the door. "Open up."

He panicked. "Just a minute."

Bumbling blindly, he shuffled toward what he thought was the corner with the stool. If he could ease himself onto it, maybe he could work his elbow out of the shirt without tipping over. But he miscalculated.

Thud.

The door handle jabbed him in the hip, and the latch released under his weight. Hannie seized the opportunity and pushed against the door. She gasped as he stumbled backward. He could imagine her face. He couldn't see it, but he could imagine.

"Gerrit, my goodness."

If he hadn't been so flustered, he would've been mortified. "Help."

Calm, cool fingers prodded his chin where the shirt was wedged tight against his face. "Hold still."

It sounded like she was smiling.

He held still. She worked her fingers under the fabric and got ahold of a button.

"You're hopeless, you know that?"

She was definitely smiling.

Once she got the button free, the shirt slid easily over his head with her assistance. He breathed a sigh of relief as he shook it off his arms. But his relief turned to chagrin when he saw Hannie's face.

"I . . . um . . ."

She started to laugh. A whole-body, lyrical laugh that filled the tiny dressing room and rushed over him like a waterfall of delight, leaving tingles on his skin.

He blinked. "Thanks for your help."

She covered her mouth with one hand, her eyes dancing. He chuckled at first, then a full-on laugh worked its way up from his bare-naked belly to his mouth and burst out like a long-forgotten song. Hannie shrieked and slapped her other hand over her mouth as well, trying to contain her amusement.

For a moment, as face muscles he hadn't used since who-knew-when were brought back to life and Hannie's face shone like a bride on her wedding day, he almost forgot he was only half wearing pants.

She poked him in the ribs with a wicked grin. "Looks like you need new underwear, too."

CHAPTER
TWENTY-ONE

Gerrit pulled into the Greenville Community Church parking lot at 2:51 wearing his old worn-out jeans and a brand-new polo shirt. Hannie had been unable to convince him to try on another pair of pants after what happened with the first pair, but they were going to the mall again in a few days because she insisted he needed new shoes. Maybe he'd give the pants another go. He'd have to stretch out before leaving the house this time.

He checked his watch. 2:52. Community Hope started at three.

He looked over at Daisy. "Should we wait or go in early?"

She undoubtedly had an opinion but didn't offer it. He tapped the steering wheel. It had been an agonizing decision, whether to bring the dog. It was ridiculous, and probably sacrilegious, to bring a dog into a church. Plus, he didn't want to get her hair all over his truck. He'd only barely gotten rid of all the feathers from when Bernard and Mr. Whiskers went a couple of rounds. But in the end, he'd pictured Morgan's face and hoisted Daisy into the passenger seat.

This should teach that kid to make a snap judgment. Gerrit *wasn't* unreliable and disappointing. He could come through for people.

As he was still trying to decide whether to wait for the clock to strike three, he spotted Rae heading for the front door of the building with some boy. They sure looked cozy, walking so close together. All smiley. Hadn't she said she didn't have room in her plans for a boyfriend?

He carefully slid out of the truck, mindful of his still-tender back, and walked to the other side to open the door for Daisy. He hadn't even thought to bring a leash because she minded so well, but now he wondered if he was breaking some kind of doggie protocol by letting her walk about freely in public.

Too late now.

Daisy loved every minute of it as they entered the building and made their way to Room F. She held her head high and sniffed the air as if it had recently rained prime rib.

Gerrit made a mental note to make Hannie prime rib for dinner this weekend.

In Room F, Mark greeted him with wide eyes. "You're here."

Gerrit nodded.

"And you brought a dog."

"She's real good." He scratched the back of his head. "She won't cause any trouble."

Mark clutched his clipboard to his chest. "But . . . dogs aren't allowed in the building."

At that moment, Rae noticed him standing in the doorway.

"Hey, Gerrit!" She hurried over to him and knelt beside Daisy, cupping the dog's face in her hands. "And look who came along. Good girl."

"Cool, a dog." The girl who had been pouting during Gerrit's previous visit joined Rae on the floor. "She's so cute."

Rae scooted over to give the other girl a chance to pet Daisy. The dog ate up the attention as if she'd been in isolation for a month.

"Daisy, this is Taylor." Rae made a show of introducing her. "Taylor, meet Daisy."

The girl leaned in, and Daisy gave her a tiny lick of appreciation.

Taylor squealed with delight. "She can be our mascot."

Morgan slipped into the room and froze in his tracks at the sight of Daisy. He stared at her, and a small smile formed on his face. This was only the second time he'd seen Morgan, but Gerrit guessed he didn't smile much.

Gerrit raised his eyebrows at Mark, daring him to put his foot down and ban Daisy from the building now.

Mark laughed and waved his clipboard toward the room in a grand gesture. "Well, Daisy, I guess it's nice to meet you. Welcome to Community Hope."

DAISY HAD ALREADY become a celebrity by the time Gerrit made his way to the back of the room, where Morgan sat hunched over a notebook. Everybody's new furry best friend pranced right up to the kid with the black hair and nudged his knee with her nose.

Morgan pulled little speaker thingies from his ears. "Hello."

Gerrit almost replied before he realized Morgan was not talking to him. How come Daisy made friends so easily?

He eased himself into a chair two seats away from Morgan to give him some space but not too much. Then he sat back to observe. Ha. This kid thought he'd never see him again, and here he was, *with a dog*. He folded his arms across his chest in a self-satisfied way.

Morgan closed his notebook and set it on the table. He tucked his earphone things into the pocket of his sweatshirt. He had to be overheating wearing that. It was a perfect spring day in the best of all places: the Pacific Northwest. Why didn't he take it off?

Morgan put a hand on Daisy's head and began a conversation, murmuring low enough that Gerrit couldn't catch it over the din of the wild animals in the room around him. Gerrit didn't interrupt. He waited.

Daisy listened intently, and if Gerrit didn't know better, he would say it looked like she nodded once in a while, urging Morgan on. After a few minutes, Morgan moved both hands to Daisy's back and gave her a good hard rub.

"I think she likes that," Gerrit ventured.

Morgan kept his eyes on the dog. "Yeah."

Gerrit scowled to himself. Would it kill the kid to show a little appreciation? He opened his mouth to say something else but nothing came out. What were teenage boys interested in? He had no idea. But this after-school program was meant to help kids with their homework, right? So they wouldn't be held back? Maybe he should start there.

"How many classes are you failing?"

Morgan looked at him, a challenge in his eyes. "What makes you think I'm failing any?"

Gerrit sputtered. "Well, Rae said—"

"Rae talked about me?"

"No, not really. She talked about the program. How it's for, uh, kids who need . . ."

Morgan glared. "I'm not stupid."

Gerrit's heart stopped beating. His lungs suspended their life-giving work. And the rectangular white table turned into a square wooden one where a young boy sat swinging his feet. Noah must've been about eleven. Hadn't gone through his growth spurt yet. The fridge in the calf barn had gone on the fritz, and Gerrit had run home to put a box of Ultravac in the kitchen fridge before the vaccines could get too warm and would need to be thrown out. Noah had been working on math homework.

"Dad, can you help me?" he'd asked.

"I gotta get back."

"But I don't understand this."

"I won't be able to explain it to you."

Noah's face had fallen. *"I'm not stupid."*

That wasn't what Gerrit had meant. Math was his nemesis, and he'd never been able to explain math concepts to anyone. Luke was the only reason he'd passed math. He'd stayed up late quizzing him and helping him work the problems out more nights than Gerrit could count.

But Noah just looked at him with hurt in his eyes, and Gerrit had steeled himself. *"Ask your mother,"* he'd said, then went back to the farm.

The rectangular white table returned. A pack of prepubescent boys roared with laughter at a table behind him. Daisy flopped on her back, inviting someone, anyone, to give her a belly rub, and Morgan leaned down to oblige.

Gerrit shook his head. Of course his son wasn't stupid. He'd never once thought that.

He decided to try a different approach. "What are you working on in your notebook?"

"Nothing."

So that's how it was going to be.

"What grade are you in?"

"I'm graduating the end of May."

Gerrit's eyebrows rose. This kid didn't look old enough to be graduating high school and going out into the world. Then again, there was something in his eyes that spoke of a maturity beyond his years.

"What do you plan to do after that?"

Morgan gave Daisy's belly one last rub and sat back up. He glanced at the red notebook lying on the table. "I don't know."

Gerrit had always wondered what it would be like to be young and facing a future full of unknowns and possibilities rather than one that had been planned out for you by someone else since before you were born. He'd always figured it would feel like adventure and freedom, but looking at Morgan's face, he wasn't so sure.

"You going to college?"

Morgan shrugged. "What do you care?"

Gerrit sat back, hard. "I care."

It wasn't lost on him that he'd said those same two words to Evi only a few days before. She hadn't believed him then, and Morgan probably didn't now. Why didn't anyone think he cared about anything?

He didn't want to delve too deeply into that.

"There are some good community colleges around here." He tried to sound casual. "Maybe that'd be a good place to start."

"I don't think I'm cut out for college."

Oh, the pain cut deep. This kid sure knew how to hit him where it hurt the most. Those were the same words he'd said to Luke a hundred times. But his big brother had refused to take no for an answer. He'd been determined to get Gerrit through college if it was the last thing he did.

He found himself borrowing Luke's reply. "Says who?"

Morgan's eyes flashed. "My dad. My teachers. Everyone."

"What do *you* say?"

Morgan leaned his elbows on the table, his notebook between them. He put his head in his hands. "I don't know."

"Oh, come on. That's a coward's response. You do know."

Morgan's head shot up. "You don't know anything about me."

Gerrit's face remained stoic, but his innards churned. Daisy sat up and scooted between them as if to play mediator.

"Who do you think you are, anyway?" Morgan demanded. "You're only here because you're Rae's grandpa."

Gerrit huffed. He wasn't old enough to be her—okay, maybe he was. But still. "Rae's my neighbor. That's all."

"Then why are you here?"

Yes, why? That was the million-dollar question. He looked down at Daisy, who was swinging her head back and forth between them as if following the conversation. He wasn't sure why he'd come. He'd mentioned it to Hannie, and she'd said it would be a great activity to keep him busy. Yet boredom alone couldn't explain why he was sitting at a table with some angsty kid and a pesky dog, trying not to look like an idiot.

All he knew was that he hadn't been able to get Morgan's face, and that expression that reminded him of Evi, out of his mind.

"I don't know."

Morgan's face turned smug. "Who's the coward now?"

Gerrit laughed. He couldn't help it. It bubbled up and

spilled over, and he couldn't have stopped it if he wanted to. "I guess we both are."

The ghost of a smile flashed across Morgan's face. Gerrit looked around at the dozens of kids caterwauling around the room. He had nothing to lose. "Fine. I'll tell you the truth, if you tell me the truth."

It was a scary thing, holding an offer like that out there.

Morgan narrowed his eyes. "You first."

Fair enough.

He cleared his throat. "I've got two kids. They're grown now."

Morgan waited.

"You remind me of them. And of myself, when I was young. That's why I'm here. Besides, you said you loved dogs, and I've got a dog."

Daisy laid her head on Gerrit's knee. Aw, shoot. He'd claimed her as his own. She'd never let him forget it.

Morgan nodded slowly. "Okay."

Gerrit let out a long breath as his shoulders drooped. This whole thing was exhausting. "Your turn."

Morgan picked up the notebook and gripped it with both hands. The cover was worn. The spiral stretched out on top. "I want to be a songwriter."

It took a minute for the words to sink in. A songwriter? Did people go to school for that sort of thing? He had no experience with any form of creative endeavor. Didn't know anyone like that.

Except Hannie. His mind flashed to Hannie at her shop, carefully arranging her bouquets, and it smacked him like an errant hoof upside the head that it was more than a job to her.

She was an artist.

"What does that mean?" He was way out of his element here. "What do songwriters do?"

He braced himself, half expecting Morgan to snap at him with the obvious *They write songs, dummy*. But he was looking for more than that, and Morgan seemed to understand.

"They usually go live somewhere they can meet a lot of other songwriters and singers. Then they pay their dues."

"Dues? Is it expensive?"

Morgan leaned closer. "It's not money. It's time. You have to put in the hard work, start from the bottom."

"Where's the bottom?"

"The bottom is on a street corner in Nashville, playing for quarters dropped in a guitar case."

Gerrit tried to picture that. "You got a guitar?"

Morgan hesitated. "It's my dad's."

"And you're a singer?"

Morgan shook his head. "I just want to write the songs. But I'll sing if that's what it takes."

"Oh." Gerrit clasped his hands together, trying to concentrate. "Do songwriters go to college?"

Morgan looked away from Gerrit and stared at the wall on the other side of the table, a wistful expression on his face. "Sometimes."

"Seems like a good place to start."

"I've already got a few college credits." Morgan shrugged. "From summer school."

"You're well on your way, then." Gerrit smacked the table with his palm. "You don't want to waste those credits."

It was all but decided, as far as he was concerned. Morgan could sing on as many street corners as he wanted once he graduated college.

His work here was done.

Morgan hung his head. "It's not that simple."

Gerrit's confidence deflated. Few things ever were. He should know that better than anyone.

"Five minutes until closing time," Mark called from the doorway.

Daisy's ears perked up.

Morgan smiled at her. "She's ready to get out of here." He leaned his face close to hers. "Aren't you, girl?"

She licked his chin.

Gerrit rose from the table. "Well, I guess I'll see you later."

"I'll be here Friday," Morgan offered. "It's something to do after school. Wish they had it every day, but . . ."

"You could always come to my house." Wait, what was he saying? This kid was going to think he was a psychopath. But Morgan looked at him like the offer was worth considering.

Emboldened, Gerrit forged ahead. "Rae hangs out there sometimes."

Morgan tensed, his eyes flicking around the room. "Um . . ."

Gerrit cringed. There went his big mouth again. Bringing Rae up wasn't going to put Morgan at ease.

Morgan tucked the red notebook into his backpack and zipped it shut. "I'll have to think about it."

Gerrit wasn't the brightest or most perceptive man to ever walk the earth, and he'd never claimed to be. But even he could tell what Morgan meant was *no*.

CHAPTER
TWENTY-TWO

Gerrit could not stand the awful racket another second. He stomped to the back door, grumbling to himself, and flung it open.

"Enough!" His shout carried across the drive and echoed off the barn. "Shut your beak, or I'll shut it for you."

From the fence post where he was perched, Bernard the Terrible cocked his head to the side to stare at Gerrit with one beady eye. Then he dug deep and let out another deliberate squawk. Gerrit winced. Ugh. He'd been putting up with this for almost two weeks now. It was worse than nails on a chalkboard.

He glared at the bird. "You're doing it on purpose."

Bernard redoubled his efforts. Daisy hid behind Gerrit's legs and whimpered.

Gerrit slammed the door and kicked the wall, his foot narrowly missing the blue-and-white suitcase that stood sentinel over him whenever Hannie was away, reminding him of how much he didn't know. He wanted to throw it into the driveway and run it over with his truck, but something held him back. Something told him its continued presence in the mudroom was a test.

He looked at Daisy. "I've got to get out of here."

Besides the rooster driving him nuts and the suitcase mocking him, he had Luisa on his mind. He hadn't seen her since signing the farm papers, but he'd been thinking about her a lot, ever since he'd gone into the pony barn and seen the boxes of Luke's things. She was an independent woman, sure—Luke would've never fallen for her otherwise—but if he didn't check in on her once in a while, who would?

Careful not to strain his back, he slowly pulled on his shabby tennis shoes. Hannie might be right about his needing a new pair. The rubber on the bottoms was beginning to separate from the rest of the shoe, and the laces were dingy as dishwater.

Daisy whined and butted his knee with her head.

"You'll be safe in the house." He struggled to tie the laces with his oversized, gnarled hands. "Bernard can't get you in here."

Her liquid brown eyes stared up at him.

"I only brought you the other day because Morgan wanted to see you."

She scooted closer.

"There's no reason for you to come this time."

That face. How could a dog be so expressive? Regardless, he wasn't going to give in this time. He'd been spending way too much time with Daisy.

He rose to his feet. "Not today. And that's final."

He grabbed his keys and hurried out the door without looking back, so he wouldn't be tempted to change his mind. He was a grown man. He could not—would not—allow a four-legged fur ball to dictate his decisions. It was time to put his foot down.

Gerrit was positive the clamor Bernard subjected him to as he got in his truck was rooster-speak for a string of obscenities. He considered answering Bernard in kind but held his tongue. Like he said. He was a grown man.

The drive to Luisa's house was quiet. No animals, no Rae, and he kept the radio turned off. He hadn't even brought his phone. He couldn't afford any distractions because he needed to think. What was he going to say to her?

She was the only person Gerrit had ever had to compete with for Luke's attention. Luke had been a sworn bachelor for fifteen years. He'd said if Gerrit alone could have a wife and family, he'd be content with that. *"And where would I meet a girl, anyway?"* he'd say with a smile. *"In the milking parlor?"*

One day, Luke had gone to the feed store for Calf-Manna and chanced upon Luisa buying a forty-pound bag of wild-bird seed. He'd helped her carry it to her car. Gerrit would never forget the look on his brother's face when he told Gerrit about the "Italian angel" he'd met. Gerrit knew Luke was a goner from that moment. No matter that Luisa was almost twelve years younger and didn't speak much English. No matter that neither of their parents approved. He'd fallen hard and fast.

Gerrit parked along the road in front of Luisa's bright blue ranch-style house. He never could decide whether he was pleased she hadn't remarried or whether it was a shame. She was a nice-looking woman. Fiery and confident. She could've found another man. Still could. But what she and Luke had together . . . well, you don't find love like that twice.

As he walked up the path to her door, he noticed her

gutters dripping over in a few places from the rain that morning. When was the last time they'd been cleaned? And her screen door had a tear in it. He had a utility knife in the truck but hadn't brought a spline roller. There was a hardware store nearby. He could run and get one.

He stuck his finger in the tear. Was it small enough to patch or should he replace the whole screen?

The door opened. "Are you coming in, or do you plan to stare at my door all day?"

Gerrit pulled his hand back as if he'd been caught stealing a cookie. "Your screen's ripped."

"Oh, that." Luisa waved a hand. "I was carrying a bunch of things into the house a couple weeks ago, and I got caught on the screen."

"You should've called me."

She pulled the door wide and ushered him in. "It's nothing. And you're here now, aren't you?"

She was a diminutive woman, dark hair and distinctive features. Her personality always made her seem bigger than she was, and the wisdom and grief in her eyes made her seem older.

She urged him into the kitchen and pulled open the fridge with a flourish. "What can I get you? Iced tea? Milk?"

He'd seen and hauled and cleaned up enough milk to last a dozen lifetimes during his years on the farm, but he'd never grown tired of it. "Milk, please."

She poured him a tall glass of milk and set it in front of him, along with a small white plate piled high with Oreos.

He picked up a cookie. "No *pizzelle*?"

He couldn't remember a time Luisa had no homemade pizzelle on hand.

She threw up her hands. "And who would eat it? There's only me. I grow tired of eating all the pizzelle."

Her accent thickened when she was agitated. He ate three Oreos in silence and took a long draught of milk, the wheels in his mind turning, turning. Should he bring up the boxes or leave well enough alone?

She wiped the immaculate countertop with an equally immaculate dishcloth. "You're not here to get the pizzelle. And you didn't come to fix my screen door."

He kept his eyes on the counter. "I haven't seen you since Jim's office. I wanted to check on you."

She held her arms out and spun in a circle. "See? I am fine."

Her parents had both died years ago. She had no siblings or children. She'd never returned to her homeland, where she'd lived the first twenty years of her life. But apparently she was fine.

"How is Hannie?"

He flinched. "Good. Busy."

"Yes, yes. I go visit her in the shop sometimes. Such beautiful arrangements. And how are the kids?"

He wouldn't know, yet he didn't want to tell her that. "Fine."

She gave him a knowing look. "Good."

"I was in the barn the other day." He gripped his glass in one hand and rubbed at the condensation with his thumb. "Luke's boxes are in there."

"So that's what this is about."

He kept staring at the counter.

She sighed. "Did you open them?"

"No."

"I think you should."

He looked up. "Why?"

Her eyes had a faraway look. "It's good to remember."

He wasn't so sure about that. There were a lot of things he'd rather forget. "I could bring them here."

"I kept all of Luke's things from our time together." She put a hand to her cheek. "They keep me company. But those things are yours. From before there was me."

When Luke married Luisa, he took nothing from the tiny apartment over the garage on the farm except a few clothes. Not much had been in there, anyway. Almost everything from his younger years had still been in his old bedroom in the house they grew up in.

Their father had moved everything left behind in the apartment into his own house so he could rent out the space to migrant workers. But after Luke died, their father had demanded Gerrit remove everything from the house that might remind him of his oldest son. His pride and joy. And then he never spoke another word to Gerrit again, aside from the logistical communication necessary between two people running a farm together.

"Did Luke ever show you his old stuff? The yearbooks or anything?"

Luisa shook her head. "He said he started a new life the day he met me and none of that stuff mattered to him anymore."

"Would you like to see it?"

A wistful look softened her face. "Maybe. If there were old photos, baby pictures . . ." She paused and smiled. "Yes, I would like to see that."

He nodded. "Okay."

Rising from his stool, he set his empty glass in the sink. "Thanks for the milk and cookies."

"Where are you going?"

"To get the ladder from the garage. Gotta clean out those gutters."

GERRIT'S BACK ACHED as he climbed down the ladder for the last time. There. Luke couldn't have done it better himself. Not a single leaf remained.

Luisa pulled her car into the tidy garage as he was setting the ladder back in its place. She had offered to run to the hardware store for a spline roller once it had become clear Gerrit would not leave until he took care of the torn screen.

She hopped out and waved the roller in the air. "I got it."

He grunted and took it from her. "Just have to find that roll of screen."

"A thank-you would be nice." She put her hands on her hips.

He stared at her in surprise. He was doing *her* a favor, not the other way around. "Thanks?"

"No wonder Hannie says you're impossible." She pointed a finger in his face. "You've got no manners."

Hannie said that? To Luisa? What else had they talked about? His stomach twisted. Had Luisa known Hannie had planned to leave him?

"You don't look so good." Luisa touched his elbow. "Are you sure you want to fix my screen door today? It can wait."

He shook off her hand, shook off the question. "It will only take a few minutes."

He found the roll of screen, grabbed the utility knife from his truck, and set to work. It had turned into a beautiful day, despite the earlier rain, so he did all the work outside, letting the sun warm his back. Luisa carried a patio chair over from the backyard and sat nearby to watch him.

"You have talked with Jakob lately?" she asked.

With his back to her, Gerrit scowled. Jakob was the last thing he wanted to talk about. Now that the farm was gone, he had no reason to waste another minute of his life thinking about his younger brother. Surely, Luisa knew that.

"He took it hard, I think," she pressed. "Losing the farm."

Gerrit's shoulders tensed. *He* took it hard? How could she say that to him? Jakob hadn't set foot on the farm since Luke's accident. Hadn't lifted a finger to help since two years before that. He'd made it clear he wanted nothing to do with the place.

"Haven't seen him," he replied.

Luisa was quiet for a moment, and he glanced over at her. Her eyes were sad, seeing right through him.

"He's your brother, Gerrit. Your flesh and blood. You know what I would give to have a brother?"

"He made his choice." Gerrit struggled to line the screen up with the frame, his hands trembling. "I've got nothing to say to him."

It shouldn't have surprised him when Jakob abandoned him and Luke to chase women and booze. Nor should it have surprised him when their father made excuses for Jakob and continued writing him a paycheck even though he never showed up for work. But it had. Even after all the years his father had favored Jakob, the son born ten years after his other sons even though the doctors had said no more children would come, Gerrit had still been surprised.

Luisa sighed. "Luke would tell you to forgive."

Gerrit's nostrils flared. He didn't trust himself to speak. He would never forgive Jakob.

176

"God gave Luke only forty years on this earth." Her voice grew louder. Sharper. "Forty short years. Look how many you've had, and you would waste them in bitterness?"

A growl erupted from his lips. "You don't know anything about it."

She knew nothing of the times Jakob had gotten himself into trouble on the farm and blamed him. Nothing of how Jakob had turned their parents against him and only worked when someone was watching, until he stopped working all together. Nothing of the thousands of dollars his father had spent trying to buy Jakob's way out of his gambling debt. And then when Gerrit needed help financing the property he and Hannie wanted so they could have a place of their own—away from the farm, away from his father's relentless scrutiny—where had his father's money gone then?

Gerrit clenched his fist. He knew exactly where it had gone.

Luisa stood and picked up the chair to carry it back to its place. She gave him a solemn look. "I know about needing to forgive, Gerrit."

She turned her back on him. Her words struck like an arrow and sunk into his side. Not a mere flesh wound. No. That arrow had pierced straight through to his heart.

Luisa's words still reverberated through Gerrit's soul as he pulled into his driveway. Words about forgiveness and a wasted life. Words he could not bear.

He heard the commotion before he even opened the truck door. Bernard the Terrible was at it again. The stupid rooster was at the back door, feathers ruffled, wings half raised. He charged the door repeatedly, screeching the whole time. Inside the house, Daisy howled.

"Cut that out!" He slammed the truck door and strode toward the house, waving his arms. "Get away from there, you little—"

Crunch.

Who would be coming over right now? He spun around and swallowed hard. A police car drove deliberately up the drive, an officer with a serious face at the wheel. Glaring at him. *Oh, God. Hannie.* His heart dropped to the ground, and he stumbled over it as he met the officer at the driver's door. Something terrible must have happened.

The young man's expression gave nothing away as he slowly got out of the car. This couldn't be real. Gerrit's mouth went dry. No words would come.

The officer cleared his throat. "Mr. Laninga?"

Gerrit nodded dumbly, his throat constricting. A black hole opening up in his stomach. *Not Hannie. Oh, not my Hannie.*

"I'm Officer Denway." The officer crossed his arms over his chest and glanced at the house. "I'm here about a noise complaint."

Gerrit watched the man's mouth move but couldn't process his words as fear roared in his ears. How could he go on if something happened to Hannie? How would he tell the kids? And Daisy would never understand. She'd surely blame him.

Officer Denway cleared his throat, and Gerrit blinked, the man's words finally penetrating. A noise complaint? He was here about a noise complaint?

"I just got home." He rubbed his forehead. "The rooster was badgering the corgi, but I'll take care of it."

Officer Denway narrowed his eyes and tucked his thumbs into his belt loops. "I see."

Relief flooded Gerrit's veins like morphine from an IV, and his arms tingled. *Thank you, God. Thank you, thank you.* Then a movement over at the neighbor's property caught the corner of his eye.

George.

A spark ignited in his chest. "Who called you about this, anyway? It's the middle of the day."

Officer Denway didn't budge but gave him a condescending look. "That is confidential information, sir. During daytime hours, complaints can still be made for unreasonable noise."

The rooster brought an end to his siege on the house and began making a wide circle around the police car as if casing it. He was silent now.

Gerrit glared at the foul fowl, trying to contain the anger expanding in his chest. "He gets worked up sometimes, but I won't let it happen again."

Because he was going to chop his filthy head off with an ax. He'd have a hard time disturbing the peace with no head.

Officer Denway nodded. "I'd appreciate that. I'm not going to write up a citation or anything this time, but I don't want to get called out here again, okay?"

He acted like he was doing Gerrit some sort of big favor. How old was this guy? Thirty-two? Where did he come off talking to Gerrit as though he were a little kid? Couldn't he see Gerrit was twice his age?

Gerrit's fists clenched, but he grunted his agreement and took a step back so Officer Denway could climb back into his patrol car. No use causing more of a scene. Hannie would kill him if he got arrested.

As the officer turned the patrol car around, Gerrit silently willed him to run the rooster over, but Bernard nimbly avoided the vehicle's tires.

Gerrit waited until the police car drove away, then raised his voice. "What's your problem, George? You had to call the cops because of my rooster?"

George slid out from behind a tree where he had no doubt been watching the whole time. "The noise was out of control, Gerrit. The rooster wouldn't stop. And my daughter's here visiting, trying to rest."

Gerrit took five menacing steps toward his neighbor. "You couldn't just ask me to shut him up?"

George didn't flinch. "You weren't home."

"You could've called. I would've come back."

"I tried."

Gerrit's hands curled into fists again. His phone. He'd left it sitting on the kitchen counter. "You knew I'd be back eventually."

"I didn't know when." George shrugged, unfazed. "And Mallory needed to take a nap. Her doctor says she's been spending too much time on her feet. It's not good for the baby."

George's defense of his daughter did nothing to cool Gerrit's anger. It was bad enough the way they'd ended up as neighbors. Bad enough George had never once said he was sorry for what had happened that day at the farm. Now he would stoop this low to pay him back for the way Bernard ran him off the other day?

He glared at his neighbor.

"Maybe you should bring Daisy with you next time you're out so this doesn't happen again." George smiled. "You're supposed to be watching her, aren't you?"

He lifted a hand in farewell and hurried back to his house before Gerrit could respond. Not that he wanted to. Mere words would never be a strong enough reply for today's indignity.

Only actions would even the score.

CHAPTER
TWENTY-THREE

R
ae covered up a yawn. It was her own fault she had to be at school by six-fifteen on a Monday morning. She'd had to settle for the last available drive time.

"You're going to do great." Her mom pulled into the school's lot and put the car in park. "Remember what Dad said about being confident."

Rae nodded. She remembered. She also remembered the meaningful look Dad gave Mom when he said it, as if he held her personally responsible for Rae's success—or lack thereof—behind the wheel.

"Did you remember to grab your lunch? I set it by the door."

"Yes, Mom."

"Your hair's a little bumpy." She smoothed her hand over Rae's head. "Do you have time to redo your ponytail?"

Rae resisted the urge to roll her eyes and remind Mom she was almost sixteen. "I'll fix it after the drive."

"Okay." Mom leaned over and kissed her on the forehead. "Have a good day. I love you."

"Love you too." She grabbed her backpack and climbed out of the car. She should be thankful. Mom only wanted what was best for her. That was the whole point of The Plan, wasn't it? But sometimes she wasn't sure if the person Mom and Dad saw and the person staring back at her in the mirror every day were the same. Sometimes both seemed like strangers.

The Driver's Ed. car idled in front of the main entrance, and Mr. Fletcher stood beside it, arms crossed. The two other students who were supposed to drive with them this morning had not yet arrived.

"Good morning, Miss Walters." The sour look on Mr. Fletcher's face made it clear he was not a morning person. "Any idea where your fellow classmates might be?"

She shook her head. It figured she would be stuck standing here with this grump, waiting on Rob and Izzy. They probably couldn't stop making out long enough to drive over here.

Mr. Fletcher drummed his bicep with his fingers and scowled at the road. She tried to avoid eye contact, not wanting to accidentally start a conversation. As she examined the school, as though greatly interested in its architecture, a dark figure lurking around the side of the building caught her attention. She turned to look closer, and he slipped around the corner and disappeared. But not before she'd gotten a pretty good look.

Morgan. It had to be him. Who else wore that hoodie every day? Who else walked hunched over like that?

What was he doing here this early?

The slam of a car door drew her attention away. Rob saun-
tered toward her and Mr. Fletcher. He was wearing a T-shirt
and jeans and had one arm draped over Izzy's shoulders.

"You do know your driver's permit requires you to have an
adult in the car when you drive, right?" Mr. Fletcher waved
an arm at Rob's car. "The rules are there for a reason."

It was a favorite saying of his. He and Dad would get along
well. Izzy elbowed Rob's ribs and giggled, brushing her long
blond hair back over her shoulder with a flick of her hand.

Rob gave their intrepid instructor a lazy smile. "I know,
Fletch. But nobody was home. I had no other way to get
here on time."

"It would be generous to say you're on time, Mr. Harris."
Mr. Fletcher checked his watch. "And the next time I see you
driving without an adult in the car, I'm going to call the police.
But we better get going. Mr. Harris, why don't you go first
since you already had a warm-up this morning?"

Izzy giggled again. Rob shrugged and held the back door
open for her, watching appreciatively as her miniskirt-clad
behind wriggled into position. He reached in and made a
show of securing Izzy's seat belt, which allowed him to graze
her breasts with his arm. Izzy smiled.

Rae made a face she hoped portrayed her utter disgust.
So immature. And embarrassing. And gross. No wonder her
parents didn't want her to have a boyfriend.

She slid in next to Izzy in the back while Mr. Fletcher took
the front passenger seat, a clipboard in hand and instructions
ready on his lips.

"Check your mirrors and—"

Rob didn't need any helpful hints or reminders. He pulled
onto the road like he'd been doing it for years.

Rae forced a smile as all eyes turned on her.

Mr. Fletcher repeated himself. "Your turn, Miss Walters. Up you go."

Her legs shook as she got out of the back seat and took the keys from Izzy's outstretched hand. Rob's and Izzy's drives had gone off without a hitch. Rob had even pulled off a textbook parallel park downtown, and Izzy had remembered to yield to the car on her right when the two cars arrived at a four-way stop at the same time.

But Rae was certain her drive was not destined to go as smoothly.

The car was centered perfectly in a parking space in front of the post office, which hadn't opened yet. She climbed into the driver's seat and adjusted the rearview mirror, buying time. So far, Gerrit was the only one who knew she was a terrible driver. And who would he tell? But now the world was watching.

Behind her, Izzy slid over to the middle seat, because an arm's length away was apparently too far to be from her boyfriend. Rob placed a hand on her bare knee. Maybe they would be too enamored with each other's presence to notice if she turned the wrong way on a one-way street or backed over a curb.

But Mr. Fletcher would notice.

She started the car and awaited his instructions.

"Check your mirrors and look behind you before backing up."

While no one would be around this early in the morning, she checked and double-checked before grabbing the shifter, pressing down on the brake with her foot, and trying to put the car in reverse. The shifter wouldn't move. She wiggled it, pulling harder. Nothing.

"Ahem." Mr. Fletcher made a note on his clipboard. "You have to press down on the brake pedal to shift gears, Miss Walters."

Rob and Izzy chuckled behind her. Heat crawled up her face from her neck. So that was why the engine was revving.

She lifted her foot off the gas pedal and depressed the brake. "There we go."

She slid the shifter in reverse and inched her way out of the parking space, swiveling to look all around and behind her the whole time.

Izzy leaned close to Rob and whispered, "She drives like my grandma."

Rob snickered. Rae tried to ignore them. Once she had room, she straightened the car and drove to the end of the parking lot but stopped short of pulling onto the road. She gave her left a long look. Then her right. The road stretched before her like a long list of expectations and demands.

"Every assignment is major, Rae."

She clenched the wheel. She couldn't give her parents any reason to be angry with each other or throw blame around.

"I've never seen a kid so dedicated."

"I don't need to remind you how important this is."

She had to succeed.

"What are you waiting for?" Mr. Fletcher asked. "There's no one coming."

Focus. Focus.

"Which way?" The pitch of her voice was too high.

"Turn left." Mr. Fletcher pointed. "We'll head down to Fifth and hit a few stoplights, then drive over toward Howard Elementary, where they have that roundabout."

Rae gulped. A roundabout? Might as well rip up The Plan right now. She was doomed.

Mr. Fletcher drove the car back into the school parking lot about ten minutes before the first bell. Rae slumped in the seat next to him. As far as she knew, no one had ever been asked—er, *commanded*—to give up the wheel halfway through their drive and let the instructor take over.

Rob and Izzy murmured to each other in the back, and she could only imagine what they were talking about. Even they had stopped nuzzling each other's necks and come up for air when she ran a red light and that SUV almost hit them. She hurried out of the car without looking back. Thank goodness Mr. Fletcher had made them all put their phones away for the drive, or who knew how many videos Izzy could've posted to social media by now.

Inside the building, a hooded head that looked like Morgan's bobbed among the swarming masses at the other end of the hall.

"Morgan," she called. "Hey, Morgan, wait up."

He ducked into the bathroom. Had he been too far away to hear or was he avoiding her? She was pondering the likelihood of the latter when Kylee appeared.

"Where's your usual Monday morning cheer?" Kylee folded her hands under her chin and gave an exaggerated smile.

Rae frowned. "I'm not that bad."

"Didn't you have a drive this morning?"

Rae looked away. "Yes."

"How'd it go?"

Fibbing or changing the subject crossed her mind, but Rae knew Kylee would find out sooner or later. Rob and Izzy were known for a lot of things, but keeping gossip to themselves was not one of them.

"I bombed big-time."

"Uh-huh." Kylee smirked. "Sure."

"Mr. Fletcher wouldn't even let me drive back to the school. He told me I was 'a menace to society.'"

"Is he allowed to say that?"

Rae shrugged. "He said it."

Kylee gave her a sidelong look. "So it really was bad?"

"Yep. You might have to eat that salad, after all."

Kylee grabbed her arm. "You wouldn't do that to me, would you?"

Rae hung her head as they walked down the hall. "Can we talk about something else?"

A wicked grin split Kylee's face. "Like David? Oh, look. Speak of the devil."

He burst between them, flinging an arm around each of their necks.

Rae looked up, her face suddenly warm. "Hi, David."

He smiled. "Good morning."

"Ew." Kylee shook him off. "You're one of those cheery Monday people, too. Gross."

He let Kylee distance herself but kept his arm around Rae, giving her his full attention. "How was your drive this morning? I had my fingers crossed for you."

Kylee scowled. "Oh, please."

Rae's heart squeezed. "Um, it was . . ."

"She ran over two puppies and a nun." Kylee pointed a finger at David. "You better watch out."

"Kylee." Rae gave her the look. "Don't you have government first period?"

Kylee tugged at the oversized metal skulls hanging from her ears. "So?"

"So aren't you going the wrong direction?"

Kylee gave an exasperated sigh. "Fine." She turned to go. "I guess I'll see you guys later."

As her friend walked away, Rae became instantly and acutely aware of David's arm still hanging over her. She pictured Rob and Izzy and pulled away.

David didn't seem bothered. "You going to Community Hope today?"

"Of course."

"Then you have Driver's Ed.?"

He already knew she did. She nodded.

"I guess you're pretty busy these days, huh?"

She tucked her hair behind her ears and shrugged. "Isn't everyone?"

"Yeah, but even straight A students should have some fun once in a while."

He gave her an intent look, and her heart began to hammer. What was he getting at?

His smile grew. "What are you doing on Saturday?"

The color drained from her face. At least she was pretty sure it did. Not that she could feel her face, because her whole body was suddenly numb. She concentrated on the floor in front of her. Was he . . . ?

"Um . . ."

He slowed his pace. "I was hoping maybe we could go to a movie."

Her eyes widened.

"Or something else, if you want." He held up his hands and laughed. "I'm open to suggestions."

This was not how she imagined it. She never thought that when the day came to stick to The Plan and turn some poor schmuck down, it would be someone she actually cared about.

"David, I—uh—can't."

His confident smile wavered. "Hey, no big deal. If you're busy this weekend, we can try next weekend instead. I'm flexible."

"No, I mean . . ." Her heart did this kind of weird squeezing thing that felt like dying. "I can't go out with you."

"You can't?" A flicker of pain flashed in his eyes. "Or you won't?"

She never should've let it get this far. Never should've encouraged him to volunteer with her or let him sit with her at lunch. See where that sort of thing led?

"My parents don't allow me to date. They want me to focus on my schoolwork."

"You have all A's. I don't think schoolwork is a problem."

"Yes, but—"

"Can't you talk to them about it? I just want to spend time with you. It's nothing serious."

She looked into his face, so hopeful and eager and sincere. Her parents hadn't brought up the boyfriend issue since the beginning of the school year when they gave their annual obligatory "Keep your eyes on the prize" speech. What would they do if she brought it up now? They might change their minds if she begged. But given their strange behavior lately, and the hard set of their faces, she had her doubts.

"I don't know. . . ."

"Oh." He came to a full stop now. "Okay. I get it."

He turned to go.

"David, wait." She grasped for his arm, but he was already out of reach. "You don't understand."

But something about the way he continued walking, as if he hadn't heard her, and the way he hung his head, the set of his shoulders, told her maybe he did understand. He understood exactly what had just happened.

She had turned him down.

CHAPTER
TWENTY-FOUR

Gerrit crossed to the other side of the truck and let Daisy out. He hadn't left the house without her since The Incident. She hadn't complained, but he felt self-conscious driving around town with a dog. And a corgi at that. Not even a manly dog.

He glanced around the yard. Bernard the Terrible was nowhere in sight. It was almost as if he'd been avoiding Gerrit since last week. Or waiting for the ideal time to cause more trouble. Hannie had found the whole story about the police officer highly amusing and had wondered aloud if maybe Bernard was worth having around, after all. But Gerrit had already determined the rooster's days were numbered. As soon as he could figure out a way to utilize the evil monster for one more payback on George, the creature would be gone for good.

He lumbered to the mailbox and pulled out a couple of envelopes. One was a monthly account statement from the bank. He didn't have to open it to know what it would say. That they'd been withdrawing almost a thousand bucks a month from savings for expenses. That his nest egg was already being eaten away by groceries, insurance, taxes, and prescriptions.

A quick calculation told him it would be gone in ten years. He'd need to die when he was seventy-three. Then his life insurance policy would buy Hannie a few more years. But what about a new car for her? A boiler for the shop? Thinking about spending money on those things felt like taking years off his life. And what if he or Hannie got sick? Or, heaven forbid, Evi decided to get married, and they had to pay for the wedding?

Luke would tell him to have some faith. *"God will provide,"* he always said. Well, Gerrit wasn't going to count on that. He would provide for himself.

Daisy ran a circle around his legs, then set a course for the barn. Gerrit grunted. Rae must be in there. When he saw her Monday at Community Hope, she'd hardly said two words to him the whole time, and yesterday wasn't any different. Morgan told Gerrit about all the famous songwriters he knew of until he was blue in the face, while across the room Rae had looked like she had a Supra Sulfa calf bolus the size of his thumb stuck in her throat.

He poked his head in the barn and squinted in the gloom. He had moved one of the deck chairs into the barn for Rae to use, and there she sat now, her raggedy cat in her lap.

"Why don't you turn on the light?"

She didn't look up. "Oh. Sorry. I forgot."

He pushed the door open all the way. "You forgot?"

For a minute, he stared at Rae's face. Only, it looked a lot like Evi's. He'd seen that look on his daughter a thousand times but never understood it. Never asked about it, afraid she'd bite his head off if he tried. Ignoring it had seemed like a safer strategy at the time.

He needed to call her again. Memorial Day weekend was just three weeks and two days away.

Daisy sniffed at Rae's sleeve as if she had a dog treat hidden up there.

Rae didn't try to push her away. "She smells the puppies." Her voice was quiet and lifeless.

"What puppies?"

"Kylee's stepdad's dog had puppies, and I went to see them."

"Oh." He rubbed the back of his neck. Why would she be upset about puppies? "Okaaay."

Daisy satisfied her curiosity and then curled up at Rae's feet, resting her head on her paws. Rae hardly noticed. She just kind of sat there, slouching. The whole scene was rather pathetic.

"What's your problem?" He gulped. That hadn't come out right. "I mean, is everything okay? You look disturbed."

That wasn't much better. Rae scowled, and his shoulders tensed. No wonder he'd never tried this with Evi.

Rae wouldn't look at him. "I'm fine."

He wouldn't have guessed that, but what did he know? Maybe girls looked like this sometimes. About once a month or so. But she didn't sound fine. She sounded like she wanted to be left alone.

He rocked on his feet and knocked a fist against the wooden door twice. "All right, well, I'll be in the house if you need anything."

Her head snapped up. He froze like a deer in the headlights. The light in the barn was dusky, yet he could still see that her eyes were suspiciously damp.

"That's it?"

He stammered. "Wh-what are you talking about?"

She wiped a sleeve across her face. "When someone says they're fine, but they're obviously not fine, you say something like 'No you're not.' Or 'Do you want to talk about it?'"

He took a step back. It made no sense. If she wanted to talk about it, why would she say she was fine? And how would he know if she was or not? If she was and he said she wasn't, wouldn't that make her mad?

She sighed. "My grandpa always used to say, 'If you're fine, then I'm a monkey's uncle.'"

He fought the urge to flee. This girl's problems were none of his business, and he was *not* her grandpa. It's not like he was going to talk to her about *his* problems. But she looked at him expectantly.

"Um . . ." His throat went dry, his mind blank. Then Evi's face popped back into his head, and he forced the words out, "Do you want to talk about it?"

Rae sniffled. "No." Her voice was high and strained.

Of all the most ridiculous, nonsensical, childish—

She burst into tears.

Oh, this was bad. He held a hand out as if to pat her back, but he was too far away. What should he do? Maybe he should run away. Her sobbing intensified, and his stomach lurched.

If there was a God, if He cared about Gerrit at all, as Luke had always claimed, He would do something. Right now.

Gravel crunched. He spun toward the sound.

Hannie.

He let out the breath he'd been holding.

Salvation.

"Now he won't even talk to me." Rae cried into her hands as Hannie rubbed her back gently. "And if I don't do well on my drive tonight, Mr. Fletcher says he's not sure he can pass me."

Gerrit stared in wonder at the miracle unfolding. Somehow, Hannie had led Rae into the house and coaxed the whole story out of her. About her parents, The Plan, and a guy named David. Also her last day of Driver's Ed. and something about her teacher telling her she was dangerous. Which, frankly, did not surprise him.

He hadn't spoken a word, but he felt like he'd been through the wringer. He couldn't remember the last time his nerves had been this shot.

Rae pressed her fists into her eyes. "What am I going to do, Mrs. Laninga?"

From what he'd heard, the answer was clear. He held up a finger and opened his mouth to offer the obvious solution, but snapped it shut again when Hannie shook her head.

"Call me Hannie. And it depends." Her voice was low and soothing. "Do you have feelings for this boy?"

Rae sniffed and nodded.

"Then you're going to need to decide whether you think the relationship is worth saving." Hannie gave a reassuring smile. "And if you do, there's some work that needs to be done."

Gerrit's brow furrowed. That was not even close to what he had planned to say.

"What about my parents?"

Hannie sighed and leaned closer to Rae with a twinkle in her eye. "Parents do tend to complicate things, don't they?"

Rae sniffed again, and a smile began to form. "Yes, they do."

"I'll tell you what." Hannie rose from the table and clapped her hands together. "Why don't we all"—and at the word *all* she eyed Gerrit as if trying to decide whether he was included—"think the problem over while we have dinner and then come back to it. We'll feel better after we've had something to eat."

Rae pulled out her phone. "I'll have to let my mom know. And I've got to be at the school by seven."

Hannie patted her shoulder. "That gives us just enough time."

Gerrit stood rooted in place, dumbfounded. Rae was staying for dinner? How had that happened? Why was she smiling all of a sudden? She was sobbing only a minute ago. He didn't know how long he could stay on this roller coaster.

Hannie clapped her hands again. "Come on, Mr. Big Shot Cook. Get to work."

"But it's leftover night."

"Then I'll heat up leftovers"—she put her hands on his shoulders and steered him into the kitchen—"while you whip up some more of those caramel brownies you made the other day."

He glanced at Rae, who was talking on the phone in a hushed voice. "Now is hardly the time to be worrying about brownies, is it?"

"Oh, my dear man." Hannie patted his cheek with a grin. "Now is exactly the time."

RAE PILED HER plate with food. Leftovers or not, she was starving.

Hannie slid the glazed carrots closer. "Here, have some more."

Gerrit reached for the bowl. "Don't mind if I do."

Hannie slapped his hand away. "I was talking to Rae."

Rae grinned and served herself another spoonful. "Thank you."

"I'm hungry, too," Gerrit muttered.

"But you're not a growing teenager." Hannie smirked. "So, Rae, tell me about this Community of Hope thing."

"It's Community Hope." Rae sprinkled salt on her carrots. "We meet every Monday and Wednesday and help kids with their homework. Kids who are struggling in school."

"How nice." Hannie glanced at Gerrit. "I've been so curious about it."

Her voice was thick with meaning, and Rae caught Gerrit looking down at his plate. Interesting.

"Daisy comes, too," Rae added. "She's like the mascot."

Hannie's eyebrows rose. "Is that right?"

Rae nodded. "Even Morgan likes her, and he doesn't like anyone. Well, except for maybe Gerrit. He's the only person Morgan'll talk to."

Hannie glanced at Gerrit again, and Rae didn't miss the enigmatic expression on her face. What were all these looks about?

"It all sounds wonderful," Hannie said. "I'll have to stop in sometime."

"Good idea." Rae took another bite. "Not many adults come around."

Hannie refilled Rae's glass with water from the pitcher. "What about your parents?"

Rae stiffened. What about them, indeed? They weren't acting like themselves. They thought she hadn't noticed. There was a growing fear in her bones that she would come home one day to the worst kind of news. But she couldn't say any of that.

She felt Gerrit's eyes on her, but she avoided them and lifted one shoulder. "They're both busy."

"What does your father do?" Hannie asked.

"He's a lawyer. My mom doesn't work, but my grandma's not doing well, and Mom has to take care of her."

"I see." Hannie reached over to squeeze Rae's hand. "They must be very proud of you."

Rae brought her glass to her lips and paused. Proud of her? Only if she kept up with The Plan. Then Dad wouldn't have any reason to blame Mom for anything, and Mom wouldn't have to feel guilty about helping Grandma Kate. Sticking to The Plan would keep everything from falling apart.

"Sure." She said it with more conviction than she felt. Much more. "Can I have some more potatoes, please?"

SOMEWHERE TO HIS left, the bushes rustled as daylight faded, and Gerrit tensed. From his favorite chair on the deck, he shot the most intimidating glare he could muster in that direction. The last thing this moment needed was an ornery rooster.

The noise moved deeper into the woods, and he let his shoulders relax. Good. No interruptions. Just him and Hannie and the sunset.

Hannie leaned her head back in her chair and sighed. "The brownies were even better this time."

His lips twitched. She was right. They had been delicious. But then why had she insisted on sending the rest home with Rae? He rubbed his belly and frowned. Oh. That could be why. He was decidedly rounder now that his farming days were done.

Hannie, on the other hand, had never looked better.

"I bet they'd go over well at the shop, too." Her voice held weight and meaning that hadn't been there before. "Just like the éclairs."

He couldn't decipher her words. Her tone hinted at an invitation, yet what would she want with his baked goods at her shop? Sure, they were tasty, and he enjoyed making them. But people visited her store to buy flowers, not brownies.

"Of course, we'd probably have to hire an extra person if we added a coffee-and-pastry bar."

His forehead wrinkled. A coffee-and-pastry bar? *We?*

"I've been researching the commercial-kitchen requirements," she continued as if they'd had this conversation before. "There's a bunch of forms to fill out and a permit fee to pay, but it looks doable."

He looked at her from the corner of his eye. She looked so peaceful and content, the golden light from the setting sun softening her features and granting youthfulness to her face, but then warnings wailed like sirens in his head. What she was talking about sounded expensive. Commercial-kitchen requirements? Permit fees? If he agreed to all that, he'd only have a couple of years left to live.

But her face . . .

She was happy. Hopeful. A surge of unfamiliar emotion pulsed in his heart. Maybe it would be worth the shorter life-span to give her what she wanted.

No. He couldn't risk it. It would be foolish to do something like that at their age. He was too old to start a new adventure.

She smiled. "You don't have to say anything right now. Just think about it."

His eyes widened. This was why he loved her so much. Why he fell for her all those years ago. She knew him better than he knew himself. Knew what he was thinking. What he needed. She was the other half he couldn't live without.

Surely she would understand about the money. Understand they weren't kids anymore. Didn't have that kind of freedom. But he wasn't willing to ruin the moment. Better to talk about something else.

"So . . ." And what else was there to talk about again?

"Isn't it exciting about Mallory's baby?"

He was happy for a change of subject, but not *that* subject. He grunted. "I guess."

She yawned and closed her eyes, sinking lower in her chair. "Agatha is beside herself to become a grandma."

"Well, I'm excited, too."

She opened one eye and peeked at him. "You are?"

"About Memorial Day weekend."

The eye shut again, and she blew out a breath through pursed lips. "Oh." Her tone was guarded. "Have you talked to the kids lately?"

"I left another message on Evi's phone a couple days ago." He covered one hand with the other and squeezed to crack his knuckles. "She hasn't called back."

"I'm sure she will."

"She acts like . . . like . . ."

"Like what?"

"I don't know." He set his hands back on the arms of his chair in frustration. "Like nothing's changed."

Hannie was silent for a minute, and he stared down the hill

at the activity going on at the farm below. Of course things had changed. Everything had changed. The fact that he was sitting here with Hannie watching his old life hum along without him was proof enough of that, wasn't it?

"It's great that you've been spending time with those other kids." Hannie proceeded slowly, with caution. "And that you've been helping out around the house and everything. But none of those things change the issues between you and Evi."

He thought back to the strange look Hannie had given him when Rae had talked about Community Hope. He'd brushed it off at the time, unsure of what it meant. Now, though, he pulled it back out and examined it. Had Hannie been thinking about Evi?

"How is anything supposed to change if she won't talk to me?"

Hannie opened her eyes and sat up. Wisps of her hair fluttered in the evening breeze. "I'll talk to her about coming." She gave him a half smile. "As you have already seen today, I still have a few tricks up my sleeve for dealing with young ladies."

He smiled back. "You came along just in time. I was going to leave her crying in the barn."

"No you weren't." Her voice was tender. "You're getting soft in your old age."

Her tone, her teasing, the soft, rosy glow of her skin all pulled at him, capturing him. He lifted his hand and moved it slowly, warily, to cover the distance between their chairs. It came to rest on hers, her warm, silky skin like fresh cream skimmed off the top of an unstirred milk tank.

She sank back in her chair again. Closed her eyes once more. And didn't pull away.

CHAPTER
TWENTY-FIVE

Kylee crumpled a Snickers wrapper and threw it at Rae's face. "Why do you keep looking over there?"

Rae jerked her head back toward the lunch table, heat rushing to her face.

Kylee turned around and made a show of scanning the room. "Who are you staring at?"

Rae sucked in her lips and stared at her turkey sandwich. It hadn't been David she'd been watching. She hadn't talked to him in over a week, except for an awkward hi or two in passing. No, she'd had her eye on Morgan. He was an enigma she couldn't help but ponder.

"I was just thinking."

Kylee smirked. "Okay, sure."

Rae snuck one more glance at the boy with the black hair. She'd tried talking with him at Community Hope, but he never said more than two words at once. Whenever she said hi to him in the hall, he acted like he didn't hear her. What had she done that made him treat her as if she had the plague? And why was he in the program if he didn't have bad grades?

"Are you daydreaming about David?" Kylee wiped the crumbs clinging to her fingers on the sleeve of her coat. "Why won't you talk to him?"

Rae cringed. "I can't."

"He's not going to bite."

"He hates me now."

"Oh, please." Kylee waved her words away. "He still gives you puppy-dog eyes when you're not looking. You're killing the poor kid."

Rae frowned. She didn't want David to suffer. He was cute and nice and a good friend. He'd been doing his best to be a good sport and act like everything was fine between them. But she knew it wasn't. She'd hurt him. Wouldn't her talking with him make things worse? After dinner the other night, Gerrit's wife had said she might have to give David some space.

"It's a dumb rule, anyway," Kylee continued. "I had my first boyfriend when I was ten."

It wasn't so much the no-dating rule that was the problem. It was how she let David believe she didn't want to go out with him whether there was a rule or not. But after feeling like her insides were turning into a black hole every time she looked at him for the past week, she was pretty sure she did want to. Mrs. Laninga had said relationships require a lot of work, and she'd have to decide if David was worth it.

When she pictured his face, she was sure he was. But when she pictured what Mom's face would look like if she told her about him . . . her certainty wavered.

Stick to The Plan. Stick to The Plan.

"Even if I asked my parents to make an exception, it's too late." Her shoulders slumped. "He's not going to ask me again."

Kylee crossed her arms. "Then you ask him."

"But my parents—"

"Your parents don't need to know. Tell them you're going to my house."

"I'm not going to lie to them."

"Oh, like you're"—she made air quotes with her fingers— "*not lying to them* about failing Driver's Ed.?"

She hadn't technically failed. Yet. After only missing the pass mark by two points last week, Mr. Fletcher was willing to give her one more chance at her final drive tomorrow. "I haven't told them yet. It's not a lie."

"Fine." Kylee crossed her arms. "Then just be miserable. But don't come crying to me when David starts liking someone else. *I* wouldn't turn him down."

Rae sat back like she'd been pushed. She hadn't thought of that. Almost any girl in school would happily accept a date with David.

"He wouldn't—I mean, he can't—"

"You don't think he would ask me?" Kylee scowled. "I'm not his type, is that it?"

"No. I mean, I have no idea what his type is. I just never thought . . ."

"What? That a guy would choose me over you?"

Rae blinked. She was digging herself a hole with a personalized shovel. She didn't know what she thought. Or what she meant. She only knew the idea of David and Kylee together made it hard to breathe.

"It's not that." Her voice was desperate. Pathetic. "I didn't know you liked him."

Kylee pushed away from the table and looked down at Rae. "I never said I did."

A rush of air escaped Rae's lungs. This was just Kylee stirring things up, as usual. That's all this was. She preferred guys with tattoos and bad grades, like Seth. Guys who couldn't begin to charm the scales off a fish, as the saying went. Someone like David would be too boring for her, right?

Kylee marched away from the table, her words still lingering in the air, then stopped. Her eyes flashed as she turned back to look at Rae. "Then again, I never said I didn't."

RAE DIDN'T HURRY to get across the street to Room F when the last bell rang like she usually did. She couldn't work up any excitement for it. She even considered bailing and catching a ride home, but Taylor was counting on her. Rae had the feeling most of the people in Taylor's life were in the habit of letting her down. She didn't want to be one of them.

As she trudged down the hall toward the double doors at the front of the school, she saw David through the glass. He never waited for her anymore, and yet he hadn't quit Community Hope. While part of her had been afraid he only volunteered to impress her, his commitment to the kids in Room F hadn't wavered.

Her heart squeezed at the sight of him. Maybe later today she would try to talk to him.

Before she reached the door, Kylee appeared at David's side. Rae froze. What was she doing? Kylee stood close to him, talking. Smiling. Rae studied David's face. Did he look interested? He didn't look *not* interested.

Her heart pounded. Okay, she was definitely going to talk to him after Community Hope. People pushed past her on either side. She hesitated. Should she rush through the doors and interrupt them? Or walk by and ignore them?

Or wait until they were gone. Yep. Definitely her best option.

Whatever they were talking about, it didn't take long. Kylee gave David's arm a little tug that made Rae want to bang her head against a locker, and then she headed off toward her car. David walked through the mass of students loading onto buses and crossed the street.

Rae waited until both were out of sight before leaving the building, anger and confusion storming inside her. Her English teacher always warned the class about committing "assumicide"—causing yourself unnecessary trouble by making assumptions without all the facts—but how could she not assume Kylee was out to steal David from her? Not that David was *hers*. . . .

Aargh. She tucked her thumbs under the straps of her backpack and hurried over to Greenville Community Church. This was why her parents had warned her about getting involved with boys. This was why they always stressed the importance of letting nothing distract her from her studies. See? Here she was, a total mess, not caring one iota about her homework or her future goals.

All she cared about was working things out with David.

CHAPTER
TWENTY-SIX

Don't your parents wonder why you're in a program for kids with bad grades?" Gerrit asked.

Morgan stared at the table. "No."

"They don't think it's strange?"

The kid shrugged.

Gerrit rubbed his chin. He'd seen the books Morgan carried around in his backpack. AP Calculus. World Literature. Physics. Why he wanted to waste his brain singing songs on street corners, Gerrit had no idea. But even more bewildering was why his parents would let him. He exchanged a look with Daisy but didn't get the impression she was on his side.

"Do they know about the songwriting thing?"

Morgan stiffened. "It's not a 'thing.' It's my dream."

"Okay." Gerrit huffed. "Fine. Do they know about your dream?"

"My mom says she had a dream once. But then . . ."

"Then you came along and ruined everything?"

Morgan frowned.

Oops. That hadn't come out right. But if Morgan's story was going where he thought it was, he'd heard it all before. Parents blaming their kids for their problems, as if they'd asked to be born.

"No." Morgan's voice sounded far away. "Then my dad started drinking, and she had to get a second job."

Oh. That was a whole different story. One that didn't sit well at all. A man had to provide. It was his duty. "Where's your dad now?"

Morgan stroked Daisy's head but didn't answer.

Gerrit sighed. "I suppose your mom wants you to follow your heart."

"You say that like it's a bad thing."

He looked at his hands. The wrinkles. The swollen knuckles. Thought of the thousands of times he'd used them to milk a cow, throw a bale, shovel sawdust. They'd served him well as far as that stuff went, but what did he know about dreams? He knew Morgan was a smart kid. He knew he didn't want him to waste his potential on a street corner. But he didn't know anything about following your heart.

The kid's red notebook lay on the table, tattered and yet somehow discerning.

He gestured at it with his chin. "You fill that thing up yet?"

"Almost."

"Can I see it?"

He wasn't sure what compelled him to ask. He didn't know anything about writing songs. Still, he had the feeling the notebook was one of Morgan's most prized possessions. And for some reason that made him want to look at it.

Morgan picked up the notebook and held it as if calculating its weight. "What for?"

"I want to see what a song looks like when it's just starting out."

The kid hesitated. "I don't even let my mom read it."

Gerrit made a show of looking around, then held out his hand. "I don't see your mom anywhere."

Morgan's mouth hung open a little as he placed the notebook in Gerrit's hand as though he were surrendering his firstborn child. Gerrit opened it with the gentle reverence he felt was expected. Daisy inched closer, tongue lolling, as if to get a better look, and he shooed her away.

"Go bug someone else."

As the indomitable corgi trotted off to visit with other students, Gerrit flipped through Morgan's book. Some pages were filled with words from top to bottom, while others only had a few brief notes scratched out in blue pen. And some pages had rough drawings and doodles. The ones that caught his eye the most had capital letters squeezed in above the words Morgan had written.

He pointed at one of the letters. "What're these?"

"Those are the chords. For the music."

It was foreign to him but strangely beautiful. Morgan's handwriting was awful, like his. The only songs Gerrit knew were from decades ago—John Denver, Willie Nelson, and Creedence Clearwater Revival. He couldn't abide what passed for music on the radio these days. But the snatches of lyrics in this book *felt* like music. A page with the words *Anyone, Anywhere* across the top caught his eye. He squinted at the writing.

An eager face
A run-down place

Back door slamming, echoing through the night
A couple tears
Nobody hears
Swearing this time everything'll be all right
Could be anyone, anywhere

It was no CCR song, but Gerrit couldn't stop staring at it.

RAE GASPED AS Daisy whimpered and ran away. She hadn't said anything when Taylor deliberately screwed up her homework and refused to try again. Hadn't made an issue of it when Taylor yelled at anyone who tried to sit at their table, or when she called Rae that word that rhymes with *stitch*.

But kicking Daisy in the stomach was going too far.

"You apologize right now." Rae stood and pointed to where Daisy cowered behind Gerrit. "Or I'll let Mark know you won't be coming back."

Mark had made it clear at the beginning of the program that any student who was disrespectful or disruptive would be asked not to return. No one had been kicked out so far, but Rae meant what she said. And one glance at Gerrit told her if she didn't do something about Taylor, he would.

Taylor's eyes widened as she stared at Rae. Her face scrunched up.

Rae pointed again. "Now."

Taylor burst into tears. "I'm sorry." She ran to Daisy and threw her arms around the dog. "I didn't mean it."

Though Gerrit glared at Taylor, ready to toss her out on her behind if she hurt his dog again, Daisy was quick to forgive. She licked Taylor's ear as the girl cried into her neck. The hard looks on Gerrit's and Morgan's faces at Taylor's abuse gradually softened as her tears soaked Daisy's fur.

Rae knelt beside Taylor and put an arm around her shoulder. "Okay, it's okay." Her tone was soothing and gentle. "Why don't you come back to the table so we can talk about it."

Rae didn't know what "it" was, but it must be something big to make Taylor lash out at an innocent animal like that. Taylor allowed Rae to help her to her feet and guide her back to her chair. The waif of a girl dropped into the seat, folded her bare arms on the table, and laid her forehead on her arms.

"What's going on today, Taylor?" Rae pulled the other chair up close and spoke quietly. "You can tell me."

"I don't want to move again." Taylor's voice sounded muffled as she spoke into the table. "I like it here. We've lived here longer than anyplace else. But Mom says we're leaving the day after school gets out. She doesn't care."

"Where are you going?"

Taylor sniffled. "I don't know. To my aunt's, I guess."

"You guess?"

"That's where we usually go when Mom runs out of money."

"Did she lose her job?"

"She doesn't have a job."

Rae waited, but Taylor offered no further information. Rae wanted to ask about her mom's boyfriend—Steve?—yet she was reluctant to pry. It hit her like a brick, however, that she hadn't caught so much as a glimpse of Taylor's iPhone all week. Her heart sank.

"Is your aunt's house far away?"

"Yes." The misery in Taylor's tone was amplified by her voice bouncing off the white plastic table. "Idaho."

Might as well be a world away to a seventh-grade girl who finally had a place she wanted to be.

"I'm sorry to hear that." Rae rubbed Taylor's back the way Hannie had rubbed hers the other night. "Is there any chance things might change?"

"When Mom says it's time to go, we go." Taylor sighed. "At least she's letting me finish school first."

Rae was proud of what Taylor had accomplished in just a few short weeks. Every grade that had been a D or F was now a C. She'd aced her last math test. What would happen to her in Idaho? Without a program like Community Hope, would there be anyone to keep a kid like Taylor from failing out of school?

"When I grow up, I'm going to buy my own house." Taylor lifted her head and looked at Rae. "And I'll never move again."

"If you want to buy a house, you'll have to get a good job."

"So?"

"So if you want a good job, you'll have to finish school."

Taylor hung her head. "I hate school."

"I know. But promise me you'll finish school and buy that house so I can come visit you."

Taylor groaned.

"Promise me."

"Fine." Taylor sighed. "I promise."

Mark called out the end of the session, and Rae helped Taylor pack up her things, keeping one eye out for David. She couldn't let him leave without her.

As Taylor scooted out the door, Rae called after her, "See you next week."

Taylor waved.

Mark stood by the door and smiled at Rae. "You're good at this, you know."

Rae shrugged. "At what?"

"Helping kids. You ever thought of becoming a school counselor or something? Social worker maybe?"

Ha. Rae tried not to laugh out loud. She could only imagine what Dad would do if she told him she wanted to be a school counselor. *They'll call you "Counselor" in court,* he'd probably say.

She shrugged again. "Not really."

"Well, you should think about it. More importantly, pray about it. There aren't many people who know how to help hurting kids. It takes a special kind of person."

The words buzzed in Rae's ear. *Hurting kids. A special kind of person.* What would that future be like? Papa Tom's favorite saying flashed in her mind. *"God's got big plans for you."* What had he meant? What kind of future had he been thinking of? She'd never thought to ask Papa Tom for specifics—definitely never thought to pray about it—but it didn't matter.

Her future was set.

Mark turned away to talk to some other kids, and Rae walked back to her table for her backpack. Gerrit and Morgan were deep in conversation in the corner as if oblivious to the fact that their time was up. Was Gerrit that special kind of person, too?

Out of the corner of her eye, she saw David sending the last of the middle schoolers from his table off with a fist bump and a smile. Her pulse quickened. Oh, that smile. She'd missed having it trained on her. Was this her chance?

Her stomach flip-flopped. Maybe it was too soon. Maybe she should wait until she knew what to say. Maybe . . .

Someone cleared his throat. She turned to see Gerrit watching her, a knowing look on his face. Her ears burned. He nodded in David's direction. The implication was clear.

And here she had thought she would be the one bugging Gerrit about *his* relationships.

When she turned back, David was walking out of the room. She hurried into the hall after him. Her mom had gone to Riverton to check on Grandma Kate after receiving a call from a concerned neighbor about Grandma wandering her front yard in her pajamas, so she wouldn't be here to pick her up until 5:20. That gave Rae ten minutes.

"David, wait."

He looked over his shoulder in surprise. "Oh. Hey, Rae."

She caught up. "Can we talk?"

He slowed his pace. "Sure."

She couldn't decipher his tone. Couldn't tell if he wanted to bolt out of the building, spit in her face, or hear her out like the gracious, sweet, and reliable guy he was.

Probably that last one.

"I wanted to say I'm sorry. About last week. You caught me by surprise."

He held the door open, and she stepped outside, hoping she wasn't making a big mistake. What had he been talking with Kylee about? What if she was too late? She searched his eyes for a clue as to what he was thinking.

He met her gaze. "I'm sorry, too. I didn't know about your parents' rule. I just thought . . ."

She waited, breathless. What he thought was suddenly the most important thing in the world.

"I thought we would have fun." He gave a small smile. "I like hanging out with you."

She floated on air, joy and relief buoying her above mere earthly concerns. "I like hanging out with you, too."

His smile wavered. "I thought maybe you liked someone else. I've seen you talking with Morgan a lot—"

"We're just friends. Sort of."

"But when I asked you out, you seemed terrified."

Her feet returned to solid ground. Looking at him now, standing this close, it was hard to remember why she'd freaked out. She just hadn't been prepared.

"I've got a lot going on right now." She thought of her parents. "And this Driver's Ed. thing has me super stressed out."

He scrunched up his face. "Isn't Driver's Ed. over?"

"It is, but I didn't exactly pass. I have to retake the final drive tomorrow. I'm really nervous."

He gave her a sidelong glance. "I heard you ran a red light and almost got T-boned. Is that true?"

She groaned. "Yes."

"I'm a good driver."

"You don't have to rub it in."

He gave her a bashful smile. "I just thought you might want to know, in case we ever did go out. The offer still stands, I mean, if you can get your parents to change their minds."

Happiness bubbles swam around inside her like a school of minnows. It was all she could do to keep from throwing her arms around David right then and there. But the thought of her dad telling her mom she didn't take Rae's future seriously enough held her back. And the sight of a dark blue Ford Explorer stopped her cold.

For a minute there, she'd almost forgotten about The Plan.

"Maybe when school lets out." Only a few short weeks remained before summer break, but it should be enough time to figure something out. To talk to her parents. "Maybe then . . ."

David grinned. "Okay."

Mom pulled up in front of them and rolled down the window, looking at David with suspicion. "Hi, guys."

Rae turned her back to the car so her mom couldn't see and mouthed the words, "We cool?"

David nodded, eyes sparkling, and waved as she hurried to get in the car before Mom could say anything embarrassing. She waved back.

"I'm sorry I had to be late, sweetie. Did you have a good day?"

Rae struggled to wipe the giddy look off her face. "Yeah. How's Grandma?"

"I coaxed her into the house with a Hot Pocket, if you can believe it. Was that David Reynolds?"

"Yeah." She had to play it off. Had to be cool. "He volunteers too. We're, uh, friends."

"I see."

But it was clear she didn't. Rae's stomach tightened. What would happen if she revealed her feelings to Mom and Dad? Was David worth listening to her parents argue? Worth the accusations she feared would come? She didn't know. And she didn't know how to know.

Kylee had always been the boy-crazy one, not her. And as far as she could tell, The Plan had no room for feelings. It was about the future. About her career, success, and holding her family together. But what kind of plan made no provision for the heart?

And what had Kylee been talking to David about?

CHAPTER
TWENTY-SEVEN

The noises coming from George's shop set Gerrit's teeth on edge. Every pound of his neighbor's hammer, every buzz of his Skilsaw, made Gerrit want to fill one of his gardening gloves with rocks and slap George across the face with it. And that radio station he was blaring? Christian music.

Blech.

The sounds mocked him, reminding him over and over that George had a successful business. Reminding him over and over of George's smug face. Reminding him one hammer blow at a time of the day he'd come out of the farm shop to find his father shaking George's hand to seal the deal on a large loan of money that should've been his. Money he and Hannie had desperately needed.

"You don't know anything about it," his father had said when Gerrit confronted him. *"You'll find another way to build that house you want."*

"But I'm your son."

"And George has got nobody."

His father's eyes flashed, daring him to disagree. When George's dad died of cancer a couple of years before, Gerrit's father lost his only friend. And George was left an orphan, as his mom had run off on him and his dad long ago.

"So you'll help him, but you won't help me?"

Betrayal had stabbed at Gerrit, lending a sharp edge to his voice.

His father had turned away. *"You don't need any help."*

Gerrit blinked at the flower bed and the roots in his hands. His father had been wrong. And Gerrit was hardly getting any weeding done.

A shot of pain made him groan as he pushed himself up off his knees. Sweat poured down his face from the midday sun. He couldn't sit out here listening to George make a racket for one more minute. And was that Mallory's red Jetta parked over there? Oh, so George could make all the noise he wanted when his daughter was around, but Bernard was too loud?

Unbelievable. George thought he was so much better than him—bragging about becoming a grandpa, calling the cops on him as if he were a criminal—but he wouldn't even *have* a furniture business if it wasn't for Gerrit's father.

There had to be something he could do to hit George where it hurt. Something to get back at him for his stunt with the police. But what?

It was cool inside the house. Gerrit pulled a Pepsi from the fridge and took a long, satisfying swig. Daisy watched him with longing in her big brown puddly eyes.

"Not a chance, girl." He made a show of gesturing at her water dish. "You have your own."

The dumb dog crept closer, pleading. Licking her chops.

"Your mother would kill me."

She realized he was serious and slumped to the floor in defeat, resting her chin on her front paws. He took another drink and set the can down on the counter.

A shrill ring nearly made him jump out of his skin. The landline. "For crying out loud."

It rang again, and he hurried to check the caller ID. It was probably a telemarketer, as usual, but he wanted to make sure. He grabbed the receiver and squinted at the screen. *Unknown Name, Unknown Number.* Bah. No way was he answering that.

He set the receiver back on its base as the ringing stopped. Good. Then he gave the contraption another look.

Hold the phone. What if . . . ?

Their home number was unlisted and appeared as *Unknown Name, Unknown Number* when he called someone, too. Which meant if he were to call George's work phone to, say, place a custom furniture order using fake information, George wouldn't know who it was. And if George were to complete the order and try to contact his fake customer for pickup, Gerrit and Bernard would be avenged.

He pulled up George's cell number from his own cell and considered what he was about to do. He wouldn't order a five-piece living room set or anything. He wasn't a monster. But a nice little end table that wasted an adequate amount of George's time and money would be just the ticket.

His conscience flinched, but he quickly ignored it. Yes, part of him knew it was childish. But another part remembered the self-righteous look on George's face as he shook his father's hand. The indignation in his own heart when he learned George had purchased the lot right next to the one he himself planned to buy. Not to mention the humiliation he'd suffered at the hands of that snot-nosed officer who had talked down to him.

George had brought this on himself.

He punched in the number and hit send. It rang once. Twice.

"Hello, thank you for calling Sinnema Custom Woodwork. How may I help you?"

Gulp. He hadn't counted on Agatha answering the phone. What was he doing? He was in way over his head. He should hang up right this second and cut his losses.

"Yes, hello." He purposefully lowered the tone of his voice, making it sound gravelly so she wouldn't recognize it. "I'd like to place an order."

"Wonderful! Can you describe what you are interested in?" Agatha's cheerful voice gave him fresh resolve. This woman had never suffered a day in her life. She had no idea what he had been through. What her own husband had put him through.

"An end table."

"What kind of end table do you have in mind?"

They went back and forth, discussing the details. The dimensions of the table. Which kind of wood he would prefer. How long it would probably take. Gerrit was glad it wasn't the sort of business that required your credit card number up front.

By the end of the conversation, Gerrit's throat hurt from talking funny the whole time, causing him to cough into the phone.

"Sounds great," Agatha finally said. "George will get to it as soon as possible."

"Uh, thank you. I'll be in touch."

"You have a good day now."

He hung up the phone, his heart pounding with self-satisfaction. He'd pulled it off. He'd gotten revenge on George, and the best part was George would never know who had made a fool of him. It was an age-old prank. A little juvenile, maybe, but effective.

After finishing his Pepsi, he slipped his gloves on and went back outside. There were still hundreds of weeds to pull, and he had a feeling the noises from the workshop weren't going to bother him nearly as much now. Daisy followed him to the small bed of geraniums on the southeast corner of the house and plopped down in a shady spot to watch him work.

Though the sun was hot on his back, he didn't mind. It felt good. He was riding high. Before long, he even found himself whistling. If only he could be there to see George's face when he realized—

"Ho, there."

He stiffened. Speak of the devil.

He rose to his feet. "What do you want?"

Turning to face his neighbor, he tried not to grimace at the pain in his lower back. Didn't want to show weakness. George stood in the driveway, smiling. *Smiling*, for goodness' sake.

"I had a question about your order." George adjusted the safety goggles on the top of his head. "Agatha forgot to ask you about the feet."

Gerrit gaped. What—? How—? "I . . ."

"I usually do a plain tapered foot on a table like that, but some people like a pedestal corner. It's a little fancier."

Heat burned Gerrit's face. His mouth went dry.

"Wh-what are you talking about?" he stammered. This

couldn't be happening. There was no way George could know it had been him who called.

George raised his hands. "Don't worry. I won't say anything to Hannie. I know you're probably planning a surprise for her birthday, right? I'll give you a discount."

The fact that George knew his wife's birthday was coming up felt like salt in an already-gaping wound. He didn't need a discount from George, and no, he *wasn't* planning a surprise. He'd forgotten all about it until right this minute. His face must've looked perplexed.

"You know what?" George waved a hand. "Don't worry about the feet. When I get to that point, I'll have you pop on over and take a look at it, and you can decide then. We'll do it when Hannie's at work. She'll never know."

Gerrit stared dumbly. "I . . ."

"Guess I'll be talking to you soon." George turned to go, then spun back around as if remembering something. "Oh, and Agatha says to tell you to take it easy with that cold you've got. She heard this bug that's going around is especially hard on the elderly."

He strode away, and Gerrit stood as if paralyzed, incredulity roaring in his ears. Of all the—! How could he—? What was he—? Fury and shock raged through his body, alternating hot and cold. Fire and ice. Then dribbled down to his toes to form a pool of disgrace and indignation at his feet.

Bested again.

And how was he going to pay for the table? A month of his life, gone.

Hannie must *never* know about this.

CHAPTER
TWENTY-EIGHT

Gerrit's eyes flew open. He sat up with a gasp. The cows. He was late. They were waiting.

He panted as he struggled out of his recliner, grunting as his back protested. It was past four in the morning. He'd better hurry.

His arms groped in the darkness. Why weren't his coveralls next to the chair? He shuffled around the room, panic rising in his chest. What were these fuzzy things on his feet? He needed his boots.

Adrenaline buzzed in his ears as reality struck. He wasn't late. The farm was gone. All that was over.

Hannie had bought him these slippers at the mall.

He stumbled to the back door and flung himself out onto the deck, sucking the crisp, fresh air. The coolness sharpened his senses, and he peered down the hill at the soft glow of the milking parlor. The faint bellow of a heifer drifted through the quiet early morning, urgent and yet peaceful. A cow seeking relief. Waiting her turn at the stanchions.

His hands gripped the deck rail as something raw and

overpowering boiled up from within, burning his chest and throat as it spewed from his mouth. A strangled cry. An answering bellow.

Tears stung his eyes. He blinked them back, ashamed, but the weight of all he'd lost forced them down his face. The farm was gone. Luke was gone. All the memories, the long hours, the backbreaking labor. The years spent trying to make his father proud. Lost in his brother's shadow.

And for what?

His heart slowly returned to a normal pace as he took a deep breath, then another. Then another. He had always loved the land. Loved the smell of fresh-cut fields and the roar of a cab tractor. Loved the freedom of working outside, away from the insistent demands of a desk or a phone or a client. But somewhere along the way, the farm had become a millstone around his neck rather than a refuge.

Maybe it was when Luke died. Or maybe . . .

A movement caught his eye. He blinked in the darkness and squinted. "Well, look who it is."

He hadn't seen the rascal in several days and had begun to believe he was rid of him. But Bernard the Terrible perched on the far end of the deck, roosting for the night. With how poorly roosters could see in the dark, he wouldn't be going anywhere until sunrise.

Gerrit inched closer. "Can't sleep either, huh?"

Bernard tilted his head to look at him with his right eye.

"You're not nearly so scary when you're stuck."

The rooster puffed up his feathers.

"Not that I was ever scared of you."

Gerrit stopped about three feet away, well out of reach, and leaned against the rail. The sky was still dark, but too alive to be called black. It looked rich and velvety, an indigo cushion spotted with stars that he was sure, if he reached out, he could press his hand into.

"Luke believed God made that sky." He glanced at Bernard, who bobbed his head as if urging him on. "Made everything. He used to say, 'God doesn't make mistakes.'" He squared his shoulders in an imitation of his brother and tried to copy his voice, but the effort was lost on Bernard.

Gerrit's shoulders sank back down. "Maybe that's true. I don't know. Maybe God doesn't make mistakes."

He took one last, long look down the hill. "But I sure do."

CHAPTER
TWENTY-NINE

Rae had never seen Gerrit so animated. She kept sneaking glances at him as she helped Taylor with her homework. The way he talked with Morgan, it was almost like he was excited about something.

Taylor's work took until the end of the session, but as soon as Rae helped her pack up and sent her on her way, she hurried over to where Gerrit and Morgan sat. Since David wasn't able to make it to Community Hope today, all her focus was on finding out what was up with Gerrit.

She approached him at the table and tried to act casual. "Hey, guys."

Morgan ignored her, but Gerrit smiled. An actual real smile. She narrowed her eyes. Something was definitely going on.

Gerrit stood. "What are you doing for Memorial Day?"

"We always go to visit family in Cedar Springs. Why?"

"I was just inviting Morgan here to my house for a party, and I thought maybe you could come, too."

"Oh." She eyed Morgan, who appeared to be listening while trying hard to act like he wasn't. "A party?"

"Evi and Noah are coming for a visit." Gerrit's face grew a little more serious. "My kids."

The plot thickened. This did not sound like a party she wanted to miss. What better opportunity to get to the bottom of Gerrit's relationship problems? But visiting Aunt Joyce and Uncle Jerry on Memorial Day was a tradition.

Morgan slunk from his chair and edged past her. "I gotta go."

"May twenty-seventh. Three o'clock." Gerrit slapped Morgan's shoulder as he went by. "Don't forget."

Morgan didn't answer but instead raised a hand in farewell. Rae watched him go. She couldn't figure him out. It was like he couldn't stand the sight of her.

Gerrit headed for the door, too, and Rae followed. "So your kids, huh?"

His face retained a hint of a smile, but then something in his eyes made her think of Mr. Whiskers during a thunderstorm hiding under the bed.

"They finally agreed to come. I haven't seen them in . . . well, in a while."

"That's great!" Her enthusiasm was genuine. "Are you inviting a lot of people?"

They reached the end of the hall and stepped outside. "No. Just us and the kids and Morgan, I guess, if you can't come. Maybe Luisa."

"Who's Luisa?"

He flinched. Or maybe he was just squinting in the sun. Regardless, he didn't answer her question. This was more like the Gerrit she knew.

"Are you making a cake?"

He hesitated. "A cake?"

"Yeah. Every good party has a cake, doesn't it?"

He rubbed his chin. "I was going to grill ribs and make pasta and pie."

"Pie's good, too." She wanted to be encouraging. This could be a turning point for him. "What about decorations?"

He reached his truck and draped an arm over the hood, staring down at his boots as if deep in thought. "No."

"It wouldn't have to be anything fancy. Maybe some streamers and balloons?"

He shook his head.

"Well, what about flowers? Your wife works at The Daisy Chain. She could make a centerpiece or something."

He raised his head and gave her a fierce look.

She swallowed hard, her stomach sinking. "What?"

"That's a good idea."

Sheesh. Way to give a girl a heart attack.

He opened his truck door. "Hannie would probably like that."

"Maybe you could even order a bouquet for your daughter."

He tensed and muttered, "She'd throw it in the garbage."

Yikes. So that's how it was. "Well, maybe just a bouquet for Hannie, then. Women love getting flowers."

He appeared to think that over. "I can't get her flowers from her own shop. It wouldn't be a surprise."

"Wait, you mean she *owns* The Daisy Chain? I thought she just worked there." Rae couldn't believe it. Why did it have to be so hard to get information out of this guy? "I suppose you could get them from some other place."

"I couldn't do that." Gerrit's lip curled like he smelled a rat. "That would be helping the competition. She might get mad."

Mom's Explorer pulled into the parking space next to

229

Gerrit's truck, and Rae held up a finger to let her mom know she was almost ready to go. "I could help you."

"How?"

"I could order them. Like, in secret."

"I suppose that could work." He nodded at the Explorer. "You better go."

"What's her favorite flower?"

He slid into his truck, a shadow passing over his face. "We'll talk about it later."

"If I'm going to order her—"

The truck door slammed shut, and the engine roared to life. Rae took a step back as Gerrit put the truck in drive. Okay then.

She hopped into the passenger side of the Explorer, and Mom gave her a questioning smile. "Do you want to drive home today? You've got to get those practice hours in."

Rae winced. Of course Mom had to bring that up. She'd been distracted by everything going on with Grandma Kate lately, but Rae knew she couldn't keep her driving struggles a secret from Mom forever. Dad would've noticed her serious lack of practice by now if he hadn't been working such long hours on a big case.

"No, that's okay, you're already buckled in."

"Nonsense." Mom unbuckled and opened her door. "Let's switch."

Oh, great. While she'd known this day was coming, it still made her breathing shallow and strained. She slowly slid out of her seat and walked around to the driver's side. As she settled in behind the wheel, Mom was grinning from ear to ear.

"This is fun—you driving me for a change. I'm sorry I haven't had time to do this with you before."

Rae forced a smile as she fastened her seat belt. "It's okay."

"Now that Driver's Ed. is over, we'll have to call and sched-ule an appointment for you at the DMV."

Rae grasped the wheel with clammy hands. She had passed her second final drive attempt a few days ago, this time scor-ing two points above the passing mark instead of two points below. She was getting better at the whole driving thing—on the outside. But inside? She was still a mess.

She put the car in reverse and begged her heart to calm down. If only there weren't half a dozen kids loitering in the parking lot. She didn't want any witnesses.

"No David today?" Mom asked.

Rae shrugged. She couldn't think about the weight of Mom's words right now. The meaning behind them. She needed to focus on driving.

"Okay, well, I circled some Help Wanted ads in the paper for you this morning." Mom's voice was chipper. "Summer's only a few weeks away. If you keep putting off applying, all the good jobs will be taken."

Rae eased the Explorer out of the parking space, hoping her inner panic didn't show. "Mark said the church is planning to do a summer program for fifth through eighth graders, if they can get enough volunteers. I was thinking—"

"You've already put in a ton of volunteer hours this year, sweetie. And that's great, but it's not going to help you reach your career goals. You need some actual work experience."

"But—"

"We'll probably want to avoid fast food, but there were a couple of openings for cleaning jobs and four or five desk jobs. One of them is even at a law firm. Wouldn't that be perfect?"

A law firm? The idea should excite her. What better way

to impress the law school at Columbia than to have law-firm experience already under her belt? But the thought of working at a firm sat like a rock in her gut. She was only fifteen. She had her whole life to work in law.

"I don't know, Mom. Maybe a cleaning job would be better. Keep me active."

"That's true." Mom tapped her bottom lip with her index finger. "It would show you're not afraid of hard work."

Rae drove past the loitering kids, careful not to make eye contact with any of them. "Community Hope is hard work."

Mom gave her a tolerant half smile. "That's not *real* work, Rae. We've only got two more years until Columbia. You know what your father would say. We've got to follow The Plan. Besides, you'll need to earn some money if you're going to pay for car insurance."

Rae nodded, but words of agreement stuck in her throat. Helping kids wasn't real work? Mom couldn't mean that. Maybe she was only referring to the fact that it didn't pay.

She pondered Mom's money statement. Her parents had agreed to buy her a car when she turned sixteen, if she paid for the insurance and kept her ranking as number one in her class. With Dad's job, they could afford her insurance themselves, but they said they wanted to instill in Rae a sense of responsibility by having her pay for it. And it wouldn't hurt to mention on her college application that she paid her own bills.

Volunteer work wouldn't pay for her car insurance. But she couldn't worry about that right now. There was a more pressing matter at the moment.

She pulled onto the road, trying to play it cool. Trying to drive smooth and easy so that Mom wouldn't know how stressed out she was. If she just focused on the road, gave all her attention to her surroundings, did everything right, and kept everyone happy—

"What are you doing?"

Rae started and hit the brakes. Her head and Mom's jerked forward. "I—I'm driving."

Mom smoothed her blouse, flustered, and pointed her thumb over her shoulder. "We live *that* way."

It was going to be a long drive home.

CHAPTER
THIRTY

Hannie gave the pan of scotcheroo bars an apprecia-
tive sniff. "Are these a thank-you?"

Gerrit nodded, though his heart wobbled a little.
She had managed to convince Evi and Noah to come for
Memorial Day weekend, and he was grateful. Yet his initial
excitement at having the family all together was wavering. He
only had ten days left to prepare. What if it was a disaster?

He'd whipped up the peanut-butter Rice Krispie bars with
chocolatey butterscotch topping after returning from Community Hope because they were fast and easy. But now he
realized he couldn't remember whether Hannie even liked
butterscotch. What if she hated it? He sure did. Butterscotch
was the worst.

He should know if there was a food she hated, but he didn't.
Which reminded him of Rae's question.

"What's her favorite flower?"

Hannie loved flowers, he knew that much. She had them
growing all around the house in every variety imaginable.

She worked with them every day at her shop. Her car smelled like them. Her skin reminded him of them. But did she have a favorite? The thought of asking opened a cold, dark pit in his stomach.

"I can't wait to see them." Hannie cut herself a square piece from the pan of scotcheroos. "They haven't been home in ages."

He looked away. The Christmas after Noah left home to try a community college in Seattle was the last time he could remember all four of them being together in this house. He'd missed opening gifts Christmas morning because a cow had gone into labor. It was a difficult birth. The heifer's first. He'd arrived home just in time for the Christmas dinner Hannie had planned for noon so it wouldn't interfere with the second milking.

After hurrying to clean himself up, he joined them at the table but struggled to keep his mind from wandering. The heifer had been in bad shape when he'd left. What if she didn't make it? Finances were tight. Money was scarce. Cows were money. A two-year-old heifer was worth her weight in gold if she could produce good milk.

He'd left the house less than two hours later to check on the mother and didn't return until everyone was asleep. The kids hadn't been back for Christmas since.

"I'm sorry."

The light in Hannie's eyes dimmed. He could practically see the wheels turning in her mind as she chewed, see her searching for a response.

"It's okay."

He hung his head. No, it wasn't. But he couldn't change the past.

"It's not fair you never get to see your—*our*—kids."

Hannie set her bar down on the counter. "I used to go down to Everett almost every weekend to see Evi. Sometimes Noah would drive up and meet us."

He looked up. So that was where she would disappear to. What would they talk about together? How much had he missed?

"We'd go to that Mexican restaurant on Washington Avenue," Hannie continued. "You know the one with the giant sombrero hanging over the door? That's their favorite place."

His heart flumped like it had a flat tire. "But you don't go down anymore?"

She leaned against the counter, staring past him at the window. Hesitant. Troubled. "No."

"Why not?"

But he knew why. Because he was around now. She was afraid he'd tag along or felt bad about leaving him alone or something. He sighed. He'd ruined everything when he was never around and still managed to ruin everything when he was.

Hannie wiped at the crumbs on the counter. "Evi's been busy."

In that moment he loved his wife more than he'd ever loved her before. She was lying to him. Her crow's feet confirmed it. And yet she was also giving him a gift. Whatever he'd ruined in the past, he had to make sure he didn't ruin anything else.

He shuffled closer to Hannie, longing to brush her arm with his as he stood beside her at the counter. Longing for the right words to say.

She let him off easy. "You know you're going to have to

clean the house from top to bottom, right? Since this whole thing was your idea? And the kids' rooms need fresh linens."

He grunted, but a smile tugged at his lips. "I know how to clean."

Her eyes twinkled. "I'll let you handle it, then."

He cut himself a small bar from the pan. "I was hoping you could make a centerpiece for the party." He scraped the hardened chocolate-butterscotch mixture off the top, concentrating on it to avoid her eyes. "I mean, I want to order one. From your shop."

She stiffened. "Really?"

His ears tingled. Was she happy or mad? He was afraid to look.

"A big fancy one for the table here." He swallowed. "I thought it would be nice."

He looked. She smiled. He managed to breathe.

"Sure, I could do that. What kind of centerpiece would you like?"

There were *kinds*? "Uh . . . whatever you think is best. You choose."

That seemed to please her. She tucked her hair behind her ear, the wheels in her mind already turning. He could practically see the flowers swirling in her brain, arranging and rearranging. He'd never appreciated what a talent she had. To him, a flower was just a flower.

"Okay, I'll come up with something festive." She nudged his shoulder with hers and grinned. "If you were baking goodies for my shop, you know, I could give you my employee discount."

Oh.

Oh, goodness.

He smiled back and nodded, as if her words hadn't turned his stomach to ice. As if it made perfect sense for a used-up old man like him to invest his life savings to join his wife at her shop and make cookies for strangers. As if her offer wasn't a lifeline he didn't deserve.

As if it didn't scare him half to death.

CHAPTER
THIRTY-ONE

Rae studied herself in the mirror. Was it okay to wear skinny jeans to a job interview? They were black at least. Looked pretty nice with her green-and-purple blouse.

"Rae." Mom knocked on the door. "You almost ready?"

She cringed. "Yes."

Mom poked her head in the room. "I'd like to be a little early."

"I'll be right there."

Mom scrutinized her outfit, nodded her approval, and shut the door.

Rae plopped onto her bed. "What am I going to do, Mister?"

Mr. Whiskers moved his head onto her lap and began to purr. She rubbed his ears. Once her dad had gotten wind of the job opening at the law firm, he'd insisted that was her only option. He'd even "made a call" and then informed her she all but had the job. The interview was merely a formality.

"It's not that I mind filing papers." She rolled her head back and forth, trying to loosen the tension in her neck. "I just . . . I don't know."

How could she explain it? Working at the Schultz and Hardy law firm would be a great experience, and their office was close by. Taylor would be moving away soon, so she wouldn't be attending Greenville Community Church's summer program, anyway. But for some reason, Rae had that same awful feeling from her driving nightmare when she was barreling down a hill out of control. And she hated it.

She glanced at her phone. Time to go. She nudged Mr. Whiskers off her lap and stood. "Look what you did, you big lug." Clumps of gray fur stuck to her black pants. "That doesn't look very professional."

He was unconcerned. She swiped at her pants to remove the fur and hurried out of her room. Mom was waiting at the door with the car keys in her hand.

She held them out. "You need to practice. We've got plenty of time to get there."

Rae groaned inwardly. "Not today. I don't want to show up to the interview all stressed out."

"You've got to get a handle on this, sweetie." Mom crossed her arms. "Why didn't you tell me you were having so much trouble?"

"It's not a big deal. I'll figure it out. But not today." Her voice came out much harsher than she'd intended. What was her problem?

Mom frowned. "Then when?"

She covered her face with her hands. "I don't know."

"Rae, you're going to need your license if you want to get a job."

"I can walk to the office, Mom." Her voice rose in intensity. "It's not that far."

"Does this have anything to do with that boy? David?"

"What?" Rae was shouting now, but she couldn't stop herself. "No. This has nothing to do with him."

"Boys are a distraction. Ever since you started volunteering at that church with him, you've seemed different. Are you seeing him behind my back?"

"Oh my gosh, Mom. No. We're just friends. But why is it such a big deal? What's so terrible about boys?"

"We've had this conversation. Boys aren't terrible, but you need to stay focused on your goals. I would hate to see you throw your future away for some crush."

"You sound just like Dad." She hardly recognized her tone of voice. It was prickly and wild, like poison ivy. "Do you really believe having a boyfriend would ruin my future?"

"Look, young lady." Mom's face was grave. "I don't know what's gotten into you, but you're about one word away from being grounded."

Rae knew better. She did. She'd gone fifteen years and eleven months without ever being grounded. But the last few weeks of stress and fear and wondering what was going on in her family spurred her onward.

"And what word is that, Mom?"

Mom's nostrils flared. "Your father and I will discuss your attitude tonight when he gets home. In the meantime, you're driving to the office."

Rae ignored the keys hanging from Mom's outstretched finger and opened the door. "I'll walk."

"Rae."

She shut the door behind her and stomped to the sidewalk,

not looking back. If she hurried, she'd still make it in time. Not that she cared. She didn't want the job. But a lifetime of high expectations and overachievement had conditioned her to recoil at the thought of missing an appointment. So she would go. At least it got her out of the house.

Mom didn't follow or yell after her. Rae wasn't sure what that meant, but it probably wasn't good. Part of her wanted to run back to the house and throw herself at her mom's feet. Instead, she strode purposefully to Parker Street and turned right. It was too late now. She'd done what she'd done.

Oh, heavens, what had she done?

The law office was easy to find. Businesses of all kinds lined Parker Street, their names etched proudly on windows or displayed in giant block letters above doors. She stopped in front of the office and straightened her blouse. Patted her hair. Hopefully the sweat she was feeling under her arms wasn't showing up on her sleeves.

If Kylee were here, she would say to forget the interview and do something crazy instead. Something unexpected. Rae was already in trouble, anyway, and didn't want a job her father had lined up. But what *did* she want?

The question frightened her. Without The Plan, her future was nothing but a scary swarm of unknowns. A place with more questions than answers. A place she did not want to be. She looked through the window at the people busy at work inside and heard her father's voice. *"Without faithful law practitioners,"* he always said, *"justice is just a pretty word."*

She believed that. She believed in what Dad did for people. Yeah, maybe he was overbearing sometimes, but he'd helped hundreds of families live better lives. The times she'd watched him in court during big cases had been some of the proudest moments of her life, the way he fought for truth and justice. If she stuck to The Plan, she could do that one day, too.

Maybe she'd overreacted earlier.

She checked the time on her phone. Five minutes early.

She opened the door.

RAE LEFT SCHULTZ and Hardy with more confidence than when she went in. The interview had been brief. To the point. They knew her father was a lawyer, knew she planned to attend Columbia and then apply to Columbia Law, and they wanted her to start this summer the day after school got out. They were nice, appreciated her timeliness, and were impressed she already understood most of their legalese. Dad had taught her well.

Maybe the job wouldn't be so bad. It would be nice to earn some money. That was the point of The Plan, wasn't it? But she wasn't ready to face her mother after the way she'd behaved.

She turned the opposite way of her neighborhood and walked. It was overcast but warm, the earthy scent of mid-May permeating the air. She was surprised by how busy it was in this part of town on a Thursday afternoon. Parker Street met Fifth, and she turned, moving farther and farther from the problems that awaited her at home. It was only four-thirty. She could put off her return a little longer.

The houses grew smaller and older the farther she went down Fifth. She rarely saw this part of town. Not that Greenville was a big city or anything. It had grown a lot in the past five years but still had a small-town feel. Her family lived in the newest subdivision, called Evergreen Terrace, but she was pretty sure none of the neighborhoods in this area had names.

One front yard had a rusty old car sitting up on blocks. Another had a fierce-looking dog chained to a fence, a Rottweiler that growled and snapped his jaws at her as she passed. She walked slowly, taking in every detail, observing as Dad had taught her. Everything here was less glossy than she was used to. If there was grass in the yard, it had brown patches. If there was a car in the driveway, it was dinged up. The paint on every house was faded.

She reached the edge of town and turned around with a sigh. Five o'clock. Time to head back and face the music. Her stomach twisted. When was the last time she'd been in trouble? No wonder she avoided it. It felt gross. But even if she was in trouble, she didn't want to miss dinner. She was starving.

Plus, she was banking on Mom and Dad feeling far less angry once she told them she got the job.

On her way back up Fifth, she neared a droopy gray house with dented gutters dangling from the roof. Shouts echoed through the air from inside. A man hollered a string of bad names she'd never even heard before. When she'd almost reached the house, the front door flew open and someone stumbled out as if they'd been pushed. A boy with black hair.

Morgan.

The yard had a waist-high chain link fence all the way around. With his head down, Morgan scrambled to the front gate and pushed it open, nearly slamming it into Rae's legs. The hinges squealed, and she inhaled sharply.

Morgan looked up with a start. She stared at him. His eyes were red, his face drawn as if caving in on itself.

He wiped his nose with his sleeve. "What are *you* doing here?"

"I . . ."

The front door flew open again, and a burly man in grease-stained coveralls waved a fist in the air. "What's goin' on?"

"Come on." Morgan grabbed her hand and pulled. "We gotta get out of here."

He ran down the block, holding on to her tightly. When she tripped trying to keep up, he kept her from falling, then tugged her around a blue trailer house and down an alley.

"This is far enough." He panted. "Boss is too lazy to leave the yard."

She leaned her hands on her knees, trying to catch her breath. "Your dad's name is Boss?"

Morgan gave her a look she couldn't decipher. "He's not my dad."

She looked at the ground so he wouldn't see the questions covering her face. If that wasn't his dad, who was it? And what was he so mad about?

A rickety flatbed trailer surrounded by knee-high weeds was parked on one side of the alley, and Morgan sat on it. Her heart resumed its normal beat, and she straightened, studying the alley. What on earth had just happened? Morgan didn't speak, so she didn't either. If he wanted to explain, he would. Dad always said a good lawyer knew when to push for answers and when to let the answers come to him.

Morgan fixed an intense gaze on her. "Why were you at my house?"

"I wasn't." She didn't look away, though his sapphire eyes burned through her. "I was just walking. I didn't know it was your house."

He looked away then, his brow furrowed. He opened his mouth like he wanted to say something but then shut it again. She wasn't cold, yet she rubbed her bare arms and looked around self-consciously, suddenly aware of how out of place she was. Standing in an overgrown alley with a kid she barely knew, in stark contrast to him with her nice black jeans and name-brand blouse. He wore the same worn-out hoodie he always wore.

She gestured back toward Fifth and started to turn. "I should probably get going."

His expression changed. "Wait."

She stopped.

He kicked at the flatbed's cracked tire, avoiding her eyes. "You're not going to tell anyone, are you?"

Instead of leaving, she took a step closer to him. Drawn by his vulnerability. "No. I promise."

"He's only like that when my mom's not home."

She took another step. "Boss?"

"Yeah, he's my mom's boyfriend. Or something. His real name is Gary."

He must've seen the question in her eyes.

He shrugged. "Everyone calls him Boss."

She hesitated, then sat down on the edge of the trailer. Morgan tensed but didn't move.

"Will your mom be home soon?"

He scooted back onto the flatbed and pulled his knees up to his chest. "I don't know. Sometimes she works late at Della's, and sometimes . . ."

She wanted to say she was sorry or something but it didn't feel right. He wouldn't like that. Instead, she sat there, rubbing her palm over the smooth, weathered wood. Boss must be the reason Morgan attended Community Hope even though he was acing his classes and graduating early. Might even be the reason he hung around the school early in the morning.

She checked her phone. A text from her mom asked where she was. It was almost five-thirty, and she still had to walk home.

She stood. "My parents expect me for dinner."

Longing glinted across Morgan's face like a flicker of flame, then was gone. Snuffed out. "You're lucky, you know."

She remembered Boss's face and the words he had shouted. "You can come with me, if you want."

He laughed a humorless laugh. "I'm sure your parents would love to see me show up on your doorstep."

"What's that supposed to mean?"

"Never mind. You better get going."

"No. I want to know. You think my family's a bunch of snobs or something?"

He shook his head, and his shoulders slumped. "You just live in a different world from me. You don't know what it's like to wish . . ."

As his voice trailed off, she thought of her parents and a car flying wildly down a hill. Whatever it was he didn't want to say, she had a feeling maybe she did know.

CHAPTER
THIRTY-TWO

Gerrit shifted in the hard plastic chair, his muscles complaining. Who knew scrubbing floors and lugging laundry up and down the stairs could be such hard work? He was wiped out, and Daisy hadn't lifted a paw to help.

But Evi and Noah were coming in five days, and the house was going to shine if it killed him.

"Rough day?" Morgan asked.

Like this kid had any clue about rough days. Well, maybe he did. A little.

"This chair is uncomfortable."

"Why are you in such a bad mood?"

He wasn't in a bad mood. He was worried. What would it be like to have Evi and Noah around? He didn't know what to talk to them about. What if he messed up the ziti?

"You're coming on Monday, right?"

Morgan nodded, one hand on Daisy's head, the other on his red notebook.

"Where are those papers I gave you?"

"In my bag."

"Get them out. We can work on it."

"I'll do it at home."

Gerrit narrowed his eyes. He'd stopped at the public library—the *public library*, for crying out loud—on his way here to use their computer thing and print an application to Everett Community College for Morgan. He'd tried to print it at home, but Hannie always did that for him. He couldn't figure it out.

"We've got time now."

Morgan pushed his hair out of his eyes. "What's the point? I don't want to go there."

Gerrit grabbed Morgan's backpack and shoved his hand inside. His fingers found the packet of papers, and he pulled them out and slammed them on the table.

"Got a pen?"

Morgan covered his notebook with his arms and scowled. "No."

Gerrit moved to dig back into the pack.

"Okay, fine." Morgan pulled a pen from the spiral of his book and held it out. "Here."

"I don't want it." Gerrit held up his hands. "You do it. Start with your name."

With a sigh, Morgan filled out the first couple of lines, mumbling, "It's a big waste of time."

"No it's not. You'll have no trouble getting in. You said you get straight A's."

Morgan looked up, fire in his eyes. "Do you have any idea how much it costs to go to college?"

Gerrit looked in the boy's eyes and could see him wrestling. Hope and fear and desperation all battled for position. Was that what his face looked like when he and Luke had this same conversation forty-some years ago?

"Community college is cheaper than a university. And the libraria—uh, some lady was telling me about this thing called FAFSA."

"I know what FAFSA is."

"Then you know you can get money for school."

Morgan dropped his pen on the table and sat back, his black hair falling back across his face. "Even if I could get tuition covered, where would I live?"

"You can commute. It's not that far."

"I don't have a car. And why would I do that?" Morgan's face twisted like he'd stepped in a cow pie. "The whole point of graduating early is to get out of my house."

Gerrit grunted and leaned his elbows on the table. Luke had struggled to convince him to attend college because what would be the point if he was going to spend his whole life on the farm? His future was already set. And deep inside, maybe he'd been afraid to go because he thought it would be easier to stay if he never knew what it was like to leave.

"You'll have the same problem if you move to Nashville. No place to live. No car."

"I could work."

"You could work here."

Morgan leaned over and scratched Daisy behind the ears with both hands, staring into her eyes like he might find the answers there. For a long minute, he gave her all his attention as if Gerrit didn't even exist.

When he finally spoke, his words were quiet but resolute. "Nobody's gonna hire me around here, Gerrit. I've got to get out of this town."

"Why not? You know how to work, don't you?"

"Yes."

"Then why wouldn't anybody hire you?"

Morgan kept his eyes on Daisy, maybe so he could pretend he was talking to her instead. "I've done some things. Stupid things. I kind of have a record. And my dad . . ."

Somehow the words he didn't say told Gerrit more than the ones he did. The weight of a father's influence, good or bad, could be staggering. He might just know something about that. The weight of bad choices in the past that stuck with a person . . . well, he might know something about that, too.

Uncomfortable feelings pushed at his rib cage from the inside. He couldn't let Morgan run off to Nashville by himself. He was just a kid. As he watched Morgan and Daisy, an idea struck. That boy needed his own dog. Maybe if he had a dog to take care of, he wouldn't be so eager to leave town.

"Whatever happened to Fangs?"

Morgan stiffened. "What?"

"You said she didn't die. What happened to her?"

"She ran away." Morgan rested his head on top of Daisy's. "My mom's boyfriend got real mad one time and started kicking and screaming, and it scared her. I looked everywhere, but she never came back."

Gerrit looked at Daisy. If she were to run away, it wouldn't bother *him* any, of course, but Hannie would be devastated. She would probably mope around and post fliers and all that. And he would probably become desperate to make her feel better and do something dumb like get her a new puppy.

Hmm.

GERRIT SPUN AROUND when he heard his name. Rae was jogging up with that David guy close behind. He opened the truck door for Daisy to hop in and gave the boy a hard look.

"I haven't talked to you since last week." Rae came to a stop in front of him. "How are your party plans coming?"

Terrible. Horrible. There wasn't enough time. He was caving under the pressure. The whole thing was a stupid idea.

"Fine."

"Are you excited?"

One side of his lip curled. "I'd be a lot more excited if I could figure out how to make a piecrust that comes out flaky but doesn't burn too fast."

She laughed. "I can't help you with that."

Why had he said that? His mouth must get a kick out of making him look stupid. But the pie problem had been bothering him for days.

"The secret is temperature."

Gerrit and Rae both looked at David.

He shrugged and smiled. "Keeping the butter and dough cold before baking it is the secret. You gotta use cold water. That's what my grandma says."

Gerrit stared at him. What did he know? The little punk. But it did make sense. If the butter got too soft before the pie went into the oven . . .

"I'm David, by the way." The boy held out his hand. "I don't think we've officially met."

Gerrit glared at the hand and glanced at Rae. Her cheeks appeared a little rosier than usual. She nodded toward David.

Fine.

He shook the kid's hand. Hard. This guy had already made Rae cry once. If he ever did it again—

"How's Bernard?" Rae asked.

"Still a rooster."

She gave him a long-suffering look. "About those flowers for your wife."

"What about them?"

"You never told me what her favorite flower is."

He didn't want to admit the truth, but apparently she could read it all over his face.

"Do you at least have a guess?"

He huffed. "I don't know."

"You must. Just think about it."

"Any flowers will do."

"It has to be her favorite. It's important."

He wanted to believe she was wrong. What difference could it make? Flowers were flowers. But something deep down told him it *was* important, like Rae said. Maybe they could order a bouquet with so many different kinds of flowers, one was bound to be her favorite.

"We've still got time," Rae continued. "Think about it and let me know."

The concern on her face made him nervous. He nodded. "I've got to get Daisy home."

He climbed in the truck and leaned an arm out the open window. It'd been warm lately, and he'd discovered the cab could get a little, er, *aromatic* if he left it shut up when it was sitting in the sun. He'd never noticed the smell before. Had it always been this strong? He started the truck.

"See you soon, Gerrit," Rae said with a grin.

He gave a half smile in return, then shifted the Dodge into drive and hit the gas.

David waved and called over the roar of the engine, "Nice to meet you."

Gerrit pretended not to hear the boy as he drove off.

CHAPTER
THIRTY-THREE

Gerrit shaded his eyes with his hand. The sun shone bright and cheerful. The temperature was warm but not too warm. If only this weather would hold through Monday afternoon. He wanted the party to be perfect.

Given all the things he'd messed up in his life, maybe that was asking too much. Regardless, he had to try. For Evi and Noah. For Hannie.

After putting a pork roast in the Crock-Pot—what a great invention *that* was, right?—he'd spent all morning and afternoon cleaning up the yard. He'd mowed, trimmed bushes, even wiped down the outside of the windows on the first floor. Daisy had loved every minute of it, rolling in the grass and chasing butterflies.

He put the last of the tools away in the shed at the back of his property and pulled off his work gloves. Sweat dripped from his forehead, and his stomach grumbled. The smell of the roast through the open kitchen window had been driving him crazy for the past two hours, but Hannie would be home any minute. He would wait. Besides, she usually came home a little early on Tuesdays.

He wiped his face with his sleeve and called for Daisy. When she popped out from the rhododendron bush near the mailbox, he remembered he hadn't checked the mail yet. He trudged down the driveway, muscles stiff and tired, and paused in the shade of the pony barn. He'd talked to Luisa about going through the boxes in there, about showing her Luke's old pictures.

Dust mites danced through the rays of light when he cracked open the barn door. No matter how vibrant the air was outside, how much was going on, inside the barn was always still. Undisturbed by the world going on around it, as if frozen in time. And maybe it was. Frozen in a moment of joy and expectancy. He could almost hear Luke's laugh as he stepped back for a good look and said, *"We did it."* Could almost feel Luke's hand slap him on the shoulder for a job well done. See the twinkle in Luke's eye as he shouted that they should celebrate.

Those weren't memories. Those were pieces of him. He shut the door. The boxes weren't going anywhere.

A cacophony of bangs and whirs and squeals shot over the fence from George's oversized garage. Gerrit scowled in that direction as he continued toward the mailbox. George had hardly missed a minute of *his* children's lives, running a business from his own shop. All that custom furniture and whatnot. Mr. Skilled Craftsman. Mr. Father of the Year. Mr. Soon-to-Be Grandpa. He didn't have to count the money left in his savings account as if it were years left in his life.

Gerrit's neck muscles tightened. What kind of man stole another man's birthright and then called the cops on his rooster? He glanced around but saw no one except Daisy. Edging closer to the fence, he took a good look at the trees between the two properties. There were some on both sides, and a couple of the oldest ones branched out over property lines.

He rubbed his chin. That cottonwood there on George's side, it had seen better days. Some of the branches looked dead and reached their wooden fingers awfully close to George and Agatha's RV. One big windstorm and that RV could be in danger, especially if those dead branches had been tampered with.

He leaned over the fence, peering up at the tree. No, he couldn't. Not that he wouldn't love to see George's RV crushed by a cottonwood, but—

"What are you doing?"

He spun around, his shirt snagging on the top board of the fence. "Oh, hi. I didn't hear you pull up." He hoped his face didn't look as sheepish as he felt.

Hannie eyed him with suspicion through the open window of her Toyota. He walked alongside as she pulled up next to his truck, parked, and got out of the car.

"You're up to something." She studied his face, glancing over at George's house once or twice. "Am I going to be getting a call from Agatha?"

Gerrit huffed. "No."

Hannie shook her head. "Don't you think this has gone on long enough?"

He kept his mouth shut.

Daisy ran around Hannie's legs, making her laugh. "Hello, sweet Daisy."

Gerrit looked back at George's shop one more time.

Hannie peeked at him from the corner of her eye. "Evi called me today."

Oh no. She had canceled. She was probably moving out of the country. She never wanted to speak to him again.

"She was wondering if Travis could come to the party, too."

Oh. That.

"Travis? Who's Travis?" As if he didn't know.

"The boy she's been seeing. I've only met him once, but it must be serious if she's talking about bringing him here."

He looked at the ground and shook his head. He didn't want to meet Travis.

"I told her it was up to you since it's your party."

Oh, great. Now he'd be the bad guy if he said no. But how could he say yes? He hadn't talked to Evi face-to-face in almost two years, and now she wanted to ruin their special weekend by bringing some loser here with her? Sparks burst in his brain. If he saw that kid touching his daughter . . .

Hannie patted his shoulder. "Why don't you take a day to think about it."

He'd think about it all right. In fact, he'd probably spend the whole night *thinking* about it. Pfft. Thinking about wringing that kid's neck. This whole thing was probably his idea.

Hannie moved toward the house, but looked back at him. "I talked to Luisa today, too. She said you were there."

He followed her, trying to dispel the image of his fist slamming into Travis's face. "Yeah. A few weeks ago."

Hannie stopped at the door. "She said you talked about Jakob."

His nostrils flared. First they had to talk about George, then Travis, and now they had to talk about Jakob? "*She* did."

"She's hoping—"

"I don't care what she's hoping." He didn't mean to shout, but the words flew from his mouth like bullets, propelled by the feeling in his gut that he was on a speeding train with no brakes. "It's none of her business."

Hannie flinched. "She thinks it'd be good for you to talk to him. She doesn't want to see you like this."

His fists clenched. "Like what? Going on with my life without having to worry about that—that *moron* taking any more of my money?"

"Like *this*, Gerrit." She tried to put a hand on his arm, but he jerked away. "Letting anger control you. Ruin your life. I don't want to see it, either."

"He already ruined my life. There's nothing more to talk to him about." It was more than a shout now. It was the cry of a wild man. "And you don't know anything about it."

He'd said the same thing to Luisa, but he knew it was different with Hannie the second the words escaped his mouth. She did know. She'd been there.

Moisture brimmed in her wounded eyes. Aw, shoot. The boiling in his veins cooled. What had gotten into him?

He reached for her, but she shook her head and stepped into the house.

"I don't know what got into me, thinking we could ever work together." Emotion strangled her voice. "I thought maybe things could be different, maybe you could change, but . . ."

He was on her heels, inside the door, desperately scouring his mind for something to say. Things *were* different. He *could* change. She took a ragged breath and looked down. He followed her gaze to the blue-and-white suitcase leaning against the wall like a prophet of doom.

No.

No!

They stood close enough that he could smell lilies and roses and pine. *Say something, you idiot.* He opened his mouth, but then she looked up, face twisted, tears imminent.

"You don't know how many times I've stood here at this door, trying to walk out on you. Trying to hate you and your useless cows."

His eyes widened, and he inched closer, drawn by her despair. She never talked like that. The desire to pull her into his arms was like a tsunami, washing over him without mercy.

She struggled to speak. "Now that you're here, it's almost worse, because there's so much more to hope for. At least when you were gone all the time, I could pretend . . ."

It was one of his greatest fears. That once he was around, once he left the farm and faced the world, she would realize he wasn't who she'd thought he was. Before he could think, he reached out with hesitant fingers and touched the ends of her hair. He could hardly feel it, so callused were his hands, so unfit to touch something soft and feminine. But it stirred something in him. Something lost. Something unfamiliar and long buried. The gentle weight of her hair in his hand was like a boulder crushing his heart.

A heifer, he knew how to handle. Knew what she needed and where she should go. But a woman?

"I love you." The words were like a foreign language on his tongue, but that didn't make them less true. His parents never used the words, never talked about feelings or hopes or dreams, never fixed him with a gentle, affectionate gaze. But he knew what love was.

She'd taught him. She and Luke.

He put his hands on her shoulders and pulled her to his chest.

"I love you." He said it with confidence this time.

She sobbed into his shirt then, her arms reaching around his waist and holding on for dear life. He braced her up, his own throat constricting. This woman—this woman who had endured years of suffering for his sake, the mother of his children whose favorite flower he couldn't even remember— she belonged with him. And he would do whatever he had to do to prove it.

Even the one thing he swore he'd never do.

"I'll talk to him."

She buried her face in his shirt, her shoulders shaking, and clung to him. She didn't respond, didn't look up, but it was enough.

He didn't know how he could ever deserve her. Didn't know where they would go from here. Yet he knew one thing for certain.

He wasn't about to let go.

CHAPTER
THIRTY-FOUR

From her locker, Rae watched Morgan slink through a mob of junior girls and into a classroom. Not much had changed since their accidental encounter at his house. He still avoided her at school as if she had lice. Still gave one-word responses when she tried to talk to him at Community Hope. Still refused to acknowledge her open invitation to join her and Kylee at lunch. But she had noticed one little difference.

He didn't seem afraid of her anymore.

Annoyed? Sure. Reluctant? Absolutely. But when she did happen to catch his eye, which wasn't often, he didn't look like he was terrified of what might happen.

"You're an idiot, you know that?" Kylee slammed Rae's locker door shut, and Rae jumped.

"Hey, I wasn't done." Rae opened it again. "What's your problem?"

Kylee stared her down. "I'm sick of watching you pine after some other random guy while stringing David along, that's all."

Rae frowned. Things had been kind of tense and awkward between her and Kylee ever since the day she saw Kylee talking to David after school, but neither of them had brought it up. Rae had been trying to act like nothing had happened. Like nothing had changed.

"I'm not pining after some random guy."

"Oh, really?" Kylee crossed her arms. "Then why are you always watching that kid with the black hair? Morgan, or whatever his name is. Why do you always talk to him at lunch?"

Rae didn't want to rat Morgan out. Didn't want to tell Kylee that he went to Community Hope to avoid his mom's boyfriend or that she'd been there when he got run out of his own house. She'd promised him she wouldn't say anything.

This time *she* slammed the locker shut. "He's just a friend. Am I not allowed to be friends with boys? You're the one who always makes fun of me for not talking to them."

"Oh yeah, I'm sure you're just"—out came the air quotes—"*friends*." Kylee leaned closer and lowered her voice. "And meanwhile, David's still waiting for you like a love-sick puppy."

"That's not true."

"It's not fair to him."

Rae narrowed her eyes. She hadn't had the guts to confront Kylee about talking to David that one day or about saying she would go out with him. Hadn't thought it would be worth it after she talked with David, and they'd reached an understanding. But now she found herself wondering again what Kylee had said.

Rae wasn't leading David on because she'd asked him to wait, was she? It wasn't like they needed to dive right into a serious relationship. They were only high schoolers.

Kylee's eyes flashed. "Go ahead and say it."

"Say what?"

"Whatever it is that's got you looking like there's a scorpion in your mouth."

"Fine." Rae slid her arms into her backpack and squared her shoulders. "What did you say to David after school a couple of weeks ago? After you said you would go out with him if he asked?"

Kylee looked away. "Nothing."

"Didn't look like nothing. I saw you through the glass doors."

"Is that why you've been acting so weird?"

Rae threw up her hands. "You're the one who's been acting weird. And you're avoiding the question."

Kylee huffed. "I said it was nothing. And that has nothing to do with the way you're treating David now."

Rae checked the time. She needed to get to class, but her feet remained rooted in place. She and Kylee had never been at odds like this before. Despite their many differences, they tended to get each other. But Kylee wasn't making any sense.

A flicker of anger sparked in Rae's chest. "Why do you care about me and David? Are you hoping I'll screw it up so he'll run to you? Is that what you were talking to him about?"

She shouldn't have said it. She knew it as soon as the words came out. But Kylee always did know how to push people's buttons.

Kylee took a step back, hurt streaking across her face like paint on canvas. "I told him he'd be an idiot not to give you another chance."

Rae's heart sank. "What?"

Kylee opened her mouth as if to speak, then spun on her heels and walked away. Rae watched her friend go, her words

drum-drum-drumming in her head. *Give you another chance.*
Give you another chance.

Oh no. What had she done?

RAE WANDERED ROOM F aimlessly, unsure what to do with
Taylor absent. Taylor's homeroom teacher had told Mark that
Taylor was sick today. Rae had spent a few minutes here and
a few minutes there with other students, helping them solve
math problems or practice spelling words or organize their
backpacks, but she missed Taylor. What would happen to
her young friend when Taylor moved away? What if all the
work they'd done the past couple of months, all that Taylor
had accomplished, was for nothing?

Her heart twinged as if she were alone in a dark alley. Even
David's smiling face across the room couldn't cheer her up.
Not having Taylor to focus on left her with too much freedom
to think about her own problems. Her parents. The Plan. And
what had just happened with Kylee.

"Having a hard day?" Mark appeared beside her, his beard
newly trimmed.

She chewed her top lip. "You look different. Got a hot
date or something?"

He touched his face and laughed. "My mother strongly
suggested I clean myself up a little. Apparently some of the
ladies in her canasta club have been talking."

"Oh." Rae nodded. "Moms."

"Yep. But you didn't answer my question."

She didn't want to. At least not with the truth. Mark didn't
need to know about her problems with her best friend or her
ongoing worries about whether she could keep her family

from falling apart. But he might be able to help with the other issue bothering her.

"Do you ever wonder if it's worth it?"

He scrunched his face, obviously confused.

"All of this." She swept her arm out, indicating the whole room. "Are we making any difference here?"

A smile slowly spread across his face. Not a silly smile or even a happy one, really. A smile filled with peace and confidence.

"Yes." He looked around the room. "It's worth it."

She narrowed her eyes. How could he be so sure? Did he not see that half the students here only came for the food?

"But what about Taylor? I'll probably never see her again, and what if no one cares about her after she moves? What if I helped her pass seventh grade only to have her fail eighth?"

Mark bobbed his head, his self-assurance undeterred. "So what? That wouldn't mean—"

"Wouldn't it prove I wasted my time here?"

Maybe Mom had been right about volunteering. It was great for college applications and everything, but it wasn't "real work."

Mark's expression turned pensive. "Have you ever read the Bible, Rae?"

She looked at the floor. "No."

"There's this part that says, 'Let us not become weary in doing good, for at the proper time we will reap a harvest if we do not give up.' What do you think that means?"

She shrugged. What did harvesting have to do with anything? There were plenty of farms around here—plenty of fields so fertile you could accidentally sneeze a seed into them and it would grow—but she had no plans to work in them.

Mark slid his phone from his pocket and glanced at it. "It's five o'clock. I gotta get these kids out of here. But think about what I said."

She resisted the urge to roll her eyes. Churchy people thought they had all the answers, didn't they? "I don't understand."

"Pray about it." He grinned, his eyes twinkling. "See what happens."

He turned and cupped his hands around his mouth. "You don't have to go home . . ."

As the students shouted back the expected reply, Rae mulled over Mark's suggestion. He'd already encouraged her to pray about whether she should look into becoming a social worker or counselor or something, but she hadn't done it. What was the point when law was already in her future? But now he wanted her to pray about understanding what the Bible said. As if prayer were the solution for every problem.

"God's got big plans for you."

Papa Tom's words popped into her head and sank like teeth into her brain. If God really did have big plans for her, how would she know what they were? *"Let us not become weary in doing good, for at the proper time we will reap a harvest if we do not give up."* That sounded like something Papa Tom would say.

As she waited for David to say good-bye to his students so they could walk out together, she stared at her phone. A goofy picture of her and Kylee making fish faces stared back. If she mentioned her fight with Kylee to Mark, would he say to pray about that, as well?

She studied the photo, smiling wistfully to herself at Kylee's wild, hot pink hair and ridiculous amounts of facial jewelry.

Her teal-blue leather jacket from the Goodwill. Her sharp edges that kept most people from seeing the softness of her heart.

Rae swallowed hard. How could she have believed . . . ?

She had no idea what praying about the situation with Kylee might accomplish. Or the situation with her parents, for that matter. But it couldn't make things any worse.

CHAPTER
THIRTY-FIVE

Cinnamon. How could they be out of cinnamon? Gerrit slammed cupboard doors and jerked open drawers, muttering to himself. Evi and Noah were coming in two days, and how was he supposed to bake a Dutch apple pie with no cinnamon?

It had been Hannie's idea to make a list of everything he needed for the party. He'd scoffed at first. How hard could it be to go to the grocery store if he needed to? But then he'd had a nightmare about a gallon of milk being so curdled it turned into cheese, and he changed his mind about the list.

Everything else seemed to be in order. He had the ribs. The pasta. The ingredients for the sauce. Food for the other meals besides the big party. He had vanilla ice cream to go with the pie and had even bought a half gallon of almond milk, though he still wasn't sure how it was possible to milk an almond. Almonds don't have nipples.

But there was no cinnamon to be found.

Daisy perked up when he strode to the back door and grabbed his keys. He held open the door. "Hurry up."

The drive to Olsen's Meat & Market was deafening as doubts and questions squabbled in Gerrit's head. Why had he agreed to let Travis come to the party? What if he forgot something else important? Evi wasn't going to be impressed by his efforts. She would just hate him more for trying. Who did he think he was, anyway?

By the time he pulled up to the market, his knuckles were white from gripping the wheel. He unclenched his fingers and gave Daisy a pointed look. "Stay."

She frowned.

"I'll be back in five minutes."

It was busy in the market for a Thursday afternoon. He kept his head down. He didn't know many people in town anymore unless they were old fogies like him, but he didn't want to take any chances.

He'd become familiar with the store since taking over dinner duty and found the cinnamon easily. Though the price was high, he'd have to drive to the Walmart over in Riverton for a better deal, and that wasn't going to happen. He grabbed the plastic container and headed for the checkout.

Oh, look at that. A box of cream cheese Danishes on sale for $2.99. He'd better grab one of those. The kids might like them for breakfast on Sunday. He could make scrambled eggs to go with it. Did he have enough eggs? Better grab another dozen just in case.

A young man in a blue apron saw him precariously balancing the items in his arms. "Would you like a cart, sir?"

Gerrit huffed. If he wanted a cart, he would have a cart. He grunted and continued on. Butter was on sale? He must've missed it in the weekly ads. Butter was never on sale. He should stock up.

Another man in a blue apron stood in his path. "Can I get you a cart, sir?"

Gerrit scowled and brushed by him. "No."

He eyeballed the lines at each of the three open checkout lanes and chose the middle one. He liked to pretend he was always looking for the shortest line, but really the middle checkout lane was the one with the drink cooler. A 20-ounce Pepsi for $1.89. Nothing could beat that.

A hunched-over woman who must've been a hundred years old carefully removed five apples one by one from her basket onto the grocery belt. Gerrit shifted on his feet, feeling the weight and awkwardness of his armload. Condensation was making the butter slippery, and the lid on the box of Danishes had been knocked askew. Oh, for crying out loud. Now she was taking personal-sized cartons of yogurt out one at a time. Perspiration sprouted on his forehead. She must have one in every flavor known to man.

"Let me help you with that." He leaned in close and tried to reach into her basket while keeping the pile of groceries balanced in his arms.

He failed.

The eggs were the first to go. Then the cinnamon.

The old woman startled and put a hand to her chest. "Oh my."

He let the rest of the pile tumble onto the grocery belt, not caring if his butter got mixed up with her yogurt, then surveyed the damage. The carton of eggs had landed on its side so that the eggs not only cracked open but also rolled onto the floor. The cinnamon landed on its feet, unscathed.

He pulled a Pepsi from the cooler, twisted off the cap, and took a swig.

Daisy was not impressed when Gerrit finally opened the passenger side door and set his grocery bags on the floor in front of her. *That was more than five minutes*, she seemed to say.

He slammed the door. "I don't want to hear it."

He went to walk around the front of the truck to the driver's side but then stopped short. A tall man in a bright blue windbreaker was stumbling down the sidewalk, his back to Gerrit. And Gerrit knew only one person in Greenville who would be wandering around in a blue jacket, drunk before four in the afternoon.

"Jakob."

The man came to a swaying halt. No good could come of this. Gerrit was not prepared to face his younger brother, and Jakob was clearly not prepared to have a coherent conversation. But the image of that blue-and-white suitcase taunted Gerrit, and he held his ground.

Jakob turned to look at him, blinking against the brightness of the sun. Gerrit gestured at the empty sidewalk next to him. Inebriated as he was, Jakob took the hint and staggered over, suspicion trembling all over his haggard face.

"I see you're putting the farm money to good use."

Jakob's eyes narrowed. "Iss my money."

"That I worked for."

"I worked."

"When did you ever—?" A young mom pushing a stroller along the sidewalk turned to look when Gerrit's voice rose, so he cut himself off. He scrubbed a hand over his face, lowering his voice. "You didn't deserve a penny of that payout."

A fire lit in Jakob's glazed-over eyes. He shook his head. "You don't know nothin' 'bout it."

Gerrit's own words. Their father's words. His chest burned.

"I know I kept the farm going after Luke died. After Dad died."

"You mean after you killed him?"

Something snapped in Gerrit's brain. He pushed Jakob up against the truck and held him there with a forearm to the throat. "Don't you talk about him."

"Get offa me!" Jakob struggled against Gerrit's arm, adrenaline shaking some of the fuzziness from his speech. "'Less you want another assault charge."

Jakob had been sixteen that time Gerrit punctured his thigh with a hay hook. Criminal assault on a minor. He'd just returned home from college and found Jakob napping on a haystack while Luke and their father broke their backs in the summer heat trying to keep the corn from dying in record high temperatures. Jakob ran crying to their father, just like he always did. Gerrit escaped with a two-thousand-dollar fine after pleading guilty.

He took a step back, releasing his brother. "I don't ever want to see you again."

Jakob glared and jabbed a finger in his face. "Fine by me."

He hobbled away. Gerrit watched him go, fists balled up tight. Then he got in the Dodge and slowly, deliberately pulled on his seat belt and started the truck. He sat like that, engine idling, staring out the windshield for a long minute.

Well.

He'd promised Hannie he'd talk to Jakob, and he had.

Beside him, Daisy whined.

He finally stopped staring out the window and forced his shoulders down. He glanced at the dog.

"I won't tell her if you won't."

CHAPTER
THIRTY-SIX

That must be Bernard." Evi nodded at the rooster, strutting down the driveway as if he were the grand marshal of a parade. "Mom told me about him."

Gerrit cut his eyes toward the creature. "Bernard the Terrible."

"Is he that bad?"

He shrugged and tried to smile. "He's growing on me."

Hannie would be rushing out of the house to greet their daughter any minute. Meanwhile, Gerrit stood awkwardly in front of Evi, unable to move. The sight of her pulling into the driveway had been like the sun rising on a winter morning, bringing light and life to an otherwise dreary world. But when she'd climbed out of her car and looked at him, he'd barely been able to think, much less speak.

"Can I take your bag?"

She looked down at the small duffel in her hand. "No. Thanks."

Another car turned in, and relief flashed across Evi's smooth, fair face. Noah. Finally, Hannie came bursting from the house, grinning from ear to ear.

"Why didn't you tell me they were here?" She shot Gerrit an accusatory glance.

"I—"

She grabbed Evi in a hug, then held her at arm's length and took her in. "I love your haircut. It's adorable."

Before Evi could respond, Noah was out of his car. A greeting stuck in Gerrit's throat as he fidgeted with his hands, unsure whether to offer a handshake or what. But Hannie didn't hesitate.

"Speaking of haircuts, looks like you need one," she chided their son as she opened her arms.

Noah accepted Hannie's hug, then ran a hand through his shaggy locks. "I like it like this."

Gerrit grunted. Noah looked like a hippie, but he could hardly say anything. His own hair was brushing the back of his neck and curling into his ears. He should've gotten it trimmed up before the kids came. He glanced at Evi from the corner of his eye to see if she was surprised by Noah's hair, but she was staring at the pony barn like it was a ghost. He followed her gaze and saw that the barn door was cracked open. Rae must not have shut it all the way after her visit last night.

His stomach twisted. The barn had been built to be a sanctuary for Evi and Noah. Not Rae.

Noah looked around. "The yard looks nice, Mom. You've put in a lot of work."

Hannie clasped her hands in front of her. "That was all your father."

"Oh." Noah looked at Gerrit and nodded.

He'd never realized before how much Noah looked like

Luke. Talked like him. Moved like him. He gaped at his son as if he hadn't held him in one hand when he was born, torn between uneasiness over how different things might've been if Noah had been Luke's son, and guilt over his pride in finally having something Luke didn't have.

His arms were lead, his feet concrete, his throat a dried-up well from which no words could be drawn.

"Come in, come in." Hannie gave him an inscrutable look and waved everyone toward the house. "Are you guys hungry? Can I get you anything?"

"We're fine." Noah laughed. "It's not like we had to catch a flight to get here."

Gerrit brought up the rear as they all filed through the door. Had Noah always been so tall? His broad shoulders were thick and muscular, perfect for throwing bales. If only . . .

"Your old rooms are ready for you," Hannie said. "Dinner's in an hour."

OVER THE RED-WHITE-AND-BLUE centerpiece Hannie had made, Gerrit watched Evi pick at her salmon. He followed her movements, enthralled by her delicate fingers. She was the spitting image of Hannie back in the day, except with shorter hair. He had taken a risk serving fish—Hannie had said she ate fish *sometimes*—and it didn't appear to be paying off. Or else being back in the house was messing with her appetite.

He couldn't blame her. Having the four of them sitting around the same table was wreaking havoc on his stomach, too. She caught him staring, and he quickly looked away.

"So. Mom." Evi set her fork down. "Are we going to be able to see the shop? I haven't been there in forever."

"Sure." Hannie had no trouble finishing *her* salmon. "Maybe we can swing by there tomorrow after church."

"Did you make this?" Noah gestured at the centerpiece, burgeoning with geraniums, daisies, and sprigs of some kind of dark-blue berry. "It's amazing."

Hannie smiled. "It was your father's idea."

Gerrit had failed to manage a bouquet for his wife, but at least the centerpiece had worked out.

Silence fell. He forced a bite into his mouth. He shouldn't have added so much lemon to the sauce. And what had he been thinking making lemon bars for tonight? Lemon overload. Chef Kellan would call it an amateur mistake. Not that he'd watched *Kellan's Kitchen* every night for two weeks in preparation for this weekend.

"Evi, do you think Travis is going to make it on Monday?" The brightness of Hannie's voice sounded forced.

Evi shrugged. "We're going to see how it goes."

Gerrit scowled at his plate. What was that supposed to mean? Well, it wouldn't bother him any if Travis didn't show up.

Hannie gave Gerrit a look he hoped was meant to be encouraging. "Your father invited one of his new friends, too."

He was not encouraged.

Noah leaned close to Evi and spoke in a low, incredulous whisper. "Dad has a friend?"

Hannie was unfazed. "Morgan is a student your father met at this tutoring program he volunteers for."

"Dad tutors?"

Evi raised one eyebrow. "His friend is a little kid?"

Why did they keep talking to Hannie as though he weren't even there? He cleared his throat.

"He's sixteen." Gerrit's voice sounded gruff in his ears. "I think."

Evi looked at him then, really looked at him for the first time since her arrival. He saw questions in her eyes but didn't know what they were. Maybe she didn't, either. He wanted to give her answers, give her anything she asked for, but he didn't know if he could. Just like when *she'd* been sixteen and stood before him with those same eyes, asking if he was going to make it to her solo performance at the state music festival.

"No," he'd said. He remembered it clearly. Remembered the dismissal in his voice. *"The cows aren't going to milk themselves."*

Her eyes remained on him as she stood and picked up her plate. "I'm going for a walk. Thanks for dinner, Mom."

He watched her shove her dishes into the dishwasher and tromp to the mudroom for her shoes. *But you just got here*, he wanted to say. *It'll be dark soon.* But no one said anything.

Evi slammed the door on her way out. She knew very well he was the one who'd made dinner.

CHAPTER
THIRTY-SEVEN

Rae almost walked into a tree as she looked at her phone. Another text from David. They'd been texting every night. A smile bloomed on her face as she read the words of his most recent message. He was so funny.

She skirted the tree and slid her phone in her back pocket, fighting back a tiny flicker of guilt. Mom had no idea how much time she'd been spending on her phone. How much she'd been talking with David. But as long as she and David remained nothing more than friends, she didn't need to feel bad, did she? Mom and Dad were pleased about her job at Schultz and Hardy, and David had said nothing more about their going out on a date after school let out.

Part of her hoped he would forget. Part of her hoped he wouldn't. Another part of her wanted to run around screaming in the woods like a crazy person.

She'd never felt like this before.

The only thing that kept her feet on the ground was the thought of Kylee and how Rae had hurt her. The last couple of days at school had been unbearable, with Kylee staying as far away from her as possible. She wouldn't even respond to Rae's texts. But Rae would find a way to apologize. She had to.

When she reached Gerrit's house, she stopped short. Mr. Whiskers meowed from her left shoulder, where he was draped like a towel.

"Would you look at that." But of course he couldn't look, facing backward and all. "They came."

The two extra cars in the driveway were proof enough that Gerrit's kids had shown up for the highly anticipated weekend. Gerrit had been a wreck all week. He hadn't actually said so, but she'd gotten the impression he wasn't sure if they'd come.

It was strange seeing so many lights on in the house. Even the back deck was lit up, though the sun was just setting. She slipped into the barn without a sound, wishing she could attend the party on Monday. Boy, would she love to see that. Nothing could take your mind off your own family drama like witnessing someone else's.

The barn was peaceful and still, as always, and yet something different hummed in the air.

"Do you feel that, Mister?" She sat in the deck chair Gerrit had set up for her and put the fat cat on her lap. "There's life around here for once."

She ran her hand over the cat's soft back. Gerrit had never told her why his kids didn't come around. Why he was so nervous about seeing them again. Or why things were so strained between him and Hannie, for that matter. But it made her happy that his family was all together.

She shifted in the plastic chair, the words Mark had said the other day at Community Hope ringing in her mind. She'd never forget the look on his face when she'd asked if what they were doing was going to make a difference in anyone's life.

He'd been so sure. Like he knew exactly what he meant when he answered yes. She used to have that kind of confidence about everything in her life. Now, though, she found herself second-guessing things she never thought she'd question. Like her parents. *"Let us not become weary in doing good, for at the proper time we will reap a harvest if we do not give up."*

Give up on what? And when was the proper time?

She remembered the words clearly because she'd looked them up on her phone after talking to Mark and reread the verse a bunch of times. She was pretty sure she understood the first part: keep doing good things even if you get tired of it. But the second part? She wasn't a farmer. She had no fields. No harvest.

Gerrit was a farmer, though. Or at least he used to be. Maybe he would understand it. Maybe she could ask him.

The cardboard box nearest her chair caught her eye. It was small, not much bigger than a shoebox. The word *Pictures* was scrawled across the side.

She stood and set Mr. Whiskers on the chair. "You ever wonder what Gerrit was like when he was younger?"

If he did, the cat gave no indication.

A single piece of tape had secured the top of the box once upon a time, but it had long ago lost its stickiness. The flaps gave easily when she pulled on them. She hesitated. He'd asked her not to move the boxes around anymore. He never said anything about looking inside them.

A messy pile of photos lay in the box like they'd been dumped there unceremoniously. Some in frames, some loose. She picked one off the top and shifted so the light would shine on it.

It was a black-and-white picture. Two young boys, maybe five and six years old, in cute little suits with bow ties. Hair slicked down. The taller one had his arm around the shorter one's shoulders and peered at the camera with a serious expression, as if he'd already seen more of the world than she had. The younger boy . . . was that Gerrit?

She flipped the photo over. On the back, an unsteady hand had written a note in tiny disheveled letters. *Easter, 1961.* She set the picture down and was reaching for another one when the sound of the house door opening and closing made her look up. Someone was coming outside. She stepped away from the box and took her place back in the deck chair, sliding Mr. Whiskers onto her lap.

Footsteps approached the barn. Gerrit appeared in the doorway.

"You're here." His voice was guarded.

She nodded, trying to imagine him as the little boy she'd seen in the picture. "So are your kids."

He glanced at the driveway over his shoulder. "Yeah."

"Are you having fun? Can I meet them?"

She couldn't begin to imagine what they were like. Stoic and awkward, like Gerrit? Gentle and kind, like Hannie? Something else entirely?

Gerrit rubbed the back of his neck. "Do you have Morgan's phone number?"

She blinked. What on earth? "No."

"Hannie thinks we should push the party back to four on Monday. Instead of three."

"Oh." She raised one shoulder. "I know where he lives, but . . ."

He looked over his shoulder again. "Could you give him the message?"

He was acting weird.

She sighed. "I can try. So, anyway, I wanted to ask you about—"

"I think you better go."

Her question fell to the ground like a fly swatted out of the air. He gave her a hard look, and she cringed.

"Oh." She stood. "Okay."

A bony finger poked at her heart. She wanted to hear all about his kids. Wanted to ask him what he thought of that verse about a harvest. But he remained in the doorway, tense and distracted, as she set Mr. Whiskers back on her shoulder and turned off the light. He stood aside so she could pass. Dusk had fallen.

Outside, she wrinkled her brow at a dark figure passing by the mailbox.

"I'm sorry, I thought—"

Gerrit waved her away. "Go on now."

She turned away, stunned. Sheesh. What a jerk. From the beginning, she'd believed he wasn't the grizzly bear he appeared to be on the outside. She'd believed he was misunderstood. But maybe she was the one who had misunderstood.

"Let us not become weary in doing good, for at the proper time we will reap a harvest if we do not give up."

From the tree line, she glanced back at the barn. It didn't look like a refuge anymore.

CHAPTER
THIRTY-EIGHT

Gerrit tugged at the collar of his button-up shirt. He hadn't been this uncomfortable in a long time. And it wasn't the clothes.

The man onstage raised his hands with a smile that made Gerrit want to punch him in his big old horse teeth. "Please stand and greet the people around you while the worship team comes up."

Gerrit could not think of a worse experience than trying to greet the people around him at Greenville Community Church. Would he have to talk to everyone? Did he have to tell them his name? He considered remaining seated in protest, but Hannie tugged on his arm. Fine. He would do it for her. He was only here for her and the kids' sake, anyway.

He stood. People milled about the sanctuary, buzzing like insects. Some of them smiled in his direction with overeager faces as if they knew this was his first time. As if they knew they had him trapped.

"Gerrit?" A bearded young man approached from the aisle, hand outstretched. "Is that you?"

Gerrit shook his hand once, noting the man's pants were even tighter than usual. "Mark."

Mark waved an arm in Evi and Noah's direction. "Is this your family?"

Gerrit nodded.

Mark turned to Hannie and jerked a thumb at Gerrit. "I didn't know this old codger belonged to you. I never put it together."

Gerrit gaped, and Hannie laughed at the stupefied look on his face.

"We've known each other for years," Mark explained. "Hannie's one of my favorite people."

Hannie smiled and waved a hand. "Oh, stop." She turned to the kids. "This is my—*our*—son, Noah, and our daughter, Evi."

Gerrit's eyes narrowed as Mark held on to Evi's hand a little too long.

Evi smiled. "Nice to meet you."

Oh, sure. She was happy to talk to and smile at some guy she'd just met, but would she give her own father the time of day?

The lights dimmed, and everyone shuffled back to their seats. Gerrit sank into his chair with a huff. So many people. Staring at him. Talking.

He wouldn't have come, but Hannie had given him the look. The "You wanted your kids here so you could spend time with them—now get off your butt and get dressed" look. And she was right. By tomorrow night they'd be gone again, and he had no idea when they'd be back. He could suffer through an hour and a half of church.

He sat on the end of the row, his long legs spilling into

the aisle, knees sticking out like torpedoes. Hannie was beside him, then Noah, then Evi, as far away from him as she could get.

When she'd returned from her walk last night, he was standing in the middle of the driveway on the verge of hopping into his truck to go look for her. She'd stopped next to him on her way back to the house and stared into the dark woods. "Another *friend* of yours?" she'd said. And he'd seen the barn through Evi's eyes.

It was meant to be hers.

He was a fool. He'd blown it with Evi. And he'd blown it with Rae.

Two guys playing guitars, and a lady wearing a giant scarf that looked like it might swallow her up, sang a few songs. Gerrit stood when the congregation was asked to stand. Sat when told to sit. And kept glancing down the row at his family. Hannie often glanced back and smiled, even patting his knee once. Noah listened intently, his eyes always on the stage, his lips moving, head bobbing. Evi was hard to read.

Gerrit shifted in his seat. The preacher took the stage. He was younger than Gerrit and unassuming. He wore a sweater vest and glasses.

"Good morning." He looked out over the congregation. "Please turn your Bibles to the book of Luke. Chapter five."

Gerrit's heart squeezed. His vision blurred. A plain pine casket draped with yellow roses appeared where the preacher had stood. A framed photo of Luke and Luisa on their wedding day stood on a black easel behind the wooden box. Stifled sobs echoed through the sanctuary.

"We are here today to celebrate the life of our dear friend and brother, Luke," Pastor Randall had said, the man who'd been

leading the church they all attended back then. *"And though we who are left behind are in mourning, Luke has no sorrow today, folks. No. He is in heaven with our Lord."*

Gerrit had not been able to cry. Not been able to move. Definitely not been able to "celebrate." His big brother, his only friend, was gone. And it was all his fault.

Hannie nudged him, and he shook his head.

The casket disappeared.

The pain did not.

The man with glasses pointed to the Bible on the stand in front of him. "Then verse twenty-seven says, 'After this, Jesus went out and saw a tax collector by the name of Levi sitting at his tax booth. "Follow me," Jesus said to him.'"

Gerrit pulled his eyes from the preacher and stared at the back of the seat in front of him. *Follow me.* That was what Luke used to say. *"Let's rake the north side first. Follow me."* Or *"No, the supply store has better prices. Follow me."* Gerrit had loved his older brother. Admired him. But sometimes he'd gotten sick of doing things Luke's way, and it had cost him. Both of them.

"'It is not the healthy who need a doctor, but the sick,'" the preacher continued. "'I have not come to call the righteous, but sinners to repentance.'"

Ha. Repentance. Sackcloth and ashes, right? That was all well and good. But he could repent of his mistakes till the cows came home, and it wouldn't do any good. Luke would still be gone.

An icy hand with a steel grip squeezed his heart. He could never repent enough to be free.

But maybe . . .

He'd been bound to the farm, shackled to his duty and

his father's expectations since the day he entered the world. But if his family could forgive him—even though Luke never could—maybe that would be enough.

Forgiveness. The thought of it made the chains on his heart feel a little lighter, as if someone were lifting them off.

The preacher said, "You are dismissed," and Gerrit stood and stretched, feeling the past ninety minutes in every muscle in his back. He stepped into the aisle, eager to escape.

Something caught his eye, near the doors. A tall man in a blue windbreaker ducked out, head down. Gait unsteady. It couldn't be. But it was.

Jakob.

The chains fell back with a thud and crushed Gerrit with their oppressive weight. He grunted under the burden, staggering and then bracing himself. There would be no freedom for him. The price was too high. He might someday, if he was lucky, earn forgiveness from his wife and kids. He might be able to make it right with Rae after the way he'd acted toward her. But he could never forgive Jakob.

GERRIT PATTED HIS full stomach. Dinner had gone over well. Both vegetarian and nonvegetarian fajitas with homemade guacamole. He, Hannie, and the kids relaxed on the deck, watching the sun sink. If the backyard were a beach, it would almost be like they were on the California vacation he used to promise they would take but never did.

Noah rose from his chair and leaned on the rail, peering down the hill. "It's weird seeing the farm now."

Gerrit's senses heightened, the mere mention of the farm setting him on edge.

"Good riddance," Evi said.

Hannie reached over and covered Evi's hand with hers. "You used to love going down there."

"Maybe when I was five."

"Even after that." Hannie pushed herself up and joined Noah at the rail. "Remember the Easter egg hunts we used to have in the old barn?"

Noah nodded. "There's probably still eggs buried in there. We weren't very good hunters."

Evi stood now, too. "Speak for yourself. I was an excellent hunter."

"Only because you couldn't stand leaving a single piece of candy behind." Noah smiled. "And you always hid the wrappers in the sawdust pile so no one would know how much you ate."

Evi smacked his arm. "Did not."

"Did too."

A comfortable silence fell between Hannie, Evi, and Noah. The only one left in a chair, Gerrit looked around self-consciously. The rest of his family stood shoulder to shoulder, a united wall. Content without him. He might as well be back on the farm. Might as well be dead. He had erased himself from their lives.

Then Hannie looked back at him, an olive branch in her eyes. "Join us?"

He scrambled to accept the branch, leaning next to Noah on one end of the lineup, wondering what it would feel like for this to be the most natural thing in the world.

A warm breeze blew wisps of hair across Hannie's face. She brushed them aside. "Remember the time your father built that giant slide out of hay bales? You kids played on that thing for hours."

"It was almost two stories high." Noah laughed. "It's a miracle nobody died."

Gerrit tensed. Noah blanched and glanced over at him. Gerrit gripped the rail, staring down at the land at the bottom of the hill, wondering how one place could hold so much joy and pain. A moment passed, Noah's words suspended in the air as if waiting to see what Gerrit would do with them.

"I liked it when you guys played in the barn," he finally said. "Liked hearing you laugh."

A hesitant, hopeful smile crept over Noah's face. "Except when we stole your Pepsi out of the vaccine fridge."

Gerrit pretended to scowl. "Except for that."

The truth was if he could go back, he'd buy a whole separate fridge to stock with Pepsi for his kids to have whenever they wanted. He'd build a hundred hay slides.

"I always used to wish you liked Sprite." Evi's voice was soft. Thoughtful. "That was my favorite."

"I didn't know that."

She frowned. "No kidding."

"Evi," Hannie said.

Gerrit held up a hand. "No, it's okay." The thudding of his heart was like pounding fence posts in the back forty. "I'm sorry, Evi. I wasn't a good father."

No one disagreed. His confession staggered down the hill, tumbling over rocks and trees and coming to rest on the site of his transgressions.

When she answered, he almost missed it. "You weren't a father at all," she whispered.

His blood—or was it the past?—roared in his ears. "Maybe it's not too late."

Her head snapped up. "Maybe it is."

Noah stood between them, looking back and forth. "Come on, Evi. He's trying."

She slammed a hand on the rail. "Who cares?"

Noah moved away, unsure. "I care."

"He can't just decide to be our dad again."

Hannie reached for Evi. "Honey, your father always—"

Evi shook her off. "The only thing he *always* did was let me down."

"What is wrong with you?" Gerrit's voice was hardened with dread.

Hannie stared at him. He swallowed. That had come out wrong.

"I mean—"

"Nothing's wrong with me." Evi faced him. "I'm not the one who told his own daughter he wished she were a boy."

Gerrit flinched. He remembered that day all too well. Apparently Evi did, too. But that wasn't exactly what he'd said. He'd been desperate for help in the parlor after losing yet another hired hand, and he had asked her to pitch in. She'd refused. Said she didn't want anything to do with the farm. He'd let his anger get the best of him.

Why did he always throw words around like they wouldn't hurt?

She headed for the door, and he moved to block her retreat. "What do you want me to do? Please."

Tears brimmed in her eyes. "I don't want you to do anything. I just think . . . I don't know." She drew a shaky breath. "When Uncle Luke died, I think maybe you did, too."

She stepped to the side to go around him, but he held out his arms to stop her. He searched her face, desperate to find something, anything that would give him hope. He scoured his brain, desperate for words to make her stay. The right words this time.

He gently placed his hands on her shoulders. "Forgive me. Please." The words were raw and ragged, tripping over the lump in his throat. "Things are going to be different."

Surely they would. They had to. Nothing else mattered.

She looked down as a tear escaped, then pulled away so that his hands fell to his sides.

"I don't know if I can."

Her voice was hollow. Lost. He reached for her, but she pushed past him, opened the sliding door, and disappeared into the house.

CHAPTER
THIRTY-NINE

Gerrit scanned the sky and took a deep breath. It smelled like grass and sunshine with a hint of apples and spice from the pie he'd baked that morning. Only a single cloud loomed on the horizon, the shape and color of an elephant.

He narrowed his eyes at it. "You stay over there."

Daisy tilted her head to look at him, tongue lolling out.

He sniffed the air again. "It doesn't smell like rain."

Satisfied, he checked the yard for dog droppings one last time and returned the shovel to the shed. The ribs were already on the grill, having been marinated overnight and rubbed to within an inch of their lives shortly before going on the rack. The ziti was in the oven. He'd gotten up early and gone to town for two cases of Sprite from Olsen's and another bunch of asparagus so he could wrap the one he already had in prosciutto and leave the second one meat-free. Everything was going well.

Shrieks and laughter came from over at George's house. Must be half a dozen cars parked over there. Two jacked-up trucks. A minivan. A red Jetta. Gerrit huffed. George couldn't come up with his own ideas. Had to steal his, just like he'd stolen everything else. Then in a couple of weeks, when his granddaughter was born, he'd probably throw an even bigger bash.

Well, *his* party was going to be just as good as George's. Even better. Surely his food would be.

Hannie called from the house, "You ready to flip the ribs?"

He checked his watch. A little after three. "I'll look at them."

There were a hundred and one ways to barbecue ribs, according to Chef Kellan, but Gerrit had chosen a fairly traditional method. The trick would be to keep an eye on the meat so it wouldn't dry out.

He made his way around the house and climbed the three steps to the back deck, where Evi and Noah were hanging out. The tantalizing smell of barbecued pork was already seeping out from under the hood of his grill.

Evi pulled her phone from her ear and slid it in her pocket. "Travis is on his way."

Noah smiled. "Good. He owes me a game of cornhole."

Gerrit scowled. "We don't have cornhole."

"I brought mine." Noah waved a hand. "It's in the back of my car. Have you ever played?"

Of course he hadn't. He'd never had time for games. But admitting it felt like defeat. He shrugged.

"Who would he play with?" Evi said. "Mom?"

Noah laughed. "Mom would smoke him."

Evi gave him a look Gerrit could not interpret. "I guess he could play with his new friends."

Something about the way she said the word *friends* rolled

like a stone in Gerrit's gut. Did she not believe he could ever make a friend? No, that wasn't it. Something else.

"They're not really my friends." He didn't know how to explain. "They're just kids. It just kind of happened."

"Do you help them with their homework?" Evi leaned her back against the rail as if trying to act casual, but an undercurrent of tension droned in the warm air.

He looked at her and saw the set of her jaw and heard the real question she was asking. She wanted to know if he was giving Rae and Morgan the pieces of himself he'd never given her and Noah. The pieces of himself he could never quite spare before.

"No." Urgency buzzed in his ears. He needed her to see the truth. "I—"

"Do you go to their basketball games? Their choir performances? Take them to the movies?"

How had this become about Morgan and Rae? They weren't the kids he lay awake at night thinking about. "I don't care about them like—"

"No, Dad." Evi pushed off the rail. "It doesn't matter what you say."

"*They* don't matter." He had to make her understand. "Can't you see—?"

A clatter interrupted his explanation. He jumped and spun around to see a flowerpot tipped over and a figure in a hoodie disappearing around the corner of the house. No. This couldn't be happening.

"Morgan?" Gerrit hurried down the stairs, Daisy at his heels, and called after the boy, "Stop."

His heart raced, even as it tumbled headfirst into the big black hole he'd dug with his own big fat mouth. He wasn't expecting Morgan until four o'clock. What was he doing here? How much had he heard?

The boy ran for the hidden shortcut trail behind the barn, but then stopped with his back to Gerrit before reaching the tree line.

"Don't go." Gerrit caught up and waited for Morgan to turn around.

He didn't. "Were you talking about me?"

Gerrit's heart shriveled like petals wilting in the sun. "Yes, but—"

"I thought you were cool because you didn't seem to care about my family or my past." Morgan's fists were clenched at his sides, his voice resigned. "I thought you just liked me for me. But I guess I was wrong."

He plowed into the woods without once looking back. Gerrit wanted to run after him, wanted to defend himself, but knew he could never keep up. His body could never maneuver the roots and branches and winding trails fast enough. And Evi and Noah were at the house on his invitation, already wondering where they stood in comparison to Morgan and Rae.

He held up a hand and shouted, "Wait!" But a west wind kicked up and snatched the word right from his mouth, tossing it up into the leaves. A cloud blew in front of the sun, deepening the shadows.

He'd really done it this time.

After staring into the trees long enough for Daisy to grow restless and abandon him, he turned back toward the house. Evi and Noah stood at the end of the deck, watching him. From the looks on their faces, they must've heard everything.

"That was Morgan?" Noah asked.

He didn't need to answer.

Evi rubbed her bare arms as the wind blew harder, chilling the air. "He was early."

Gerrit hung his head.

Noah glanced at the woods. "Maybe you should call him or something."

"Can't," Gerrit grunted. "Don't have his number."

He hadn't seen the look on Morgan's face, but he had a feeling he knew it all too well. Had seen it a hundred times on Noah's and Evi's faces. On Hannie's. He lifted his own face to the sky, now gray and ominous.

"We better go inside."

Evi and Noah filed into the house, silent and solemn. Gerrit stepped in and closed the sliding door behind them.

Hannie met them in the living room with a bright smile. "Hey, guys. I was just on the phone with Luisa. She says she's going to be a little late, but . . ." Her smile faded as she noticed their expressions. "What's going on?"

Evi looked at Gerrit, but when he didn't respond, she sighed. "Morgan was here."

"What do you mean *was*?"

"I feel kind of bad," Noah said.

Hannie's crow's feet appeared as she looked at Gerrit. He looked back. She would think this was all his fault. And she wouldn't be wrong.

A knock sounded at the front of the house.

Evi perked up. "That must be Travis."

She scurried to answer the door. Gerrit's frown deepened. Bad to worse. That's how this day was going.

Hannie and Noah followed close behind Evi, eager to greet their guest. The sounds of a door opening and closing, shuffling feet, and happy voices snaked around the corner to where Gerrit stood. He frowned. If he saw Travis getting familiar with Evi, he'd need a blunt object to deal with the problem. He scanned the room for possibilities but nothing stood out.

"And here's my dad." Evi came back to the living room dragging a young man behind her. "Dad, this is Travis."

Travis was unimpressive. Barely taller than Evi, he looked like he'd never done a day's hard labor in his life. He held out a smooth, unconvincing hand, and Gerrit squinted at it. Looked like he wouldn't need a blunt object after all. His fists would be more than enough.

"Dad." Evi gave him a look.

He shook the scrawny hand. "Travis."

"Good to finally meet you, Mr. Laninga. This is a great place you've got here."

Nice try, kid.

"And what do you do for a living, Travis?"

"Dad." This time Evi's voice held a warning. He wrestled with himself. Maybe now wasn't the best time to grill Evi's—ugh—boyfriend. She hadn't even wanted to come, but she was here, and he didn't want to totally blow it.

Gerritt held up his hands. "I made strawberry lemonade."

Hannie put on a making-the-most-of-it smile. "I tried it this morning. It's delicious. Who wants some?"

Travis put his hand on the small of Evi's back as they followed Hannie to the kitchen. Like he'd done it a hundred times before. She wasn't a little kid anymore, Gerrit knew that, but he wasn't ready for this. It was like she'd grown up overnight when he wasn't looking. Which was exactly what had happened. He hadn't been looking.

His neck muscles constricted as Travis and Evi stood close to each other, sharing a glass. Gazing into each other's eyes. But he kept his mouth shut. He'd told Evi things were going to be different.

She poured more lemonade. "This is really good, Dad."

He caught her eye. She didn't smile, but she didn't look away.

He would take it.

A gust of wind struck the house, and the *plop-plop* of heavy raindrops hit the roof.

"Looks like we'll be eating inside." Hannie peeked out the window. "That blew in fast. Is the grill going to be okay?"

"Hope so," Noah said. "I'm starving."

Gerrit blinked. He'd forgotten all about the ribs. The grill was on the leeward side, tucked close to the house, so it shouldn't be affected by the wind. But he hadn't flipped the meat. Hadn't brushed it with sauce every thirty minutes. Hadn't checked the temperature.

He shuffled to the sliding door and stepped outside. Fat drops hit the deck rail with a splat, like water balloons dropping from the roof.

"You couldn't give me one sunny day, huh?" Gerrit scowled at the sky. "I go to church for the first time in twenty-five years, and this is the thanks I get?"

A headache began to grow. His back spasmed. With a growl, he snatched the meat tongs hanging from the side of the grill and threw open the lid.

"What the . . . ?"

The meat lay only half cooked on the rack, looking like a giant centipede that had been rolled over by a truck. The flame was out.

He checked the propane tank. Empty? He'd bought a new tank last week and hadn't used it once. How could it be empty?

He squeezed his eyes shut and saw red. Opened them and felt it. George. It had to be him. He couldn't leave Gerrit in peace, could he? He was still sore about Bernard. Still mad about the mailbox.

It was the final straw.

He slammed the lid shut and charged down the back steps. Into the shed. He reached for the chainsaw on the shelf. The stepladder by the door.

Wind buffeted him as he stalked down the driveway toward the tree with the dead branches.

"Don't know why you never took care of that tree, George," he mumbled to himself, rain plastering his hair to his forehead. "I always knew a storm was going to knock those branches down one day."

He reached the fence and set the chainsaw down so he could open the ladder. Then he grabbed the chainsaw and peered up into the tree. "It's a shame about your RV."

The metal rungs of the ladder were slippery from the rain, which had begun to pelt him like dirt kicking off the back tires of the silage truck. He climbed, chainsaw in one hand, until he could just reach the dead branches with the tip of the chainsaw if he leaned far enough.

"Oh my goodness! What are you doing?" Hannie shouted.

He revved up the chainsaw and reached, imagining George's smug face in the bark of the tree. Hearing his sanctimonious voice on the wind. *"You keeping busy? Other than dog sitting, I mean. I'm going to be a grandpa in June."*

Other voices joined in.

"You mean after you killed him?"

"When Uncle Luke died, I think you did, too."

"Luke would tell you to forgive."

"Get down from there." Hannie's voice was closer now. "You're going to get yourself killed."

"He sabotaged my propane tank."

"Dad! Stop."

That was Noah, shouting over the wind.

His outstretched arm trembled. Rain poured down his face. If he could reach a little farther . . .

"Your propane tank?" That was Evi. "You've got to be kidding me."

She didn't understand. Didn't know how George had been tormenting him.

He turned to explain. His foot slipped off the rung.

Weightlessness.

Fear.

A loud crash.

A rush of pain.

Each breath came in a sharp gasp, the ladder crushing his chest. The cold, wet metal like chains holding him down. Like an unforgiving vise. Like a 1976 Massey Ferguson 235.

Gerrit brought the old tractor to a stop in front of the parlor, his muscles spent and sore.

"Did you finish the north forty?" Luke asked.

Gerrit shook his head. "It's almost dark."

"It needs to get done today."

Gerrit clenched the wheel. Luke wasn't his boss. They were supposed to be partners.

Luke waited, arms crossed over his chest, exhaustion pinching his face. Gerrit left the tractor idling and hopped down to stand in front of his older brother. "Then you can do it yourself."

He could smell the grass. Feel the chill of the air as the sun set. If only Luke had gotten in his face and yelled at him. Shoved him. If only there'd been a different job to do.

Luke climbed up into the tractor's seat with a grunt. "Did you check the oil?"

Gerrit's nostrils flared. "What do you take me for?"

"Did you lock the brakes?"

"For crying out loud, Luke! I'm not a kid anymore."

He was always harping on Gerrit about those stupid brakes. About how "Page ten of the manual says, 'If traveling on a road or highway, the brake pedal interlocking latch must be engaged.'" Blah, blah, blah. Gerrit couldn't care less about page ten of the manual.

Luke drove off in the waning light without looking back. Gerrit almost shouted after him when he realized he hadn't engaged the latch, after all. Almost waved his arms to get Luke's attention when he thought of the narrow road to the north forty and the deer that liked to jump out of the ditch at dusk. But if Luke liked to be the boss so much, he could figure it out himself.

And he had.

Gerrit blinked at the somber sky, his vision fuzzy. His body screaming in agony but unable to move. Was it like this for Luke before their father found him, pinned under the 235 and bleeding out? Did he look at the sky and wonder if there really was a heaven?

"I'm sorry, Luke." His mouth moved, though he couldn't tell if any sound came out. "I'm so sorry."

Hannie's face appeared above him. "The fence is broken."

Noah's voice. "I think *he's* broken."

A blurry figure hovered behind Hannie. "Dad?" The voice was high and strained. "Dad, are you okay?"

Gerrit groaned. "Evi?"

The world would not come into focus. He squeezed his eyes shut. Opened them again. The blurry figure was gone.

A car door slammed.

He tried to sit up, but the pain wouldn't allow it. "Where's Evi?"

Hannie looked over her shoulder, then at Noah. But she wouldn't look at him. "She's gone."

CHAPTER
FORTY

Rae folded her arms across her chest and glared at the door. She had no reason to be at Gerrit's house. He'd made it clear she wasn't welcome, and her heart still stung from the way he'd dismissed her the other night. But when neither he nor Morgan had shown up for Community Hope this afternoon, a warning in her gut had rung out like an alarm.

Something was wrong.

She let out a deep breath through pursed lips. She wouldn't be able to sleep tonight if she didn't make sure he was okay. All she had to do was check, and then she'd never come back here again. She hadn't even bothered to bring Mr. Whiskers.

She knocked.

Hannie answered. "Oh. Hi, Rae, how are you?"

Rae hesitated. What if Gerrit had turned his wife against her, as well? "Fine."

Hannie's voice was serious but kind. "I suppose you're wondering where Gerrit was today."

She nodded.

"He had a bit of an accident, but he's going to be okay." Hannie stepped back and held open the door. "Would you like to come in and say hi?"

Well, not really. Gerrit's words from the other night still scratched at her. *"Go on now."* But Hannie's face was warm and welcoming, so Rae stepped inside the house.

"He's in here." Hannie motioned for Rae to follow, and they walked through the kitchen into the living room.

Gerrit sat in his recliner, pillows tucked all around him and an ice pack resting on his left shoulder. His face was gaunt and his neck discolored as if bruised. When he spotted her, something flashed in his eyes, though she didn't know what. Was he going to yell at her?

"Hey," he said.

She stepped a little closer, vaguely aware that Hannie had retreated into the kitchen. "Hey."

They eyed each other for a moment, then both spoke at once.

"About the other night . . ."

"You look like you got hit by a train."

Gerrit leaned his head back against the chair. "I feel like it, too. But it was a ladder, not a train."

"How was the party?"

"I was waiting for Evi to get back from her walk, and I was afraid if she saw you in the barn, she'd be mad."

Rae's eyebrows knitted together. "Why would she be mad?"

"Because she gets mad about everything it seems." Gerrit sighed. "And because I built that barn for her. It was meant to be our special place. But now . . ."

"Now it's a shrine to some guy named Luke."

Gerrit closed his eyes. "Luke was my brother."

"Oh." One of the chairs from the kitchen table had been

pulled up next to Gerrit, and she sat down on it. That must be why he'd always been so defensive about the barn. Maybe his behavior Saturday night had more to do with Evi and Luke than with her. "Did she see me?"

"Yes."

The tone of his voice told her everything.

"I'm sorry."

"I'm sorry, too. I don't want you to stop coming."

Rae picked at a nail. She hadn't expected this. "When you and Morgan didn't show up today, I—"

Gerrit's eyes flew open. "Morgan wasn't there?"

She shook her head.

He slammed the arm of his chair with a fist and grumbled something to himself.

Her heart sank. "Have you seen him?"

"He showed up early to the party, and there was a . . . misunderstanding."

A memory pinged in Rae's brain. Gerrit had asked her to get a message to Morgan, but she'd been so upset she completely forgot. "I never told him about your moving the party to four o'clock."

Gerrit groaned. "He heard me say something to Evi and Noah that made it seem like . . . well, let's just say I blew it big time with both you kids. He ran out of here."

"It's my fault. I forgot all about the message."

"No." He waved her words away and told her what he had been trying to say Monday afternoon. What Morgan had heard. "I wish I could go to Community Hope and talk to him. Explain. But I'm not supposed to leave this chair."

"Don't even think about it," Hannie called from the kitchen.

He gave Rae a conspiratorial wink. "Yeah, yeah."

"If you're stuck here, maybe I can find Morgan and ask him to come see you."

He looked at her long and hard. "You don't owe me anything."

"I'm worried about him." If Morgan thought Gerrit didn't really care about him—thought he didn't matter? Something inside told her Morgan might have done something foolish.

"Me too. When he left . . ." His head sank back against the chair again, his exhaustion evident.

"I better go." Rae stood. "I'll stop by his house and see if he's there. I'll let you know what I find out as soon as I can."

Gerrit nodded.

Rae said good-bye and thanked Hannie on her way out the door, all the while thinking about the time she ran into Morgan at his house. How he'd been afraid. How that man had yelled horrible things. She remembered exactly where the house was, but she was uneasy about going there by herself. What if Boss was there?

She hurried along the shortcut back to her house, weaving through trees as she pulled out her phone to text David.

> What r u doing? Can u meet me at the entrance to Evergreen?

His answer came quickly.

> I'm on my way.

RAE LOOKED AT the house, then over at David. It wasn't dark yet, but the sun was getting low.

David's smile lacked conviction. "You're sure this is the place?"

She nodded. "Thanks for coming."

He climbed out of the car, and she did the same. "Of course."

He hadn't hesitated to offer help when she'd explained the situation, even though she knew he was unsure about her relationship with Morgan. As they walked up to the dark house, she was beyond grateful for his presence.

Neither of them was eager to knock on the door.

She looked over her shoulder, glad to see several cars on the road. "It doesn't look like anyone's here."

"Only one way to find out." David banged his fist against the door and stepped back. "Here goes nothing."

Thudding sounds came from inside. They waited. A light turned on. David raised a fist to knock again but hesitated when they heard a shout.

"Who's there?"

Rae exchanged a panicked look with David. Boss. Maybe they should go.

The door flew open.

"I said who's there?"

Her eyes grew wide, and she inched away from the man peering out at them with bloodshot eyes. She looked at David, her legs ready to run.

"We're looking for Morgan," David said.

Boss wiped a hairy arm under his nose. "Ain't seen him."

"Do you know where he might be?"

Boss swore, his face turning red as he leaned closer to David with a venomous scowl. "Like I care. He's probably with his dad in jail somewhere."

"Do you have his phone numb—?"

"Look, you little punk." Boss grabbed the front of David's shirt, and Rae whimpered. Why had she left her phone in the car? "I said I ain't seen him. Now get outta here."

David stumbled backward after Boss released him. Rae grabbed David's arm and pulled as Boss slammed the door. "Come on, let's go."

David didn't protest. They dashed back to the car, not stopping to latch the gate. Rae's heart pounded. She wouldn't mind if she never saw that guy again in her whole life. She hurried into the passenger seat, and David shoved the key in the ignition.

"That guy's a piece of work."

She struggled with her seat belt, her hands shaking. "I thought he was going to punch you."

"Me too."

"I'm sorry for dragging you into this."

David took the buckle from her hand and slid it into the latch. "I couldn't let you do it alone."

For a second, she thought he might touch her hand. Instead, he shifted the car into drive and asked, "What should we do next?"

They couldn't sit outside the house, she knew that much.

"Go down that alley." She pointed. "Morgan hides out there sometimes when he's waiting for his mom."

David pulled ahead and turned left down the alley. She scanned the lengthening shadows and spotted the flatbed trailer but saw no signs of life. How long had Morgan been missing?

"Does he have any other friends?" David asked. "Any other place he goes?"

A lightbulb switched on in her brain. "Della's Diner. I think his mom works there."

David pulled onto Sixth and turned left with a flourish. "Della's it is."

She was worried about Morgan but couldn't help a small smile, their close call with Boss now behind them. David was cute when he was driving. They took Sixth back to Parker and followed Parker to I-5. Rae's palms began to sweat just thinking about having to drive on the freeway herself someday soon—everyone was going so *fast*—but David took the on-ramp and merged with ease. He hadn't been kidding when he said he was a good driver.

Della's was two exits away. Everyone knew where it was because it was famous for its blackberry milk shakes. High-school students often went there on Friday nights after football or basketball games.

If they didn't find Morgan soon, she'd have to head back home. As far as her parents knew, she was still at Gerrit's house. They would've never agreed to her driving around with David. Things would get very uncomfortable if they found out.

The conversation she'd had with Kylee about David only a few short weeks ago returned to her mind.

"Tell them you're going to my house."

"I'm not going to lie to them."

She swallowed hard. She was lying to them now.

"Don't worry." David gave her a reassuring smile as he merged into the left lane to pass a red Jetta. "We'll find him."

"What if he's not at Della's?"

"Then we'll have to settle for a milk shake and fries and try again tomorrow. Right?"

She blushed. This wasn't supposed to be a date. But she

couldn't help wondering what it would be like if he reached over and held her hand. He looked over at her and winked.

"I—" Her answer froze on her lips. Her eyes grew wide. "Look out!"

People say time slows down in an emergency. Seconds stretch like taffy on a pulling machine. As a boxy white car barreled across the median toward them, somehow Rae had enough time to look over at the car they were trying to pass and see a pretty curly-haired woman singing along to the radio in the driver's seat. Enough time to cross her arms in front of her face in terror. Enough time to replay her worst nightmare, over and over and over.

The white car struck David's hood from the side. Pushed his car into the woman in the red car. Ripped Rae's world to shreds.

She had time to wonder what station the woman was listening to. She even had time to wish her mother knew where she was.

But she didn't have time to scream.

CHAPTER
FORTY-ONE

Hannie hung up the landline and stared at Gerrit, her crow's feet deep and ominous.

His heart twisted. "Who was that?"

No one ever called this late. No one ever called the landline at all, in fact, except for the occasional telemarketer.

"That was Rae's mother." She moved closer to him. "I guess Rae asked her to call."

She was keeping something from him.

"She found our number in the phone book."

"I thought our number was unlisted." He tried to sit up. "Wait, did something happen?"

Hannie pressed her lips together. "Honey . . ."

Fear jabbed his broken ribs and wrapped its fingers around his neck. "Where is she?"

"There's been an accident."

Every fiber of his body protested as he moved to the edge of his chair. "Get my boots."

"Honey, you can't—"

"Boots. Now." She flinched, and he softened his voice. "Please."

She hurried to the mudroom and returned with his boots. "Let me help you put them on."

He didn't object. "GMC?"

She nodded, and fear's grip on his throat loosened the slightest bit. If Rae was at Greenville Medical Center, that was a good sign. People with life-threatening conditions were almost always sent to Mountlake Hospital. And if Rae had spoken to her mother, she must be okay. Unless she asked her mom to call Gerrit because she . . .

No. He wouldn't think like that.

He ignored the pain as Hannie helped him into her Corolla. Had Rae been driving? He'd never seen her go over thirty miles per hour. She couldn't have been alone.

"Did she say who else was there?"

Hannie shook her head. What if it was Morgan? What if she'd found him, and they'd both been in the accident? Oh, what had he done?

The fifteen-minute drive to GMC took about ten, and Hannie parked as close to the main door as she could. He held tight to her arm, wincing with every step as they made their way into the building. Hannie inquired about Rae at the front desk while Gerrit leaned against a pillar trying to catch his breath.

"Come on." Hannie grabbed his arm, and they took the elevator to the second floor.

The muted sounds of people talking, machines beeping, and trays clattering greeted them when they stepped off the elevator. They found the room number they'd been given and knocked on the door.

An older, more nervous version of Rae answered the door. "Yes?"

Hannie cleared her throat. "Is this Rae's room?"

The woman's eyes narrowed.

A voice from inside called out, "Mom, let them in."

The woman stepped aside, and Gerrit stumbled into the room, almost fainting in relief. Rae was sitting on a hospital bed with a black eye and a bandage wrapped around her forehead, but breathing on her own. Awake. No missing limbs. But something else was missing. The spark in her eyes.

She must've read his face. "I'm okay." Her voice was soft. Tired. "And David broke his nose. But those other people . . ."

David. Not Morgan. She read his face again.

"We never found him."

A man came around from the other side of the bed and held his hand out. "You must be Gerrit."

He dumbly shook the man's hand while Hannie stepped up and introduced herself to Rae's mother.

"What happened to the other people?"

Rae's dad sighed. "They were taken to Mountlake. It doesn't sound good. The kids were lucky."

"I need to talk to Gerrit about something." Rae sat higher on the bed. "Would you give us a minute?"

Rae's mother hesitated. "I don't know. . . ."

Hannie gave Rae's hand a squeeze. "I think I saw some vending machines in the hall. I'm going to see about a snack."

Rae's parents watched Hannie stride out of the room, then reluctantly followed. Unable to stand a second longer, Gerrit sank into the nearest chair with an oof. He could feel his pulse in his collarbone thrumming away.

"We went to his house," Rae began. "Me and David. But Morgan wasn't there. The guy he lives with is a jerk."

"Did you talk to that guy?"

"We tried." She grimaced. "He yelled at us. Practically attacked David. I'm worried Morgan might've run away."

Run away, like Fangs. And Fangs never came back.

Gerrit's stomach was a gaping hole of regret. If something happened to Morgan, he'd only have his own big mouth to blame. It felt awkward and hypocritical, but he didn't know what else to do.

God? Let Morgan be okay. Not for my sake or anything. I just . . . he's a good kid.

"His mom works at Della's," Rae continued. "We thought we'd go there and talk to her, but . . ."

"David was driving?"

She nodded.

"You could've been killed." His tone was harsh and scraped against the sterile white walls.

Tears pooled in her wounded eyes. "It wasn't his fault. That other car crossed the median and rammed us into the red Jetta."

He looked at the floor. Everything was someone's fault. Even accidents. God's, at least, if no one else's.

Rae sniffed. "The police said the guy in that other car was intoxicated. And I heard a nurse say the woman he pushed us into was pregnant. She said—" a single tear fell—"she said the baby died."

The weight of her voice was new. The girl who'd left his house earlier that evening was gone.

She tenderly touched her bandage. "This certainly wasn't part of the plan."

Gerrit sighed. What did a fifteen-year-old know about what she wanted out of life? He sat quietly for a minute, then lifted his eyes to meet hers. "You know, I used to have a plan, too, when I was your age."

She blinked in surprise. "You did?"

"Yeah." His voice took on the color of memories. "I'd lived on the farm my whole life, and I was going to grow up and take it over with my brothers. We'd run it together, and our children after us."

A long moment of silence. The bed squeaked as she shifted.

"It didn't turn out like I planned," he continued. "I'm not sure anything ever does."

"But it's what you wanted, wasn't it?"

He hung his head. "I don't know. It wasn't about what I wanted. That's just what everyone expected."

"Everyone expects me to be a lawyer like my dad."

"Is that what you want?"

When she didn't answer, he looked up. Her face was pensive.

"If you could be anything in the whole world, what would you be?" he prodded.

The corners of her mouth lifted slightly. "Professional cat sitter."

He snorted. Maybe the old Rae was still in there after all.

Her halfhearted smile faded. "I'm not sure. I like to help people. Mark says I'm good with the kids at Community Hope."

"Lawyers help people. The good ones, anyway."

"My parents act like getting into law school will be easy for me. I've always done well in school, but what if I go to Columbia and fail?"

Her words struck a chord in his heart. Hadn't he secretly feared the same thing when Luke pushed him to go to college? Farming made sense to him. He'd done it his whole life. But college? He was afraid he'd fail and waste what he thought was his father's money. Worse, let everyone down. Instead, he'd done fine in college—excelled even—but had failed to . . . oh. He could see it, finally. The reason Luke had been so insistent, going against their father's wishes the only time in his life. The reason he'd sacrificed his own college fund.

Gerrit swallowed hard.

Luke hadn't cared about managing the farm better or implementing modern practices so they could make more money. He'd hoped Gerrit would learn one simple thing: there was more to life than the farm.

He looked at Rae. "What would happen if you didn't go to Columbia at all?"

"I don't know. My parents would be mad. Especially my dad."

"I've wasted a lot of years on the wrong path." Muffled voices came from under the door. No doubt Rae's family was anxious to get back to her. Gerrit struggled to his feet. "Don't make the same mistake."

"How do I know which path is the right one?"

"I'm not sure," he said and put one hand on the doorknob, "but I know you still have plenty of time to figure that out." Gerrit looked back at her battered but youthful face and knew it was true. She had her whole life ahead of her, full of opportunities.

But what about him?

CHAPTER
FORTY-TWO

Rae stared at the ceiling, a pounding headache keeping her awake. At least that was part of it. Her conversation with Gerrit earlier was another part. How was she going to figure out what to do with her life? What had happened to Morgan? And another thing. During the accident, when her mind had flashed back to her driving nightmare, she'd finally seen with clarity who the two people were at the bottom of the hill.

Mom and Dad.

What if she made the wrong choice, and it hurt her parents?

For some reason, something Mark had said a few days ago returned to her mind. *"More importantly, pray about it."* She'd never prayed by herself before. She'd looked up that one verse Mark mentioned, but praying felt like a whole different ball game. She'd never had any reason to do it, really. But here in the hospital, in the dark . . .

God, are you there? Please help me with all this stuff.

She shifted in her bed, trying to get comfortable and

wishing the doctor hadn't decided to keep her overnight for observation. She missed Mr. Whiskers. The doctor had also issued a strict no-electronics policy due to her concussion. Regardless of that, she turned on her phone and hid it under the blanket so the light wouldn't disturb her mother. The clock said one-thirty. She wished Mom would've gone home for the night. How could she sleep in a chair like that? It looked painful.

A long string of texts from David stared back at her from her cell.

How r u feeling?

Is ur head ok?

I'm so sorry this happened.

Please text me back.

She scrolled through them for at least the tenth time. Maybe it wasn't fair not to respond, but she couldn't bring herself to write a message back. Every time she thought about David, she replayed the accident in her mind. Saw the white car hurtling toward them from the other side of the freeway. Saw the woman singing. Heard the crunch of metal, the blare of sirens.

If only he hadn't tried to pass the other car. If only he hadn't looked over at her. If only they hadn't tried to find Morgan . . .

If only.

But what would've happened to that woman if they *hadn't* been in between her and the other car? She shuddered. If she thought driving was scary before, how would she ever do it now?

Her phone buzzed, and she jumped. David must be having trouble sleeping, too.

> Hey, it's Morgan.

She gasped. Mom stirred, and Rae turned her back to her so she would think Rae was sleeping if she woke up.
Another buzz.

> Heard about the accident. R u okay? Got ur number from Mark.

Stunned, she hurried to reply.

> Yeah, I'm fine. Head injury. He gave out my number?

> Only after I promised to wait until morning to use it.

So much for that promise. But Morgan was alive! He texted again.

> I'm at the hospital. Up for a visitor?

> Pretty sure visiting hours are over.

> Wouldn't be the first time I've snuck into a hospital room. Be there in 5.

She hesitated, glancing over her shoulder at her poor mom, sleeping fitfully. That neck angle didn't look good. It would probably be doing her a favor to wake her up at this point.

> Ok.

She tucked the phone out of sight. "Mom?"

Mom's head jerked up. "What? Yes? What's the matter? What do you need?"

Her hair was smushed flat on one side. Rae couldn't remember the last time she'd seen her looking so disheveled.

"I'm hungry."

Mom rubbed her eyes. "The cafeteria's closed, sweetie. There are some crackers and candy bars in the vending machine."

Rae had to think fast. "What about the gas station?"

She'd seen the red Conoco sign across the street through her window before Mom shut the curtains for the night.

Mom ran her fingers through her hair. "Are you sure you're up to eating something? The doctor said with your concussion—"

"I just really want some ice cream. Then I can take ibuprofen for my head."

Mom stood and yawned. "Maybe the nurse will have something you can eat."

"But the Conoco always has Ben and Jerry's. Please, Mom. Chunky Monkey?"

She was wavering, Rae could tell. Time to move in for the kill.

"You know I'll puke if I take ibuprofen on an empty stomach."

"All right." Mom picked up her purse from the floor. "But don't you leave this bed. I'll be right back."

Rae smiled. "Thanks, Mom."

She did love Chunky Monkey.

Mom stumbled out of the room, still half asleep. The door clicked shut behind her.

Rae held her breath. How on earth was Morgan going to—?

The door opened again, and a dark figure slipped in.

She pulled up the light blue blanket, suddenly aware of her thin hospital gown. Why had she agreed to see him? But the room was dark, and she had no intention of turning on the light.

"Why are you so good at sneaking around?" she whispered.

He shrugged. "My mom's been in the hospital a few times."

There must be more to that story. Why would a kid have to sneak in to see his own mother?

She didn't press the issue. "My mom will be back soon."

He stood at the foot of her bed, hands in the pocket of his hoodie. "Your face looks bad."

"Gee, thanks."

"I meant—"

"Where have you been? We've been worried about you."

"Who's we?"

Her head throbbed. She adjusted her pillow so she could lean back on it without lying all the way down. "Me and David, we went to your house."

"That was a dumb thing to do."

Yes. Well. She squinted at him in the dark. "Boss was mad."

Morgan laughed a humorless laugh. "I bet he was. I can't stand that guy. I've been staying with a friend of my mom. My mom's thinking about leaving Boss and coming to live there, too."

"Oh." Her brain was firing slower than usual, yet it didn't need much spark to know what Morgan said was a good idea. "I'm glad."

"Me too."

"Gerrit told me what happened."

Morgan looked away. "He said he didn't care about me. About either of us, actually."

"No he didn't."

"I heard him."

She closed her eyes. That ice cream and ibuprofen couldn't come soon enough. "You didn't hear everything. He told me what really happened. What he was trying to say."

Morgan didn't answer, and she opened her eyes. "You should've seen him when I talked to him earlier today. He was worried sick about you. He had an accident, too, you know."

His eyes bored into hers. "What do you mean?"

"He fell from a ladder. Cracked some ribs and stuff."

"But he acted like I wasn't even supposed to be there, even though he'd reminded me about the party like a hundred times."

She groaned. "I didn't give you the stupid message. I'm sorry."

"What?"

"He changed the party from three to four. I was supposed to tell you." She yawned, causing pain to shoot down the right side of her face.

Morgan looked over at the door. "I should go."

"Don't be mad at him. He does care about you."

Maybe it was the darkness that made honesty easy, or maybe it was because she was so vulnerable herself. Whatever it was, for just a moment Morgan dropped his mask for the first time since she'd talked to him that day in Room F.

His voice was thin but heavy. "Sometimes it's easier to keep people at a distance."

She thought of all David's texts that she hadn't answered.

How he must be going crazy, wondering if she was okay and blaming himself. "I know. But that doesn't mean we should."

He slipped out the door as stealthily as he'd come in. She stared at the end of the bed where he had been, clutching her phone under the blanket. Morgan had been brave enough to open up, just a tiny bit, to someone who he was still trying to figure out. Was she brave enough to do the same?

Mom would be back any minute. She pulled out her phone and opened David's last message.

> I'm fine.

She paused, thinking, then finished and sent the text.

> But scared. Call me tomorrow.

CHAPTER
FORTY-THREE

She'd only been in the hospital for one night, but it might as well have been a whole week. Rae couldn't wait to go home and take a shower. Couldn't wait to see Mr. Whiskers.

Mom held out her clothes. "Let me help you get dressed."

"Mom, please." Rae tried to roll her eyes, but sharp pains pierced her head. "I can do it myself."

"But you heard what the doctor said. You're supposed to take it easy."

Rae snatched the clothes from her hands. "I think I can handle getting dressed."

Mom held up her hands. "I'm only trying to help. I'm worried about you."

"Worried enough for me to skip school today?"

"There's no way you're going to school." Mom put her hands on her hips. "After the weekend, depending on how you're feeling, then *maybe* you can go."

"But I have two finals today. And three tomorrow."

Mom rubbed her forehead. "I'm sure your teachers will understand. I'll call the school when we get home."

Rae pulled on her pants and reached behind her back to untie her ill-fitting gown. "I might not have time to catch up on everything before the last day of school. What about The Plan?"

"Honestly, sweetie, now's hardly the time to be thinking about that."

Rae slid her arms into her T-shirt and frowned. "Really?"

Mom's eyes widened. She crossed her arms and sputtered, "Of course. What—I—how could you think I'd care about that at a time like this?"

Rae shrugged. "It's always been the most important thing."

"No." Mom put her hands on Rae's shoulders. "You're the most important thing."

Rae tossed her gown on the bed and ran her fingers through her hair. They were nice words—something a mother would say—but her parents had always made The Plan a priority, regardless of what Rae thought. She didn't know what to make of Mom's statement.

Her phone dinged, and she checked the screen. A text from David.

Just got released. How about you?

Her stomach flip-flopped. When was he going to call her? Would she be ready? What would she say? She slipped the phone into her back pocket.

"Who was that?" Mom's voice was high-pitched and overly casual. She wasn't fooling anyone. "Kind of early to be getting a text."

"It's not that early."

"Was it David?"

Rae looked away. David was kind of a touchy subject at the moment, for both her and her parents. They weren't pleased to learn Rae had been driving around with a boy without permission. Rae shuddered to think how Mom might react if she knew about Morgan's visit to her room last night.

Mom slung her purse strap over her shoulder and motioned toward the door. "I'm not sure I want you communicating with him right now."

"We're just friends."

"He put your life in danger, Rae." Mom stopped at the door, holding it open with one arm. "And you went with him behind my back."

Tears pooled in Rae's eyes as she trudged into the hallway, her head pounding as if the hall lights were hammers and her skull was an anvil. Mom was right. Sort of. She'd gone behind her back, but had David put her in danger? It was an accident. The driver of the car that crossed the median was at fault. But Rae didn't know what to think. The pain in her head made it hard to think at all.

"Are you okay?" Mom touched her arm. "Should I call for a wheelchair?"

Rae shook her head. "I need more ibuprofen. I'll be fine."

They rode the elevator to the first floor and walked out to the car in silence.

Mom waited until Rae was well secured before starting the engine. "Do you want to stop somewhere for breakfast?"

"I just want to go home."

"I can run in at the market and grab some cinnamon rolls."

"Mom. Stop."

The harshness of her own voice made Rae wince. She was exhausted and in pain and—and—out of sorts or something. And probably would be for a while. She'd never been in a car accident before. She couldn't even think about it without freaking out. But her irritation at her mother had nothing to do with that.

"I like David, Mom. He's a good guy."

Mom kept her eyes on the road ahead. "Maybe we should talk about this when you're feeling better."

Rae didn't want to wait. She didn't know when she would be "feeling better."

"I don't know if I want to be a lawyer."

Mom's mouth opened and shut. Her expression was guarded. "You've always wanted to be a lawyer. It's your dream."

Rae looked out her window. Maybe it had been at one point. But it had been a part of The Plan for so long, she couldn't remember whose dream it really was.

"God's got big plans for you." Being a lawyer was pretty big, wasn't it? If she joined the right firm, she would be involved in cases that could make a difference in people's lives. *"Let us not become weary in doing good, for at the proper time we will reap a harvest if we do not give up."* Was being a lawyer the same as doing good? Did the verse mean she shouldn't give up on The Plan?

"I don't know anymore."

"Sweetie, you're upset. You've had a traumatic experience."

Rae twisted in her seat to stare at her. "That has nothing to do with it."

"Is this all because of David? When exactly did you plan to tell me about going out with him?"

"It wasn't a date."

Mom gave her a skeptical look.

Rae slumped in her seat, weariness hitting her like the on-coming car that would surely haunt her dreams for months to come. "There's this kid named Morgan. He goes to my school. I was worried about him because he kind of disappeared." She touched her bandage. "David said he would help me look for him. We were going to Della's to talk to Morgan's mom."

"What do you mean he disappeared? Did he run away?"

Rae shrugged. "I'm not sure. But he lives with this really mean guy, and I was afraid . . ."

"You should've told me. We could've contacted the police."

The look on Mom's face gave Rae the impression she should probably save the information that they'd gone to Morgan's house for another time. She didn't want Mom's head to ex-plode.

"I hoped it wouldn't come to that, and it didn't. Morgan's fine."

Mom sighed. "You still lied to me. You said you were at Gerrit's. When the sheriff showed up at the door—" her voice wavered with emotion—"I've never been so scared in my life."

"I'm sorry, Mom. Really. I should've told you."

Mom took a deep breath, composing herself. "We'll talk more about this once we've both had some rest."

"Okay."

Mom drove on in silence for a minute, though the air between them crackled with words still unsaid. Rae glanced at her from the corner of her eye and waited.

"And maybe it's time we talked about The Plan, too." Mom blurted out the words as if unsure how they would sound. "If you have something on your mind, I want you to feel like you can come to me with it."

Rae sat back. This was new. "What about Dad?"

"What about him?"

"He'll say I've got to take my future more seriously. He'll think—"

"He only wants you to be happy."

"I won't be happy if you get divorced."

Mom tapped the brakes as if she wanted to stop in the middle of the road. "No one's getting divorced." She put one hand to her chest. "Why would you even say that?"

Rae swallowed. She hadn't meant to bring up the *D*-word, but she needed to know. "The way you guys have been acting . . ."

"Oh, sweetie." Mom rubbed her forehead. "Yes, it's been a tough year, with your father's job and your grandmother, but it's nothing for you to worry about."

"How can I not worry about it?" All the overheard conversations, the accusations, they didn't mean nothing.

Mom sighed. "I'm so sorry you thought . . . I don't even want to say that word. It's not going to happen."

An expectant buzz of hope droned in Rae's ears, and she sat up a little straighter. All this time she'd been thinking the worst. "So you guys are okay?"

"There are some things your father and I need to talk about." Mom put her blinker on to turn in to Evergreen Terrace. "Some changes we need to make. But yes, we're okay. And the first thing we will discuss when you are up to it is The Plan. All right?"

Rae rested her head against the seat back. Wow. This was uncharted territory. The Plan had never been up for debate or open to discussion before. Then again she'd never had these doubts before, either. But if her choosing to make alterations to The Plan wasn't going to result in a divorce, then who knew what she might decide to do?

It was funny, in a sick sort of way. It had taken her almost being crushed to death in a car accident to get to the point where she could have this conversation with her mom. Relief coursed through her body. She was almost glad she'd been in the accident.

Maybe she should've asked God for help sooner.

She smiled to herself. "Okay."

CHAPTER
FORTY-FOUR

Gerrit grumbled as he shifted his weight forward. He couldn't sit in this beat-up old recliner for one more minute. He'd promised Hannie when she left for work that he would be good—and he *had* spent all morning watching *Kellan's Kitchen*—but he was antsy to get outside. He felt much better today. Walking around and visiting Rae in the hospital last night had helped in loosening up his muscles.

Now he had some unfinished business to take care of.

As he eased himself onto his feet, Daisy raised her eyebrows at him. *Don't say I didn't warn you* flickered in her eyes.

In the kitchen, he paused next to a pair of sunglasses on the counter. Evi's. He hadn't spoken to her since Monday. Didn't know what he'd say if he did. If George would've just minded his own business . . .

Harrumph. He winced as he pulled on his boots. He was going to settle this thing with George once and for all.

Daisy pouted when he told her to stay in the house, but he shut the door in her face before she could change his mind. He didn't need her running around underfoot, causing a distraction. Outside, it was clear and still, and he could hear the familiar racket of George working in his shop. He was probably building the stupid end table Gerrit had accidentally ordered. Perfect.

It was no trouble getting to George's shop, what with a gaping Gerrit-sized hole in the fence between their two properties. He slipped through and approached the building, practicing in his mind what he would say.

You've got some nerve messing with my grill after all you've done.

You ruined everything.

That money should've been mine.

I should be the one to call the cops on you.

Don't ever come near my house again.

It was a warm day. The shop door was wide open. His boots crunched on the gravel as he approached. George was wearing bulky yellow earmuffs to protect his ears, so he didn't hear Gerrit coming or turn around. Gerrit stood in the doorway, neck muscles tensing. Fists clenching. Bracing himself.

This was it. A moment thirty years in the making.

George worked with his back to Gerrit, his shoulders stooped. Wood shavings covered the floor. Gerrit stepped into the shop, anger and humiliation buzzing like a miter saw in his head, driving him forward.

Then he hesitated. An end table he knew Hannie would love sat in the corner of the shop, nearly complete. Meant for him. It was beautiful. And what was George building now? He could see only part of it as George moved around, but it didn't look like the kind of furniture that usually came out of his shop. Some kind of box? It was small, two feet long at the most.

Something about George's slow, deliberate movements

made Gerrit uneasy. He'd never seen George look so old. So weary. He tapped the nails in unwillingly yet with gentle care. It was almost as if . . .

That was when Gerrit noticed the silence between hammer strikes.

No radio.

George reached for the nail punch on the workbench beside him, revealing the project to which he was so reluctantly dedicated. The buzzing in Gerrit's head faded away. His fists unclenched. His throat tightened. A box about eighteen inches tall sat on the table, the wood sanded smooth. Two small silver handles lay beside it, waiting to be attached to the sides.

Gerrit flinched as George threw the nail punch to the ground and covered his face with his hands. He kicked at a can of wood stain beneath the table.

A low, guttural groan seeped through his fingers, thick and cold, like fog under a bridge. "Why? Oh, Lord, why?"

The despair in George's voice turned Gerrit's blood to hay hooks, ripping him apart from the inside.

"That other car rammed us into the red Jetta," Rae had said. *"The woman was pregnant. The baby died."*

He took a step back. Mallory drove a red Jetta.

Realization poured over him. No. *No, God, please.*

Another step back.

"I'm going to be a grandpa in June."

He forced himself to look away.

Staggered out of the shop.

Gulped for air.

"Isn't it exciting about Mallory's baby?"

He trudged back to the fence, the sun shining brightly on his head as if nothing had changed. Yet the pain in his chest told him everything had. George's desolate cry reverberated in his heart as he stared at the hole his ladder, his recklessness, had created.

The fence he'd broken.

The mess he'd made.

His indignation disappeared, leaving him empty. He nudged a splintered board with his boot. One hour, a couple of pressure-treated posts, and three two-by-fours and he could have the fence looking good as new.

He took a deep breath. This? This was something he could fix.

A bush rustled, and Bernard the Terrible appeared, regal with the light shining on his black-and-green feathers.

Gerrit's voice sounded small to him. "Where have you been?"

The rooster trained a beady eye on Gerrit and bobbed his head. The same low, guttural sound George had made built up from the creature's throat and let loose, a feral keening all of nature could understand.

"I know." Gerrit rubbed a hand over his face and looked at the fence. "I know."

He stepped over the broken pieces, determined. He needed to grab his dog and his keys. The hardware store closed at six. He'd better get a move on.

Maybe he could do one thing right.

And maybe he'd call Evi tonight.

As he passed his truck on his way to the house, something clicked in his heart, like a key turning to release a lock. He thought about Luke and Luisa and Morgan and Rae and his family. He thought about George's granddaughter, lost, and how much a lifelong grudge had cost compared to the money he'd thought he deserved. He thought about the words he'd spoken at the hospital.

"I've wasted a lot of years on the wrong path."

He thought about Jakob.

And he almost didn't notice the shiny new tank of propane sitting in the back of his truck.

CHAPTER
FORTY-FIVE

R ae winced as she paced in front of the rust-colored house, waiting for Gerrit to meet her. She still couldn't believe her mom had agreed to drive her here. Even more surprising was that she'd agreed to wait in the car while Rae and Gerrit attempted this important mission.

But a lot of surprising things had been happening lately. When Mom told her dad Rae might lose her number one spot at school because of missing her finals, he hadn't freaked out. "As long as you're okay," he'd said, "and in the top ten."

Her response? "Top five."

Just because she was rethinking her priorities didn't mean she wanted to become a slacker.

She continued to pace, each step echoing through her body and causing a sharp pain where her forehead had smashed into the window of David's car. A large square bandage covered the stitches, but gunk had been oozing from the wound all day. Mom had told her to "take it easy" about a dozen times on the way over.

A truck door slammed and Gerrit approached, hunched over as if each step caused him pain, as well.

She gave him a small wave. "You made it."

"I'm having second thoughts."

"Too late. Come on."

They started toward the house, and she glanced sidelong at him. "By the way, I've got Morgan's new address."

He stood up straighter. "He's okay?"

"He's living with a friend of his mom's."

Gerrit nodded. "That's good. Did you say anything to him about . . . ?"

"No." She bumped his elbow with her shoulder as they walked. "You're going to do that yourself."

"What if he doesn't want to see me?"

She climbed the front steps. "He knows you didn't mean what you said."

A glint of humor sparked in Gerrit's eyes as he followed her. "Is that so?"

She knocked on the door. "Don't forget, this was *your* idea."

Gerrit grunted and shifted awkwardly beside her. "Does she know we're coming?"

"Yes."

Though Rae still hadn't spoken to her, Kylee had texted when she got home from the hospital to make sure she was okay. Rae had taken that as a good sign. And when she'd asked about the puppies at Gerrit's request, Kylee had agreed to let them come over.

The door opened.

"Hey." Kylee's hair was green now. She leaned against the doorframe and eyed Rae's forehead. "You look terrible."

Gerrit snorted.

Kylee raised one eyebrow at him. "You don't look much better."

Rae smiled. "It's good to see you, too."

"This way to the little monsters." Kylee stepped aside and swept her arm out. "They just ate so they're hyper."

Rae followed Kylee to the laundry room at the back of the house, Gerrit close behind. He bumbled along like an elephant on a tightrope, and she shook her head. He was probably twice the size Papa Tom had been, and twice the trouble, but she was starting to love him almost the same. She couldn't help it.

With a flourish, Kylee swung open the laundry room door, revealing five black-and-white puppies yipping at, stumbling over, and head-butting each other in a roiling, furry mass of ears and limbs and tails.

Gerrit's eyes grew wide, and he took a step back. "They're so small. And noisy."

"They're eight weeks." Kylee shrugged. "Ready to go to their new homes. I'll let you get acquainted."

She waved Gerrit into the room and closed the door after him, locking him away with the puppies so none of them could escape. The two girls stood alone in the hallway. Kylee turned to face Rae and waited.

Rae's heart suddenly beat a little faster. So many things to say. So many regrets.

"Green, huh?"

Kylee touched her hair. "It turned out way darker than I expected."

"I like it."

"Thanks."

"Look, Kylee, I—"

"I shouldn't have been so hard on you." Kylee threw up her hands. "I'm sorry."

"No." Rae waved her friend's words away. "I'm the one who's sorry. I know you would never go behind my back and try to steal David. I was stupid."

Kylee rolled her tongue ring around in her mouth. "I was only trying to help."

Rae hung her head. "I know."

"You were different with him. Happier. Like all that stuff with your parents and"—air quotes again—"*The Plan* wasn't so important anymore."

Rae rubbed her temples, a headache forming. She needed to get home soon and rest, but not before she said what she came here to say.

"I'm starting to realize The Plan isn't all I thought it was." She met Kylee's gaze. "Instead of making my life easier, it made it way more complicated. And you're my best friend, Ky. I've been miserable without you. Please, will you forgive me?"

Kylee scrutinized her for a long moment, then nodded. "So." She grinned wickedly. "Have you kissed him yet?"

Rae huffed in exaggerated exasperation. "You've got to be kidding me."

"You have, haven't you?"

"No."

"But you want to."

Rae made a face. She'd had several long talks with David since the accident, and each one had put more butterflies in her stomach than the last. They'd agreed to take their relationship slow—*very* slow—but . . . "Maybe."

"I knew it," Kylee shouted in triumph. "I'll turn you into a normal teenager yet, Rae. Just wait and see."

Rae smiled. It was what she had prayed for last night. That Kylee would be willing to accept her apology and that they could pick up where they'd left off. Maybe it had worked. Maybe this was what that whole "harvest" thing meant. That you get out what you put in. If you plant anger and suspicion, you harvest misery. Yep. She'd experienced that firsthand. And if you plant reconciliation, forgiveness, hope—there was no telling what good things might come out of it.

Rae glanced around the house. "Your parents out of town again?"

"Yeah. My stepdad doesn't really like me tagging along on their little adventures, so . . ."

"So dinner at my house tonight?"

Kylee hesitated.

Rae folded her hands under her chin and batted her eyelashes. "Please?"

"You're such a dork." Kylee laughed. "Okay, fine."

A yelp came from the laundry room, and Rae and Kylee exchanged a look. It was impossible to tell whether the sound had come from a puppy or Gerrit.

"Do you think they're okay in there?" Rae asked.

Kylee shrugged. "He's really getting a puppy for that Morgan kid?"

Rae nodded. "You would like him. Maybe we could all hang out sometime. Me and you, David and Morgan."

Kylee gave her a long look before cracking a half smile. "Maybe."

Another yelp made Rae jump, and she jerked her chin at the laundry room. "We better go check on them."

Kylee opened the door, and Rae giggled. When was the last

time she'd actually giggled? Gerrit was sitting on the floor, his long legs stretched awkwardly in front of him, five puppies crawling over him like he was a jungle gym.

His hair stuck out in all directions, and panic flashed in his eyes. "Help."

She and Kylee gently nudged the puppies off him and helped him to his feet. He appeared thoroughly terrorized.

"What do you think?" Kylee asked.

He brushed himself off, muttering something about sharp teeth.

Rae picked up the puppy with the chubbiest belly and nuzzled its face. Who could resist that puppy smell? "I think they're cute."

Gerrit protested. "They're nothing but bullies."

Kylee smirked and moved toward the door. "Well, if you don't want one . . ."

"Now hold on." He pointed at the runt of the litter. "I kind of like that guy."

The puppy was more black than white and at least a third smaller than the rest, but he had shoved one of his siblings' heads into the ground with his front paws and pinned it down. Rae set the chubby one down and picked up the runt.

"This guy? He seems a little wild." He squirmed in her hands and attempted a growl. She caught Gerrit's eye and smiled. "Morgan will love him."

GERRIT BANGED ON the steering wheel and shouted, "You couldn't wait five seconds? You had to pull out right in front of me?"

The newfangled silver Prius ahead of him drove on unaffected. Gerrit grumbled. This was a bad idea. What if Morgan wasn't home?

Then again, what if he *was*?

"What street do I turn on again?" he asked himself and glanced around for the scrap of paper on which Rae had written the directions. Then he narrowed his eyes at the puppy sprawled on the seat beside him. "Don't even think about it."

The puppy looked at the scrap of paper as if it might make a good lunch. Gerrit snatched it away. The little runt growled, if you could call it a growl, and gnawed on the seat belt instead.

"Stop that."

The puppy did not stop.

"I'll make you ride in the back."

The puppy redoubled its efforts.

Gerrit reached over and tousled the black-and-white monster's ears. "You rascal. I can't believe I paid two hundred bucks for you."

He followed the paper's instructions and pulled up in front of a small white house long before he was ready. The number 713 was painted on the side of the mailbox.

"This is the place."

Everything he'd considered saying to Morgan suddenly seemed stupid. About how important the kid was to him and how sorry he was. Maybe he should leave well enough alone. Maybe Morgan was better off without him and his big mouth.

Gerrit's lip curled. Rae's description of the guy Morgan used to live with reverberated through his memory, along with Morgan's face the day Gerrit asked him about his father.

He scooped up the puppy. "Come on."

Halfway up the walk, he paused. Looked down at the little critter. What was he thinking, showing up at Morgan's door with a puppy in his arms? Maybe Morgan didn't want another dog. Maybe dogs weren't even allowed in this new place. He turned around.

"You better wait in the truck." He set the puppy on the passenger seat and pointed his finger at it. "And you better not pee on anything."

He steeled himself as he approached the front door, second thoughts—and third and fourth ones, too—swirling in his head. It wasn't too late to hop in his truck and drive away. No one would have to know.

The door flew open.

Morgan looked out at him, eyes narrowed. "How did you find me?"

"Uh . . ." Gerrit cleared his throat.

"It was Rae, wasn't it?"

"I . . ."

Morgan stepped out of the house and shut the door behind him. He wore the same ratty sweatshirt as always, and his black hair hung over his face more than ever, but he seemed different. Taller.

Gerrit shifted on his feet. "I didn't mean for you to hear—"

"Rae told me." Morgan stuck his hands in his pockets. "You were trying to explain me away to your kids. I get it."

"You don't understand."

"I don't expect you to care about me the same as them."

"But I do." Gerrit swallowed hard. "That's just it."

"What?"

"When Rae told me you were missing from school, I was

scared." It was hard to get that word out, hard to admit, yet he was knee-deep in it now. "I thought something happened to you. I was afraid you'd run off to Nashville, and I'd never see you again."

Morgan looked away. "Well, there's nothing keeping me here. Why shouldn't I go?"

Gerrit hesitated. He didn't want to come between a boy and his dreams. And what did he have to offer, anyway? Now that Morgan had graduated, a world of possibilities lay at his feet. A world far away from here.

But Morgan was just a kid. Shouldn't there be someone looking out for him?

Morgan met his eyes with a challenge. "Give me one good reason."

Gerrit opened his mouth. Closed it. Opened it again. "Okay."

He turned around and strode back to his truck. When he glanced back over his shoulder, Morgan hadn't moved from his spot in front of the door. His face was hard. Defensive.

Gerrit reached into the truck and tucked the puppy under his arm. Morgan's eyes fixed on the squirming creature as Gerrit walked back to stand in front of him. Gerrit knew that look. Was all too familiar with it. Longing.

He held the puppy out. "Who will take care of this little guy if you go?"

Morgan's sharp eyes flashed back and forth between Gerrit and the puppy, as if testing the weight and strength of Gerrit's words. As if he stood at the water's edge, unsure if it was safe to jump in.

Gerrit placed the dog in Morgan's arms, and it immediately scrambled to reach Morgan's face with its tongue.

"He likes you."

Morgan grasped at the puppy for dear life. "He's . . . he's . . ."

"He's yours."

Now, *that* was a smile Gerrit would not soon forget.

CHAPTER
FORTY-SIX

Hannie leaned against Gerrit and wept, a tissue pressed to her face. He squinted in the sun. It was the first day of June. A beautiful Saturday that smelled like clover and promised a perfect summer. But here they were.

Evi and Noah stood on the other side of Hannie, staring somberly at the tiny wooden box. George and his family were across from them, along with a handful of other family members. It was a small gathering. A small hole dug in the ground. A small comfort that the birds sang a cheerful tune.

Mallory's shoulders shook, her sobs silent but violent as the pastor asked each person to place a yellow rose on the casket. Her husband held her tightly, as if afraid she would disappear into the freshly dug grave along with their daughter if he let go. Gerrit looked across at George and caught his eye. Éclairs. When this was all over, he was going to make George some éclairs. And then pay him full price for Hannie's table.

He nodded once. George nodded back.

As he led Hannie back to their car, she clung to his arm. He relished her touch. Her nearness.

She looked over at Evi and Noah walking alongside. "I'm so glad you guys could come."

They didn't answer, but Gerrit knew Evi and Mallory had been good friends growing up. She wouldn't have missed this for anything.

"You'll come for dinner, won't you?" Hannie's voice was hopeful.

Evi looked at Gerrit. They'd spoken briefly on the phone, and he had apologized for his behavior last weekend. She hadn't said much, but he was willing to give her time. Take it slow. It'd taken him years to get himself into this mess, and he wouldn't get out of it overnight.

"Sure." Evi shrugged. "If it's okay with Noah."

Noah nodded and opened the car door for Evi. They'd driven up together and met Gerrit and Hannie at the cemetery. Gerrit noticed Travis's absence but didn't dare bring it up.

Hannie smiled. "That's great."

"Why don't you ride with the kids?" Gerrit waved an arm at Noah's car. "I have an errand I need to run real quick."

"Oh. Are you sure?"

He forced a smile. "I'll meet you at the house."

He waited until they drove away before sliding into his truck. Hannie had only agreed to let him drive to the private graveside service because she was "an emotional wreck" and could "barely see straight." She'd taken the news about George and Agatha's granddaughter hard, as he knew she would. He cranked up the Dodge and headed into Greenville.

When he was nine and Luke was ten, they'd discovered an ancient GMC truck on the edge of the back forty, covered over by years of blackberry bushes. It took them hours to hack away enough briars with their Buck knives to get close to it, but they didn't mind. It was like stumbling upon hidden treasure.

The truck was covered in rust, and the metal springs had poked out of the bench seat inside, yet to him and his brother it was better than a castle. With wonder in their eyes and scratches covering their arms, they climbed inside, and Luke took the wheel. What magic an old truck could hold for a pair of boys with wild imaginations.

He'd never forget that day. He could still smell the musty fabric of the bench seat. Hear Luke laughing as he pushed buttons on the old radio, pretending to change the station. See the sun filtering through the blackberries, dappling their make-believe world.

When they went home for dinner that night, after a long day of adventure, their father broke the news. *"Your mother's going to have a baby, and the doctor says she needs to take it easy. You boys are going to help out more around the house, you hear?"*

"Yes, sir," Luke had said. But Gerrit hadn't said anything. Somehow he'd known everything was about to change.

He parked his truck in front of the Bronze Boot and took out the keys. They were heavy in his hand, like metal regrets. He heaved himself out of the Dodge and stood in front of the building. The bar windows were tinted dark and covered in posters and neon signs, but he knew what he would find inside.

A lethargic din met him when he opened the door. Not many patrons yet, but the numbers would increase as the night went on. He walked through the haze of broken dreams and haunted memories and sat down at the bar next to a man in a blue windbreaker.

"What can I get you?" the bartender asked.

"Ginger ale on ice."

The bartender narrowed his eyes, his hopes of acquiring a new long-term customer fading. "All right."

As the man walked away, Gerrit leaned his elbows on the bar.

Jakob stared at the empty glass in his hand. "What are you doing here?"

He'd been asking himself the same question since parking the truck. "It's a free country."

The bartender slid Gerrit his drink, and he nodded his thanks. He took a sip. Looking around the dingy place, he couldn't guess what the appeal was for a middle-aged man on a Saturday afternoon. But then he never did understand his younger brother. Maybe he'd never tried.

"You talk to Luisa lately?" he asked.

"No."

"I worry about her, living alone."

Jakob tensed. He'd lived alone since his wife left him ten years ago, but that was his own doing. She'd given him far more chances than he deserved, and his legacy was a broken marriage and thousands of dollars of gambling debt. Yet Luisa had been a widow since the age of twenty-eight through no fault of her own. No one to blame but Gerrit.

Ice clinked as Jakob swirled his glass like he could coax out one more drop. "He wasn't perfect, you know."

Gerrit snorted. "Unbelievable."

Jakob slammed down the glass. "Do you have any idea what it was like, watching the two of you? Luke would do anything for you, but he wouldn't give me the time of day."

"That's not true."

"I was always on the outside."

Gerrit's hands itched to slam his own glass onto the counter. Instead, he forced his shoulders to relax. He didn't come here to start a fight. He remembered again that day in the blackberry bushes, playing with the old truck. Had he and Luke ever played with Jakob like that?

They'd never had the time. By the time Jakob was born, he and Luke had taken over almost all the household chores in addition to their farm chores, and their responsibilities only grew from there. It was all their mother could do to take care of Jakob, never mind her other two sons, and sometimes she couldn't even do that. Luke often had to get up in the middle of the night and give Jakob a bottle because their mother was too depressed to move and their father had to be in the parlor by three-thirty for the early-morning milking. Then Luke would pack their lunches, forge their mother's signature on Gerrit's homework, and make sure they didn't miss the bus.

But Jakob didn't know about any of that. He was just a baby then.

Gerrit watched condensation run down the side of his glass. "It was hard on Luke to be the oldest brother."

Jakob didn't respond. Gerrit glanced at his face and recognized the bitterness there. Felt the familiar weight of self-inflicted chains. Maybe it was hard to be the youngest brother, too. Maybe Jakob wasn't the only one at this bar in need of forgiveness.

"I'm sorry." The words hurt coming out. They lay there beaten and bloody on the bar like they'd been yanked from his chest. Gerrit made no move to put them back.

Jakob's grip on his drink tightened.

"I've been thinking of going through Luke's old boxes. They're in my barn." Gerrit took the last swig of ginger ale and slid off the stool. "Maybe you'd want to come by one day and help me."

"There's nothing in there for me."

He pulled a fiver from his wallet and left it on the bar. "You never know."

Jakob looked up with bleary eyes, desperate and broken. "Why'd you come here?"

The answer was suddenly clear. Luke's chance to live out his dreams had been cut short. Jakob's had been flushed away, one whiskey at a time. But Gerrit's? He'd almost squandered it, believing that making something of his life had everything to do with the farm, but he understood differently now. His opportunity to leave a legacy was only just beginning.

"I wanted you to know I'm letting go of the farm."

Jakob sneered. "We sold it two months ago."

"But I didn't let it go until today."

"Leave me alone."

Gerrit left the bar with the sound of chains falling to the ground all around him.

CHAPTER
FORTY-SEVEN

Rae smoothed her hand over Mr. Whiskers's back as she sat in the barn. He purred.

"When are you going to start rubbing *my* back?"

The cat twitched his ears.

"I don't think it's too much to ask after all I've done for you."

Gravel crunched outside.

"Gerrit must be home."

She'd seen Hannie's car and what must've been either Evi's or Noah's car when she got there, yet Gerrit's truck had been missing in action. A heavy door slammed. Yep. That was him.

It had taken some convincing to get her parents to let her walk over here. She'd had to beg, telling them the fresh air would do her good, which was true, and that she needed to talk to Gerrit, which was also true. For some reason, she had to see him. She'd been forced to promise she would come directly home in one hour and not talk to any boys.

Her neck and back were sore, leftover evidence of the accident. Her head felt a lot better, though. The sound of boots striking gravel drew near.

"Hey." Gerrit opened the barn door and gave her a concerned look. "I didn't expect to see you out and about."

"I walked slowly."

"How's your head?"

"It's okay."

He rubbed his chin. The bruises on his neck had faded to a light green. "Are you sure you should be walking this far?"

She smirked. "You're the one who fell off a ladder."

"You got hit by a car."

Touché. "We're quite a pair, aren't we?"

Something wistful flitted across Gerrit's face.

She eyed him curiously. "So your kids are here?"

He looked over his shoulder at the house. "Yep."

He seemed different today. Subdued. Or maybe at peace.

She pulled Mr. Whiskers tight to her chest and rubbed her face against his head. "The last Community Hope session is on Monday. You should come."

"Is that right?" He folded his arms and raised his eyebrows. "I'll have to check my schedule."

She laughed. When his eyebrows shot up like that, she was reminded again of Papa Tom. He was always making faces and telling jokes. Coming to all of her basketball games. He always said, *"Make time for family, and family will make time for you."* And he'd been right. She'd spent every minute she could with him up until he died.

"Guess you better go hang out with your kids." She stood. "I have to get home anyway."

"What are you going to do about that lawyer thing?"

"I don't know yet. But I know I'm going to pray about it."

"Huh." He stepped aside so she could exit the barn. "That's a good idea. And what about that David guy?"

She paused in the driveway. While she couldn't stop thinking about David, it was going to take some time to figure out what their relationship was going to look like. "I think he blames himself that I got hurt."

Gerrit nodded slowly. Gravely. As if he had been there.

She continued, "But it wasn't his fault. Things happen, and people have to live with the results. That's part of growing up. Part of life. It might be a while before I try driving again, though."

She pictured herself behind the wheel and, despite the accident, realized the thought of driving didn't scare her as much as it did before. Her nightmare about careering down the hill toward her parents, out of control, hadn't returned since she came home from the hospital. Maybe it hadn't been the driving she was afraid of as much as where she thought she was headed.

Gerrit reached out a hesitant hand and patted Mr. Whiskers on the head. "Don't let fear hold you back."

She looked at the house, then back at him, and thought of Papa Tom. "You either."

GERRIT WATCHED RAE disappear into the woods, gingerly maneuvering over fallen branches and around salmonberry bushes. She was right. He was still afraid of opening his heart to Hannie and the kids. Afraid they would discover he had nothing to offer them. Afraid the farm had taken more than he could ever get back.

He strode to the house and opened the door to the sound of lively voices. In the kitchen, Hannie was pulling food from the fridge, and Evi was leaning against the counter.

"Dad." Her eyes sparkled. "Is it true your rooster attacked Mr. Sinnema?"

Gerrit rubbed the back of his neck. "He happened to run in George's direction, yes. I wouldn't say he *attacked* him."

"Poor Bernie is just misunderstood, isn't he?"

"I believe so." He took the pitcher down from above the fridge. "George even called the cops on him."

Evi laughed, and it sounded like heaven. "I never heard about that."

"He asked me not to tell."

"Who? George?"

"No." He made a serious face. "Bernard."

Evi rolled her eyes. "Travis was afraid of him. Said he was watching his every move."

Gerrit smiled inwardly. He'd begun to suspect he and Bernard were kindred spirits. Now he knew for sure.

"Where *is* Travis today, Ev?" Noah asked.

"I . . ." Evi glanced at Gerrit. "Asked him not to come. This time."

Gerrit cringed. Was that his fault? Was his daughter afraid to bring her boyfriend over because she didn't know what Gerrit might do? And why shouldn't she be? He'd made a complete fool of himself last time. Only five days ago.

He steeled himself. She'd avoided him and this house for long enough. He wouldn't let anything stand in the way of her spending more time here. Even himself.

He caught her eye and forced the words out. "He's welcome anytime."

She held his gaze as if searching for something. As if holding him in a spell. But her face gave nothing away. "We'll see, Dad."

"What smells so good, Mom?" Noah asked. The spell was broken. "I'm starving."

"Just leftovers." Hannie pushed hair out of her face. "But your father's quite a cook as it turns out, so even the leftovers are delicious."

Gerrit felt his face redden as he drew a knife from the block and began cutting strawberries for the lemonade. "I only make easy stuff."

"You should taste his éclairs." Hannie set four plates on the table. "I keep telling him my customers would love them. *If* we put in a pastry bar."

Noah's eyebrows rose in surprise. "Are you thinking of expanding The Daisy Chain?"

Gerrit's stomach tightened. The last he'd heard from Hannie on the subject was that she couldn't believe she'd ever thought they could work together. He held his breath.

"Maybe." Hannie glanced at him. "It's always been my dream to add on to the shop. Turn it into something unique. Maybe even add a little stage like some coffee shops do."

"I remember you talking about it before." Evi's eyes shone. "A long time ago. Think of the possibilities. Greenville doesn't have anything like that."

Gerrit stared at the knife in his hand. When had she talked about it before? He'd been married to Hannie for thirty-five years, and he couldn't remember her saying she had a dream. Not that he'd ever stepped away from his own bitterness and guilt long enough to ask. So she'd been forced to fight and scrape to chase her dream by herself while he'd chased what he thought was his own dream only to find that it wasn't. Only to find he'd been chasing the wind. Alone.

"I think you should do it."

He was as surprised as everyone else when the words came out. Three heads turned to look at him in disbelief.

"You think I should expand the shop?" Hannie asked.

He nodded.

"Add a coffee and pastry bar?"

He set down his knife. Took a deep breath. "If that's what you want, then yes."

She moved closer to him. "And you'll make éclairs?"

"As many as you need."

She was right beside him now. "We're not exactly spring chickens anymore. It would take a lot of work."

"I have time on my hands."

Her eyes narrowed. "And a lot of money."

How many years of his life would it cost him to invest in Hannie's dream? Five? Six? He studied the tilt of her head. The spark in her eyes. Even if they never made the money back, it would be worth it to see her smile. "I happen to know where some is. Anything else?"

The corners of her lips twitched. "Don't take this the wrong way, but you could never run the counter. We'd need another employee."

Gerrit watched her face, longing, praying, hoping for all the light shining from it to be for him. "I know a kid. He's real smart and needs a job. He even sings."

She threw her arms around his neck. He stood there for a second, stunned, then reached around to hug her back. Over her shoulder, he could see the kids watching. Evi with a pensive expression. Noah with a grin.

Noah tapped the counter with his knuckles. "Can we eat now?"

CHAPTER
FORTY-EIGHT

The back deck had been built for this. For sitting next to Hannie as the sun set. For watching the fields at the bottom of the hill turn to gold. Fresh, clean water from the sprinkler system sparkled as it covered the grass in life. Promise. Hope.

Gerrit knew he could sit on this deck every night for the rest of his life and still not make up for the sunsets he'd missed. But he was here today.

Bernard strutted up the deck steps and hopped up onto the rail, ready to settle in for the night.

Hannie smiled at the foul creature. "Who invited you?"

Gerrit waved his hand at him. "You'll have to excuse him. He thinks this is his deck."

"He better not poop on it."

"He knows better." Gerrit glared at Bernard. "Don't you?"

The rooster acted like he didn't hear.

Gerrit made his voice as stern as possible but couldn't keep his lips from twitching. "You miserable thing."

Hannie gave Gerrit an inscrutable look. He swallowed

hard. She searched his face. "Something happened to you today."

"What?"

"After the service. Where did you go?"

He looked away and sank back in his chair. "I talked with Jakob."

She was silent for a minute. He could almost hear the wheels turning in her head. When she finally spoke, her voice was soft. "When you came back to the house, you looked different."

"I was." He wanted it to be true. *God, please let it be true.* "I am."

"Do you want to go to church with me in the morning?"

The golden fields turned purple. The Pacific tree frogs began their evening song. Gerrit watched the lights turn on outside the milking parlor.

"Yes." He turned his face to her. "I'd like that."

She smiled and stood, patting his hand. "Me too. And I think I'll head to bed. It's been a long day."

A long week. A long thirty-five years.

"Okay."

At the sliding door, she paused. "It's about time you slept in your own bed, don't you think?"

Every muscle in his body tensed. "I reckon."

"Okay then."

She went into the house, shutting the door behind her. He stood and gripped the rail, seeing everything around him with new eyes. Hannie had made a home here. Filled this place with beauty while he was away. Created a refuge he had never realized he needed.

He surveyed the backyard. The flower beds near the house arranged so that something would be blooming all summer long. The climbing rose entangled on a wooden trellis. A patch of daisies waving their green arms with abandon at the last rays of sunlight.

Of course.

His eyes widened as the truth hit him.

Hannie loved daisies.

He retrieved the small orange pair of gardening shears from the shed and crossed the yard to the cheery white-and-yellow flowers. With gnarled hands, he gently cut as many as he could fit in one fist.

Inside the house, he found a blue-tinted Mason jar in the cupboard by the sink, filled it halfway with water, and stuck the daisies in. It was a paltry offering maybe, but it was all he had. He glanced at his recliner in the living room, then at the stairs. His mouth went dry. Had she meant what she said?

"Here goes nothing," he whispered.

He headed for the stairs, flower jar in hand, and hesitated. Wait. There was one more thing he needed to do.

In the mudroom, by the door, he stared down the blue-and-white suitcase. It had frightened him the first time he saw it. Angered him many times after that. It had told him more than any words Hannie could've spoken. But its time was up, its services no longer needed, because he knew everyone was right where they belonged.

He bent his stiff back and grunted, reaching for the suitcase handle. His fingers wrapped around it, and he lifted.

The suitcase gave easily, swinging freely in the air.

It was empty.

A hundred memories flashed through his mind. Memories of Hannie sitting on his lap while he drove the cab tractor around the field. Of her belly swollen in pregnancy, face aglow. Of her brushing her honey-colored hair back when it was as long as her waist.

Of her tears at Luke's funeral.

Of the plates of food left for him to find long after everyone else had gone to bed.

Of her standing in the doorway, holding a blue-and-white suitcase.

He carried his simple yet profound gifts to the bottom of the stairs and looked up—yes, things were looking up.

And he smiled.

ACKNOWLEDGMENTS

Thank you to my mom for never once doubting this day would come. You're the best.

Thank you to all the men and women who have dedicated their lives and their land to feeding the world. Long live the family farm.

Thank you to my first readers, Sarah Carson and Janice Parker, and my second readers, Kerry Johnson and Emily Conrad. Thank you to Jim and Carol Ashby for your generous hearts. Thank you to my many friends in the writing community for your support and encouragement, and to my QTs for hanging out in the hallway with me. Thank you to my agent, Keely Boeving, for believing in me, and to Steve Laube for showing me the way.

Thank you to everyone at Bethany House, from those who helped me fill out paper work to those who coordinated this book's release into the world to everyone in between. Special thanks to Dave Long for giving this book a chance, and to Luke Hinrichs for pushing to make it the best it could be.

Thank you to my husband, Andy, for doing all those dishes while I worked and refusing to let me give up. I love you.

And all thanks, honor, and glory to God: Creator, Sustainer, and Author of the greatest story of all.

ABOUT *the* AUTHOR

Katie Powner grew up on a dairy farm in the Pacific Northwest but now calls Montana her home. She's worked alongside her husband in youth ministry for over a decade and is a mom to the third power: biological, adoptive, and foster. In addition to writing contemporary fiction, Katie blogs about family in all its many forms and advocates for more families to open their homes to children in need. *The Sowing Season* is her debut novel. To learn more, visit her website at www.katiepowner.com.

Sign Up for Katie's Newsletter

Keep up to date with Katie's news on book releases and events by signing up for her email list at katiepowner.com.

More from Bethany House

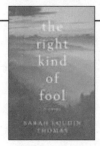

When deaf teen Loyal Raines stumbles upon a dead body in the nearby river, his absentee father, Creed, is shocked the boy runs to him first. Pulled into the investigation, Creed discovers that it is the boy's courage, not his inability to hear, that sets him apart, and he will have to do more than solve a murder if he wants to win his family's hearts again.

The Right Kind of Fool by Sarah Loudin Thomas
sarahloudinthomas.com

You May Also Like...

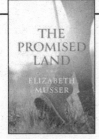

Desperate to mend her marriage and herself, Abbie Bartholomew joins her son in walking the famed Camino pilgrimage. During their journey, they encounter an Iranian working in secret to help refugees and a journalist searching for answers from her broken past—and everyone is called into a deep soul-searching that threatens all their best laid plans.

The Promised Land by Elizabeth Musser
elizabethmusser.com

In this epistolary novel from the WWII home front, Johanna Berglund is forced to return to her small Midwestern town to become a translator at a German prisoner of war camp. There, amid old secrets and prejudice, she finds that the POWs have hidden depths. When the lines between compassion and treason are blurred, she must decide where her heart truly lies.

Things We Didn't Say by Amy Lynn Green
amygreenbooks.com

◊ BETHANYHOUSE